SUSAN MALLERY

ALMOST PERFECT

ISBN-13: 978-1-61664-527-4

ALMOST PERFECT

This edition published by arrangement with Harlequin Books S.A.

® and TM are trademarks of the publisher. Trademarks indicated with
® are registered in the United States Patent and Trademark Office, the
Canadian Trade Marks Office and in other countries.

Printed in U.S.A.

To Rhinda, Nikki's "other" mom!
This one's for you.

ALMOST PERFECT

CHAPTER ONE

LIZ SUTTON HAD ALWAYS KNOWN the past would come back and bite her in the butt—she just hadn't known it was going to happen today.

Her morning had started normally enough, with getting her son on the bus to school, then going down the hall to her home office, where she wrote five fairly decent pages before stopping for some serious pacing, followed by deleting three of the last five pages. She was figuring out who to murder in the first chapter of her new book, not to mention how he or she would be murdered. Was decapitation just too predictable? Luckily her assistant knocked on her door, sparing her from making a decision.

"Sorry to interrupt," Peggy said, frowning slightly as she held out a piece of paper. "But I thought you'd want to read this."

Liz took the single sheet. It was an e-mail, sent to her Web site. There was a link there for fans to get in touch with her. Peggy handled most of the e-mails, but every now and then she found something she didn't know what to do with.

"A crazed stalker type?" Liz asked, pathetically grateful for the interruption. When the writing was slow, even a death threat was more thrilling than the current work in progress.

"Not exactly. She says she's your niece."

Niece?

Liz scanned the sheet.

Dear Aunt Liz,

My name is Melissa Sutton. My dad is your brother Roy. I'm fourteen years old and my sister Abby is eleven. A few months ago, our dad went to prison. His new wife, our stepmom, said she would take care of us, but she changed her mind and left. I thought Abby and me would be fine. I'm really mature for my age. My teachers say that all the time.

She's been gone a while now and I'm really scared. I haven't told Abby because she's still a kid, but I don't know if we can make it. I don't want to tell Dad what happened because he really liked Bettina and he'll be sad she didn't wait for him.

So I thought maybe you could help. I know we haven't met before, but I've read all your books and I really like them.

Hope to hear from you soon. Your niece, Melissa.

P.S. I'm using the computer at the library, so you can't e-mail me back. But here's our phone number. Even though the lights are off, the phone still works at home.

P.P.S. We're living in your old house in Fool's Gold.

Liz read the e-mail a second time, trying to get the words to make sense. Roy was back in Fool's Gold. Or at least he had been, before heading off to prison.

She hadn't seen her brother in nearly eighteen years. He was a lot older and had left the summer she'd turned twelve. She'd never heard from him again. Apparently he'd married a couple of times and had kids. Daughters. Girls who were living alone in a house that had been run-down and disgusting twelve years ago. She doubted there had been many improvements since.

Questions tumbled through her brain. Questions about her brother and why he'd returned to Fool's Gold after being gone so long. Why he was in prison and what on earth was she supposed to do with two nieces she'd never met?

She glanced at her watch. It was barely eleven. As it was Tyler's last day before summer vacation, he was getting out at twelve-thirty. If she got the car packed in time, they could leave directly from his school and be in Fool's Gold in about four hours.

"I need to deal with this," Liz told her assistant, as she wrote an address on a piece of paper. "Call the electric company in Fool's Gold and get the power turned back on. They should take a credit card for payment. Do the same with the other utilities. I'll call the girls and let them know I'm coming."

"Are they really your nieces?" Peggy asked.

"I guess. I haven't seen my brother since I was their age, but I can't let them stay there alone." She shook her head, determining what else had to be done. Her next book wouldn't be published until the fall, so she didn't have to worry about publicity and book tours. She could work on her new story anywhere she had her laptop. At least that was the theory.

"I don't know how long we'll be gone," she continued. "I'm guessing it will take a couple of weeks to get everything straightened out."

Peggy stared at her. "Just like that?"

"What do you mean?"

"Aren't you going to think about it? Most people would hesitate. You don't even know these girls."

True, Liz thought. But what choice did she have? "They're kids, by themselves, and they're family. I have to do something."

"Which is just like you," Peggy said. "You leap in and do what you think is right which is admirable. But not always smart."

"Someone has to take care of this." Besides, she'd grown up having to take care of things. Her mother hadn't bothered. "With luck, I won't be gone too long."

"Don't worry either way. I can handle things here."

Liz forced a smile. "I know you can. I'm going to pack and then get Tyler. We'll drive to Fool's Gold today."

"Maybe it will be nice to go home."

Liz did her best to look normal. "Sure. Okay, I'll call the girls."

She waited until Peggy left before picking up the phone. She dialed the familiar number, then let it ring eight times before hanging up. No answer. Of course, it was a weekday. The girls were probably still in school. She would try again later, from her cell.

She had to pack for herself and her son, phone a few friends and let them know she would be gone for a couple weeks, e-mail her editor and agent to tell them the same. Logistics, she thought as she collected the notes she'd made on her current novel. She was good at logistics. The ability to plan and deal with problems was part of the reason she enjoyed writing her detective mystery series. She'd always been good at the work. It was the rest of life that caused her to stumble time after time.

"Introspection later," she murmured aloud. "Action now."

She powered off her laptop, then disconnected it from the docking station. After collecting her notes, a few pens, pads of paper and her address book, she went down the hall to her bedroom.

A little over an hour later, she'd packed what she hoped was enough, loaded the car and gone over everything with Peggy. Her assistant would take care of the house and make sure the bills were paid.

"Are you all right?" Peggy asked.

"Sure. Great. Why?"

Peggy, a forty-something former executive assistant, frowned. "Just checking. This is a lot to take in." She hesitated. "You know if there's no one else to take care of the girls…"

Liz might suddenly be responsible for two nieces she'd never met. "I know. I'll deal with that when I have more information."

"Mac and I went to Fool's Gold on our honeymoon. Back when I thought marriage was a good thing. I didn't know you were from there."

No one did, Liz thought grimly. She found life easier when she didn't talk about her past. "I left right after high school and moved here. San Francisco is my home now."

Peggy smiled at her. "If you need anything, call me."

"I will."

Liz went downstairs to the single car garage and got into her Lexus. She'd packed four suitcases, a couple boxes with Tyler's favorite movies, his Xbox and a handful of books. She went over the inventory because that was easier than thinking about what she was doing. Going back to the one place she never wanted to be. The town where she'd grown up.

For a second she wondered if she really *had* to do this. Go rescue a couple kids she'd never met. Then she shook off the thought. Right now there wasn't anyone else. She couldn't leave the two girls on their own. She would deal with the problem, get it resolved and return to her life. Staying was not an option.

Midday traffic was relatively light and she made it to Tyler's school in about twenty minutes. He was talking to his friends, probably making plans for hanging out. When he saw her small SUV, he waved and hurried over.

"Jason says his family's for sure going to Disneyland in August and they're gonna call and talk to you about me going with them," he said as he climbed into the passenger seat.

"Hello to you, too," she greeted with a smile.

He grinned. "Hi, Mom. How was your day?"

"Interesting."

"Great. Now can we talk about Disneyland?"

Her son was the brightest and best part of her life, she thought as she stared into his dark brown eyes. He had her smile, but everything else came from his father. As if her DNA hadn't been strong enough to overpower his.

Tyler was smart, funny, warm and caring. He had dozens of friends, an easygoing disposition and plans to be an architect when he grew up. She knew that everyone said the early teen years were the worst with boys. That by thirteen or fourteen, he would be making her life hell. But that was a problem for another time. Today, Tyler was her world.

A world that had just been shifted off its axis and was tumbling freely through space.

"Disneyland sounds like fun," she agreed. "I'll talk to Jason's mom. If they want to take you and you want to go, then we'll arrange it."

His grin widened. Then he glanced toward the back of the vehicle.

"Whoa, are we going somewhere? Road trip?"

She pulled into traffic, heading toward I-80. She

would take it east, until she turned off to drive into Fool's Gold.

"Sort of," she said and tightened her grip on the steering wheel.

Over the years, she'd done her best not to lie to her son. Not about her past or his father. For the most part, she'd simply told him there were questions she wouldn't answer. At four or five, he'd been easily distracted. At eight, he'd been determined to find out the truth. Now he asked less, probably because he knew he couldn't wear her down. But she knew he wondered.

"I got an e-mail today," she announced. "You remember I told you that I have a brother?"

"Uh-huh. Roy. We don't ever see him."

"I know. He's a lot older and he left when I was twelve. I woke up one morning and he was gone. I never saw him again."

She still remembered her mother's sobs, made thicker and louder by the alcohol lingering in her system. From that moment on, her mother spent her life waiting for Roy to return. Nothing else had mattered, certainly not Liz.

Liz had left town shortly after graduating high school. She'd phoned home once, a few weeks later, saying she thought she should check in and tell her mother where she was.

"Don't bother calling again," had been the woman's only response before hanging up the phone.

"So Uncle Roy e-mailed you?"

"Not exactly." Liz didn't know how much to reveal. Telling the truth was one thing, but sharing details was another. "He's, um, in some trouble and I have to help. He has two girls. Your cousins. Melissa is fourteen and Abby is your age."

"I have cousins? You didn't tell me about cousins."

"I didn't know about them until today."

"But they're family."

True enough, she thought. And the word *family* implied caring and connection. Maybe in most places, but not in the Sutton household. At least not until Liz had had Tyler. She'd done everything she could think of to break the cycle of neglect. She'd been determined to be a warm, loving mother, to offer her child a safe haven.

"I didn't know where Roy was," she said. "He never got in touch with me after he left." For six years, she'd waited, hoping he would come get her and take her away. Until he'd walked out, he'd always taken care of her. Been a buffer between her and her mother. Protected her from the worst of it.

By the time she'd been old enough to go looking, she told herself she no longer cared.

"Do they know we're coming?" Tyler asked. "Do they know about me?"

"Not yet, but they will. We're going to stay with them for a couple of weeks." She didn't mention the fact that Roy was in prison. Time enough for that later. Nor did she discuss the possibility of the girls living with them permanently. Maybe other family could take care of them.

"I grew up in a small town called Fool's Gold," she said. "It's in the foothills of the Sierra Nevada mountains."

"Do they get snow?" he asked eagerly. Because at age eleven, seeing snow was about the best it could be.

She laughed. "Probably not in June, but yes, they get snow. There's lots to do there. Hiking, swimming. There's a river and a lake."

"We could go camping."

She made a noncommittal noise in her throat, mostly because the thought of camping ranked right up there with being awake during open-heart surgery. Not even thinking about it was pleasant. But then she wasn't an eleven-year-old boy. She hadn't been fascinated by worms and dirt and play cars and plastic guns, either.

More traits she knew he got from his father. Which was another problem. Not the traits, the man himself. Odds were Ethan was still in Fool's Gold. The one place he'd asked her not to be. He'd made it clear he didn't want her or his kid around.

Well, he was just going to have to get over it, she told herself. This was an emergency. She wouldn't make a big deal about Tyler being in town and she certainly wouldn't tell her son about his father. Not when Ethan had rejected them both so completely.

She would deal with the girls and get out as quickly as possible. If she happened to run into Ethan, she would be pleasant and distant. Nothing more. Because after all this time and all the ways he'd managed to hurt her, there was no way she would ever be vulnerable to him again. She'd learned her lesson. Fool me once and all that.

She gripped the steering wheel tighter and glanced at her nav system screen. It showed the way to her destination and she was counting on the little device to guide her back home when she was done.

ETHAN HENDRIX STOOD BY THE barricades between the crowd and the cyclists. The sun was hot, the spectators loud. The noise of a race was specific and not something he would ever forget. There'd been a time when he'd planned on seeing the world on the racing circuit. A long time ago, he thought, remembering the feel of the wind, the sensation of muscles burning as he dug for the will to win.

Winning had come easily. Maybe too easily. He'd gotten careless during a race. At fifty miles an hour, balanced on skinny wheels and a lightweight frame, mistakes could be deadly. In his case, he'd been left with a few broken bones and a permanent limp. For anyone else, it would have been considered lucky. For him, the injury had kept him from ever racing again.

Now, ten years later, he watched the cyclists speed past. He spotted his friend Josh, still making up time from his late start, and wondered *What if.* But he didn't have a whole lot of energy for the subject. Everything was different now and he was good with that.

He turned away from the race, ready to return to his office, when he spotted a woman in the crowd. For a second he thought he'd imagined her, that he was putting beautiful features he would never forget onto the face of someone else. There was no way Liz Sutton was back in Fool's Gold.

Instinctively he moved closer, but the road with the barricades was between them. The redhead looked up again, this time facing him. She removed her sunglasses and he saw her wide green eyes, the full mouth. From this distance he couldn't see the freckles on her nose, but he knew they were there. He even knew how many.

He swore softly. Liz was back. Except on the back cover of her books, he hadn't seen her in over a decade. As of five seconds ago, he would have told anyone who asked that he'd forgotten her, had gotten over her. She was his past.

She looked away then, as if searching for someone. Obviously not him, he thought, then grinned. Liz back in Fool's Gold. Who would have thought?

He eased his way through the crowd. He might not be able to find her now, but he had a feeling he knew where she would be later. He would meet her there and welcome her home. It was the least he could do.

LIZ KEPT A TIGHT HOLD ON Tyler's hand on their way to the local grocery store. The crowd around the bike race was big and seemed to be growing. She'd been foolish to think she could find two girls she'd never met in the throng of tourists. It wasn't as if she even knew what they looked like.

She pointed toward a vendor selling shaved iced and bought Tyler his favorite flavor. Blueberry.

All around them, groups of people laughed and talked about the race. She heard something about a new bike racing school and a new hospital being built. Changes, she thought. Fool's Gold had changed in the past ten years.

But not enough for her to forget. Despite having to detour around blocked roads, she easily found her way down side streets, and back toward the house where she'd grown up.

"You lived here before you went to San Francisco?" Tyler asked.

"Uh-huh. I grew up here."

"With my grandma Sutton?"

"Yes."

"She's dead now."

He spoke the words as information, because that's all they were to him. He'd never met Liz's mother.

When Liz had first left town at eighteen, running away with a broken heart, she'd found her way to the city by the bay, had struggled to find work and a place to stay in a glorified shelter. Then she'd found out she was pregnant.

Her first instinct had been to go home, but that initial

phone call had made her wary. Over the next year, she'd phoned home twice. Both times her mother had made it clear her daughter was no longer a part of her life. The rejection had hurt but hadn't been much of a surprise. Her mother had also taken great delight in telling her that no, Ethan Hendrix never called or asked about her.

When the woman died four years ago, Liz hadn't cried, though she felt regret over the relationship they never had.

Now, as she crossed a quiet street, she found herself in her old neighborhood. The houses were modest, two- and three-bedroom homes with small porches and aging paint. A few gleamed like bright flowers in an abandoned garden, as if the neighborhood was on the verge of being desirable again.

The worst house on the street sat in the middle. An eyesore of peeling paint and missing roof shingles. The yard was more weeds than plants or lawn, the windows were filthy. Plywood filled the space where one was missing.

She used the key she'd found under the front mat to let them in. She'd already done a brief tour of the house, to see if the girls were there. Judging from the school books piled on the dirty kitchen table and the clothes on the girls' bedroom floors, she would guess summer break hadn't started yet.

Now she walked through to the kitchen with tonight's meal. Half the cabinets were gone, as if some- one had started remodeling then changed his mind. The refrigerator worked, but was empty. There was no food in the pantry in the corner. There were a few potato chip wrappers in the trash and one small apple on the counter.

She didn't know what to think. Based on her niece's letter, the girls had been on their own for a few weeks. Ever since their stepmom had taken off. With their father in jail and no other family around, shouldn't the state step in? Where were social services?

She had more questions, but figured she would deal with them later. It was after four. The girls should get home soon. Once they'd all met, she would get more food in the house and figure out what was going on.

"Mom?" Tyler called from the living room. "May I watch TV?"

"Until your cousins get here."

Peggy had already called to confirm she'd paid all the amounts due on the utility bills and that everything should be working. Liz could see there was electricity. She turned on the faucet and water gushed out, which was a plus. Seconds later, she heard the sound of cartoons, which meant there was cable. Modern life as she knew it had been restored.

She walked back to the front of the house and took the stairs to the second floor. She made her way straight to the master. It was the only room with family photos. A wedding picture of a much older Roy standing next to a chubby blonde had been placed on the battered dresser. There were a couple of school pictures of the girls. Liz moved closer and studied them, looking for features that would be familiar.

Melissa seemed to have Roy's smile. Abby had Liz's eyes and freckles. They were both redheads, Melissa blessed with a soft auburn color. Abby was all carrot-top, which looked totally adorable. Although Liz had a feeling the eleven-year-old wouldn't appreciate her unique coloring for a long time.

She turned away from the photos to look at the room. The bed was unmade, the dresser drawers open and empty. In the surprisingly large closet, only men's clothes hung. A couple of boxes were filled with socks and underwear—most likely placed there by Roy's wife.

Memories crowded around, filling the space. They poked at her as she moved back into the hallway, then into the bedroom that had been hers, making her remember things she'd tried so hard to forget.

She heard echoes of her mother yelling, inhaled the smell of alcohol. She remembered the low voices of the men who had come and gone. Most of her mother's "friends" had stayed out of Liz's way, but a few had watched her with an intensity that had made her uncomfortable.

She went into the room that had been hers. The wall color was different. The faded yellow had been replaced with a pale lavender. While the walls were freshly painted, the baseboards and trim had been sanded, but not finished. In the bathroom across the hall, the floor had been pulled up, exposing sheets of plywood below. She'd noticed a framed room off the back, sitting on a poured foundation. So many half-started projects that gave the already old and battered house the air of being wounded.

Easily changed, she told herself. A good contractor could have this place fixed in a few weeks. Or maybe the old house should simply be torn down and left for dead.

She shook off the morose thoughts. She'd been here all of an hour and already the place was getting to her. She had to remember she had a great life in San Francisco. Work she loved, a beautiful home, an amazing son. She'd left Fool's Gold over a decade ago. She was a different person today. Older. Stronger. Able to deal with a few memories. It wasn't as if she was settling here permanently. She would find out what was going on, then either take the girls to wherever they were going to live, or pack them up and bring them back to her place. A couple weeks, she told herself. Three at most.

She went downstairs and heard the sound of excited voices. There were racing footsteps on the porch, then the front door flew open.

Two girls stood there, the taller and older one looking both scared and relieved, while the younger hung back shyly.

"Aunt Liz?" Melissa, the fourteen-year-old, asked tentatively.

Liz smiled at them both and nodded. "Hi. I hope it's okay that I let myself in. The key was right where—"

The rest of what she was going to say got squeezed out of her as both girls raced to her and hugged her hard, holding on as if they would never let go.

CHAPTER TWO

LIZ HUGGED THEM BACK, recognizing the relief and desperation in their embrace. They were too young to have been left on their own. What had Roy's wife been thinking?

She mentally added that question to the growing list she would deal with later. For now she wanted the girls to feel safe and get them fed.

"You're really here," Melissa said, looking at her. "Really?"

"Yes. I got your e-mail this morning and came right away."

Melissa, thin and nearly as tall as Liz, drew in a breath. "I'm really glad. I was trying so hard to make it okay, but I couldn't. The money Bettina left us ran out really fast."

Abby, a little shorter and also thin, bit her lower lip. "Are you our aunt?"

"I am. Your dad's my brother."

"You're famous."

Liz laughed. "Not really."

"But you have books in the library. I've seen 'em."

Abby glanced at her sister. "I don't read them because Melissa says they'll give me bad dreams."

Liz reached out and touched the girl's cheek. "I think she's right. But maybe when you're older."

"Or you could write a book for girls my age."

"Something to think about." She looked past the girls and saw Tyler standing in the doorway to the hall. "Girls, you have a cousin. My son Tyler is with me. Tyler, these are your cousins, Melissa and Abby."

The girls turned. Tyler smiled.

"Hi," he said, sounding more curious than uneasy.

"Hi," the girls responded together.

"Tyler's eleven," Liz told them. "His last day of school was today."

Melissa wrinkled her nose. "We have to go until Friday. Then we're off for the summer."

A fact that would make life easier, Liz thought. If she ended up taking the girls back to San Francisco, she wouldn't have to worry about pulling them out of school.

Abby turned back to her. "Where's Tyler's dad, Aunt Liz?"

Not a question Liz wanted to deal with right now. She saw her son's expression sharpen, as if hoping she would share some information. Not likely, she thought, wishing things had been different and Ethan had at least wanted to be a small part of his son's life.

"Not with us," Liz stated lightly. "Why don't we go into the kitchen and get you two something to eat? I picked up a cooked chicken and some salads on the way into town. Then we'll get to know each other a little and you can tell me what's been going on."

She had more to say, but both girls ran into the kitchen, as if desperate for food. Based on how they'd been living, they probably were.

She served them each a large portion of the chicken, along with coleslaw and potato salad.

The girls fell on the food, practically shoving it in their mouths. Liz poured the milk she'd bought and they gulped two glasses each. As she watched them devour the meal, she felt herself getting angry. How could Roy's wife have simply abandoned the girls like that? What kind of heartless cow left two kids on their own? The least she could have done was phone social services on her way out of town.

She decided she would find out all she could about Bettina then kill off a character just like her in her next book. The death would be grisly, she promised herself. Slow and painful.

Tyler watched the girls wide-eyed, but didn't say anything. He seemed to sense they'd been hungry for a long time, which was sad but probably a good lesson for him. Not everyone got to have three meals a day.

Liz took in their worn, not-very-clean T-shirts. Their jeans had seen better days, as well, and their sandals were in need of replacing. She knew most fourteen-year-old girls would be humiliated to be without stylish clothes and at least a hint of makeup. Was Melissa without both by choice?

When the feeding frenzy slowed, Liz settled across from Melissa. Tyler stood by Liz's shoulder and she wrapped her arm around his waist.

"How long has Bettina been gone?" Liz asked.

"A while. Nearly three months. She left us with one hundred dollars. When that ran out…" Melissa dropped her gaze to her plate, then pushed it away.

Liz thought about the potato chip wrappers in the trash. The small apple on the counter. If there wasn't any money and no one was taking care of them, there was only one way they could have survived. Melissa had been stealing from local stores.

"We'll talk about that later," Liz offered. "Privately. We can talk to the store owners and explain. I'll pay them back."

Melissa flushed, then swallowed. "I, um… Thanks, Aunt Liz."

"How about just calling me Liz? Aunt Liz is too long."

"Okay. Thanks, Liz."

"Did your friends know Bettina was gone?"

Abby shook her head. "Melissa said not to tell. She said we'd be taken away and put in different homes. That we'd never find our way back to each other."

"I wasn't going to let them take Abby from me," Melissa claimed fiercely, her green eyes flashing with determination.

An admirable sentiment, if slightly impractical when the alternative was starving. Of course Liz might be the wrong person to make a judgment on the issue. She'd adored her big brother and he'd taken off without a word, leaving her behind.

"A couple of my friends figured it out," Melissa admitted. "They would bring us food sometimes. It's been hard. I really thought I could take care of us both."

"It's a big responsibility," Liz conceded. "You did the best you could, but the situation was impossible. I'm glad you e-mailed me."

Abby grinned. "She's read all your books, just like Dad. He has them all upstairs. Can we go see him?"

"Let me find out what's going on first," Liz explained, stalling for time. She didn't even know where Roy was, let alone what he'd been convicted of or where he was incarcerated.

"Dad's really proud of you," Melissa told her shyly. "He talked about you all the time."

Liz wasn't sure how she felt about that. Roy's pride hadn't extended to getting in touch with her. As his daughters had proven, finding her wasn't all that hard.

Abby raised her face to the ceiling. "The lights are on." She grinned. "It won't be dark anymore."

"Everything's back on," Liz confirmed. "Even cable."

Their eyes lit up. "We can watch TV?" Abby asked.

Tyler looked at Liz and grinned as if to point out he wasn't the only kid who wanted to watch TV all the time.

"Not until your homework is done," Tyler informed

them. "And not every night." He sighed heavily, as if his life was pain.

Liz laughed. "It's true. I insist on reading nights every week, where we just sit quietly and read."

"I like to read," Melissa said. "But Dad and Bettina let us watch TV all the time."

An issue she would address later, Liz thought. "If you two are done, why don't you take your plates to the sink and rinse them? Then we can make a list and go to the grocery store."

When they'd rinsed their plates, she sent Tyler to see if the upstairs bathroom had toilet paper and Abby out to the garage to check if there was any laundry detergent by the old washer. She and Melissa sat back at the table and started to make a list.

"We'll get the basics," Liz began. "But not too much. I'm not sure how long we'll be here."

Melissa frowned as she flipped her long hair over her shoulder. "We're not leaving. I'm not going to let anyone separate me and Abby."

Liz touched her arm. "I'm not suggesting anything like that. But you can't stay here alone. You have to live with an adult or two. I'll talk to your dad about the situation."

"What about you?" Melissa stared at the table as she asked the question.

"I don't know. If there's other family, then we'll have options to explore. If not, then you and Abby will be coming back to San Francisco with me."

Melissa sprang to her feet. "No. We won't go. We live here. In Fool's Gold." Tears filled her eyes.

Liz rose. "I'm sorry. I shouldn't have said that. Everything is still new and we haven't even gotten to know each other. Let's not worry about anything more than today."

"I won't go. Neither will Abby." Melissa looked defiant, despite the tears. "I mean it, Liz. You can't make us."

Liz knew that if she ended up with custody of the girls, she could and would, but there was no point in pushing hard now.

"I understand," Liz assured calmly. "As I said, let me talk to your dad and figure out where we are. I won't do anything without talking to you first. Can we put this on hold for a bit?"

Melissa looked as if she wanted to argue, but nodded slowly.

Liz took her seat and turned back to the list. "Shampoo and conditioner?" she asked.

Melissa sank into the chair across from her. "We're out of them, too."

Liz made a note. "You'll have to show me what you like. What about makeup?"

It was a bribe, plain and simple, but she figured both she and Melissa had earned the break.

"I, ah, don't wear that much, but I'd like to."

Liz smiled. "We'll get mascara and lip gloss when we go out, but later in the week, we'll make a serious drugstore run and get some fun stuff to play with."

Melissa leaned close. "Do you have highlights?"

Liz fingered her layered, wavy hair. It fell just past her shoulders—a length that allowed her to pull it back, put it up or go crazy with the hot rollers and have beauty pageant curls.

"A few. Our hair is about the same color. A bit of reddish gold adds dimension." Liz shrugged. "You're pretty without any help, but in a few years, you'll be looking for more."

Melissa flushed. "Abby hates her hair. It's so red."

"She'll grow into it. When you're young, it's hard to be different."

"That's what my mom used to say." Melissa pressed her lips together as she twisted her fingers. "She died."

"I'm sorry."

"It was a long time ago. Abby doesn't remember her."

"But you do."

Melissa nodded.

Liz wondered about the woman her brother had married and where he'd been all this time. When had he come back to Fool's Gold? Had it been when their mother had died? Liz suspected she'd left the house to him. But how had anyone known how to get in touch with him? Unless he'd been in touch with their mother and she hadn't known.

More questions for later, she told herself.

Tyler clattered down the stairs. "No toilet paper," he announced. "And there isn't soap in the shower."

He sounded both shocked and delighted by the strangeness.

Abby returned to the kitchen to say there wasn't any laundry detergent, either.

"I don't know if my car's big enough for all we'll have to buy," Liz teased brightly. "We may have to tie one of you on the roof of the car to make room."

Abby looked a little startled, but Tyler laughed. "I'll do it. Tie me on the roof, Mom."

"Thank you for volunteering."

Abby glanced between them, then smiled shyly, as if getting the joke. "You could tie me, too."

"Why thank you," Liz said, touching her cheek. "That's very thoughtful of you. Okay—are we ready? I was thinking we'd have spaghetti for dinner. How does that sound?"

"My favorite," Tyler yelled.

"Mine, too," Abby said.

"With garlic bread?" Melissa asked.

"It wouldn't be spaghetti if there wasn't garlic bread," Liz told her.

Melissa grinned.

ONE SHOPPING TRIP, A DINNER and shared kitchen cleanup later, Liz supervised the kids settling in for the evening. Melissa had one last assignment for school, while Abby and Tyler sat on the sofa downstairs to watch a movie.

Liz poured herself a second glass of wine, then

carried it out front. While her nieces were great, the situation was intense and she felt the need to be alone for a few minutes.

She walked to the edge of the porch and sat with her feet on the second step. The night was clear, the stars much bigger and closer than they appeared in San Francisco. Here there weren't big city lights to dilute the heavens. She could make out the mountains to the east, rising miles into the sky. The very tops seemed to almost brush the twinkling stars.

The sound of the movie carried to her, a safe sound. Abby and Melissa were good kids dealing with an impossible situation. Her anger at the absent Bettina grew every second. How could an adult simply walk away from two girls like that? Even if she didn't want them herself, she could have done *something* to make sure they were taken care of.

Part of Liz wanted to call the police and report the woman, but she wouldn't. Not until everything was straightened out. Getting social services involved at this point was a complication no one needed. Besides, she wanted to talk to Roy first.

At dinner Melissa had mentioned her father was at Folsom. Despite the fact that Johnny Cash had made the place famous with a song, the facility was old and very much a prison. Liz had researched the prison for one of her books. She still had several contacts there which would mean getting in to see her brother would be relatively easy.

But knowing that didn't make the idea of seeing him after all this time anymore comfortable. What was she supposed to say?

She shook off the question and returned her attention to the beautiful night. That was easier than thinking about the past, or hey, even the present. After all this time, she was back in Fool's Gold. Who would have thought?

The grocery shopping had been uneventful. Only one shopper had recognized her enough to call her by name. The older woman hadn't been the least bit familiar to Liz, but she remembered enough of small-town life to pretend to be delighted at the meeting. The woman had commented on how nice it was that she'd come back for Roy's girls.

An innocent comment, Liz thought as she sipped her wine. There was no reason for her to want to snap at the other woman, ask her how it was possible that an entire town hadn't noticed two girls living on their own. Of course this was the same town that had seen plenty of bruises on her arms and legs and no one had asked any questions back then, either.

"Don't go there," she whispered. She was here to help Roy's girls and get out as quickly as possible. Nothing else.

She heard someone walking on the sidewalk. In-stinctively, she stiffened before reminding herself that this was Fool's Gold, and no one ever got mugged here. She looked up to see a man walking by. Only he didn't keep walking. He stopped at her front gate and let himself in. The wineglass nearly slipped from her fingers as she watched Ethan Hendrix stroll toward her.

"Hello, Liz."

He was as tall and handsome as she'd remembered. Broader and a little older, but only in that good way men age. It was too dark for her to make out his exact features, but if she had to guess, she would say he was happy to see her. At least he was smiling.

She blinked, not sure he was real, but the image didn't go away, which was confusing. Why would Ethan be pleased she was back in town?

She clutched her wine in both hands. Standing up made the most sense and was also polite, but she wasn't sure she could manage it. Her legs felt a little wobbly as she stared at the first man she'd ever loved. If she'd had another glass of wine, she probably would have admitted he was the only man she'd ever loved, but why go there now?

"Ethan," she said, startled to have his name on her lips after all this time. She'd yelled at him, cursed him, cried for him and begged—but only in her mind. In the past twelve years, she'd never once spoken his name. Except once…to his wife.

"I thought I saw you earlier," he revealed, moving closer and shoving his hands in his front pockets, a smile tugging at his lips. "At the race. I tried to get to you, but there was too much of a crowd. You're back." The smile turned into a grin. "You look good."

She looked what?

Gathering all her strength, she set the glass on the porch, then pushed to her feet. After crossing her arms over her chest, she realized she still had to tilt her head slightly to meet his gaze. Time had not caused him to shrink.

"It's not what you think," she began. "I'm not here to make trouble."

Confusion flickered across his face. "Why would you be?"

"I'm here because of my brother and his daughters. This isn't about anything between us."

The grin faded into a straight line. "About that," he reflected, then shrugged. "I was a kid and a jerk. I'm sorry."

As apologies went, it wasn't much of one. Not when compared to his incredible rejection of both her and their son, but Ethan had never been big on accepting responsibility for his relationships.

For him, it was all about how things looked. After all, he was a Hendrix. A member of the founding family. Upholder of all things good and right. A girl from the wrong side of the tracks was good enough to sleep with, but a guy like Ethan would never want anything more.

"Whatever," she muttered. "I didn't know my brother had moved back and I didn't know about his daughters. Until Melissa wrote me. That's why I'm here. It'll be two weeks. Three at most. I'll stay out of your way, just like you asked." Commanded was more like it, but this didn't seem like a good time to bring that up. She was tired and dealing with too much already. A fight with Ethan would only complicate the situation.

She shook her head, her temper rising just a little. "But I will point out you don't own the town, and you don't have any right to tell me where I can or can't be."

"I know," he said, moving a step toward her. "Would it help if I said I have no idea what you're talking about?"

The lazy smile returned. The one that always had the ability to make her stomach flip over a couple dozen times.

"I wanted to welcome you back," he continued. "And tell you I think it's great you've been successful with your books. Even though I'm not sure I like the part where you kill me over and over again."

Now he wasn't the only one who was confused, she thought. He wanted to talk about her *books?*

"You deserved it," she retorted. "And technically I haven't killed you at all."

"Then why do your victims always have a more than passing resemblance to me?"

"I don't know what you're talking about." Which was a lie.

"Right."

The smile left again as he took another step toward her. A step that put him a little too close.

"Eleven years ago I was a jerk," he said. "I admit it and I'm sorry. That's what I came by to say."

"What?" She dropped her hands to her hips and glared at him. "That's it? After everything that happened the last time I came to town you want to talk about *that?*"

His eyebrows drew together. "What last time?"

"Five years ago, I came back to speak to you. Instead I had a very awkward conversation with your wife. You were out of town. Then I received your letter a few days later."

The frown deepened. "What?"

She wanted to shriek. "I came here to talk to you. To tell you about Tyler. I saw Rayanne, who said you were out of town. About ten days later, I got a letter from you telling me you didn't want anything to do with either of us. To stay away from Fool's Gold and that if I came back, you'd make sure I regretted it."

The frown turned into an expression of dismissal. "I accept that what I did all those years ago was stupid and mean, and I'm sorry. As for this crap—don't bring my wife into your stories."

She stiffened. "Stories? You think I'm lying? I spoke to your wife five years ago. You wrote me a letter. I still have it."

He shook his head. "I didn't write you a letter. You didn't see—" He hesitated. "I don't know if you saw Rayanne or not. I could have been traveling. I saw you in town earlier today, so I came by to say hello and apologize. That's it." His gaze sharpened. "Who's Tyler? Your husband? You're married?"

Oh, God. Liz sank back on the step. Thoughts and

memories flooded her, making it impossible to pick just one. The early past intruded first—reminding her how much she'd once loved Ethan. How he'd convinced her to trust him, had told her that he loved her. She'd given herself to him on a starry night, by the lake. Desperate emotion hadn't been enough to make her first time not hurt, and he'd held her when she had cried.

They'd planned on her joining him at his college, because being together in Fool's Gold was impossible. Not that his family was especially rich, but because they were respectable. Something Liz Sutton could never be.

She remembered him and his friends at the diner where she worked after school. How his friend Josh had mentioned seeing Ethan with her. As clearly as if it was happening right now, in front of her, she recalled Ethan's discomfort. He'd said she was a piece of ass— but not anyone he could be interested in. He'd denied her, had denied *them.* She'd heard every word.

Maybe if she'd been older she would have understood why he'd said what he did. Or if he'd been more mature or stronger, he could have stood up to his friends. Instead he had hurt her and she'd reacted. She'd walked over to the table, picked up the chocolate milk shake she'd brought him only minutes before and thrown it in his face. Then she'd walked out. She'd quit her job, packed a bag and run away to San Francisco.

Three weeks later, she'd figured out she was pregnant. She'd returned to town, prepared to tell Ethan, only to find him in bed with someone else. She'd run again. This time she'd been determined to make it on her own. But five years ago, as Tyler had been getting ready to enter first grade, she'd decided to make another attempt to tell Ethan. Which had led to the conversation with his wife and the letter telling her that he didn't want anything to do with her and his son.

None of this made sense, she thought. Ethan was many things, but stupid wasn't one of them. He wouldn't just forget about his own child. Unless he really hadn't been told. Which meant his wife had kept the information of Liz's visit from him.

"Liz?" His voice was low. "What's going on?"

"I don't know." She pushed to her feet. "At the risk of repeating myself, Rayanne never told you that I came to see you?"

"That's right."

"You never wrote me a letter."

"No."

"So you don't know about any of this?"

"Any of what?" he asked.

She sucked in a breath. She'd known there was a good chance she would run into Ethan again. Or his wife. Or both. But she'd never imagined anything like this.

"I came back to see you five years ago," she began. "No, I came back a few weeks after I left, but you were in bed with Pia."

"What?" He stiffened. "I didn't..." He half turned away, then faced her again. "It's not what you think."

"I thought you were both naked and in bed," she said, struggling to keep her voice even. "It doesn't matter. Screwing around with Pia isn't the point."

"I didn't screw around."

"No? Then your intense and meaningful relationship isn't the point, either. I came back to tell you that I was pregnant. When I saw you in bed with Pia, I took off. I was too hurt, too angry. You'd denied me in public and then slept with one of the girls who delighted in tormenting me."

She squared her shoulders. "More irrelevance, right? The point is, I always wanted you to know. So I showed up here five years ago to tell you about Tyler. I spoke to Rayanne and told her. Then I got a letter from you saying you didn't want anything to do with me or Tyler and to stay away from town." A letter apparently written by Rayanne.

Ethan stared at her as if he'd never seen her before. Emotions flashed across his face. Disbelief, confusion, anger.

"Tyler isn't your husband?"

"He's my son. Your son. He's eleven. And he's here."

CHAPTER THREE

ETHAN HEARD THE WORDS BUT THEY made no sense to him. Son? As in a kid? An eleven-year-old boy who was his?

"You never told me."

The words came from him, although he couldn't feel himself speaking. He was still trying to make sense of the information. A baby? No. Not a baby. A child. His child.

"I did tell you," Liz reiterated, putting her hands back on her hips, looking as if she was prepared to take him on. "I just explained that. I'll admit I didn't make much of an effort when I came back the first time, but the whole naked-in-bed-with-Pia was more than I could handle. I came back a second time."

"Stop." He glared at her, anger growing. "You're lying."

"I told you—I still have the letter. I can have my assistant send it overnight. It will be here day after tomorrow."

He knew there wasn't a letter, mostly because he'd never written one.

He turned and walked back to the gate, before facing the house again. Liz stood silhouetted in the glare of the porch light. He'd been so damned happy to see her. He'd wanted to come talk to her. Now this.

"How the hell can you stand there and tell me I have an eleven-year-old son I've never known about?" He stalked toward her, fury growing. "You didn't bother to tell me that you were pregnant? What gives you the right?" He swore.

"I did try to tell you," she countered. "You were too busy screwing Pia."

He grabbed her arm. "I don't care if I was burning down the entire town. You were pregnant with my child, and I had the right to know."

She jerked free. He let her, mostly because of how he'd been raised. It was the right thing to do.

"I cared," she snapped. "I cared a lot. You were supposed to love me. You convinced me it was safe to love you back. You took my virginity, then let someone call me a whore in front of all your friends."

"None of that matters."

"Of course it matters. It speaks to who you are as a person. It's the reason I didn't try very hard."

The unfairness of the accusation burned. "I was a kid," he growled.

"So was I. Eighteen, alone and pregnant. If you expect a break, then I get one, too."

"No. It's not the same. He's my child. You deliberately kept us apart for years."

Liz drew in a breath and nodded slowly. "I know. That's why I came back to tell you five years ago."

He didn't believe the bullshit story about talking to Rayanne. He didn't care about anything except he had a son.

He pushed past her and headed for the door. "I want to see him."

"No!" Liz grabbed his arm and held on with both hands. "Ethan, wait. Not like this. You can't just walk in there and blurt it all out. He's only eleven. You'll scare him."

He could have kept walking. She didn't have the physical strength to stop him, but as her words filtered through the haze of anger and resentment, he recognized that something—or someone—was more important than both of them.

Tyler.

He stopped.

She released him, then came around so they were facing each other again. "I'm shocked, too. And sorry about all of this. I swear I thought you knew."

"I want to meet him."

"I agree. But we need a plan. He has to be prepared."

He narrowed his gaze. "You lost your right to decide what happens the day you chose to keep him from me."

She raised her chin. "That's where you're wrong. This isn't a game. We're talking about a child's life. As for rights, I'm his mother and you're not on his birth certificate."

He'd never wanted to hit a woman before. Never wanted to punish one. Intense rage grew until it nearly overwhelmed him.

"I'm not saying I don't want you to have a relationship with him," she continued. "I do. That's why I came back before. Of course I want that. I'm pissed, too. You said you loved me and yet you never bothered to look for me when I ran away. Based on what I saw with Pia, did you even miss me at all?"

"What does that matter?" He swore again, then took a step back. "You stole eleven years from me, Liz. Stole time and memories I can never get back. Do you really think hurt feelings from high school come close to measuring up to that?"

"I'll accept responsibility for the first few years," she told him. "But not the last five. Why do you refuse to believe me? I was here. I spoke to Rayanne. I'll show you the letter as soon as it gets here. In the meantime, go talk to your wife."

He stared at her. Of course. She wouldn't know. "Rayanne is dead."

Her eyes widened. "Oh, God. I'm sorry."

He glanced up at the house, wanting nothing more than to break in and take what was his. He might loathe Liz with every part of him, but she was right about one thing—Tyler was the only one who mattered in this situation. Bursting in and grabbing him would only terrify the kid. Ethan wanted a better start than that.

Not that he should have to worry about that, he

thought grimly. If he'd known about Tyler, he would have been there from the beginning. Been a father.

"I'll be by tomorrow after work," he said quietly. "I want to meet him then." He met her gaze. "No excuses."

She nodded. "I'll tell him tomorrow, prepare him."

"Going to make me an asshole?"

"Of course not."

"What have you told him before now?"

"Nothing. I wouldn't lie to him. I told him there were things I wouldn't talk about. He doesn't always like that answer, but he accepts it."

Because he didn't have a choice, Ethan thought, still fighting fury. Liz had controlled the situation, done whatever she wanted. Well, that was about to change. He would make sure of it.

"You'll be here?" he asked, not putting it past her to leave town. What was different was this time he *would* follow, chasing her to the ends of the earth, if necessary. She'd already stolen too much from him.

"I'll be here," she said. "I swear."

He gave a hollow laugh. "Because your word means something?"

She dug in her jeans front pocket and pulled out her car keys. "Want to hang on to these? Will that make you feel better?"

It might, but it wasn't necessary. "I have your license number. If you try to sneak away, I'll have you hauled back for kidnapping."

An empty threat. If she was telling the truth—if he

really wasn't on Tyler's birth certificate—then his rights were probably limited. But if she pushed him, he would do everything in his power to make it happen. Tyler was his son—and Ethan took care of what was his.

A voice in the back of his head whispered if he'd been as willing to claim Liz, none of this would have happened. He would have known about Tyler from the beginning.

A fact that might be true, he told himself, but didn't erase what she'd done.

"Ethan, please." She gazed into his eyes. "We have to work together. Make this right for Tyler."

"I agree, but don't expect me to ever understand or forgive you, Liz. You played God with my life and my son's life. I hope there's a special place in hell for you."

She flinched as if he'd hit her. He didn't care. Instead he walked toward the sidewalk, stopping when he reached the gate. "I'll be back tomorrow at six. Don't make things worse than they are."

And then he was gone.

LIZ REACHED FOR HER COFFEE. She usually tried to limit herself to one or two cups a day, but after a sleepless night, she had a feeling she was going to exceed her limit before noon.

She'd been an idiot. She accepted that. What she really didn't like was the reality that she'd been thoughtless and cruel—characteristics she would have claimed weren't a part of who she was.

Ethan's parting shot—that she'd played God with both him and her son—had been a direct hit. One she'd been unable to forget. Guilt was powerful. Despite the fact that she'd come back to tell him everything five years ago, he'd still lost the first six years of Tyler's life.

The time couldn't be made up, as he'd said more than once. And she regretted that. But now everything was worse. Apparently Rayanne hadn't told Ethan about Liz coming to town at all. There hadn't been a second rejection, this time of both her and her son. Not that it mattered. Ethan obviously didn't believe her. Still, she would call Peggy and have the letter sent overnight. An easy solution to only part of the problem. If only she could explain away the first six years as easily.

She heard footsteps on the stairs and got the milk out of the refrigerator. She'd already put a couple boxes of cereal on the table, along with bowls and spoons.

Melissa entered the kitchen first, her jeans and T-shirt clean from the loads of laundry Liz had finished the evening before, her hair shiny and bouncy. She moved to the table.

"Good morning," Liz said, forcing herself to smile. Her trouble with Ethan had nothing to do with the girls.

"Hi." Melissa moved to the table but didn't sit down. "You're still here."

"Why wouldn't I be?"

Melissa shrugged as she pulled out a chair. "You didn't sleep upstairs. In my dad's room."

The thought of sleeping in the same bed as her

brother and her mother before him had totally creeped her out. Which wasn't the point. Obviously Melissa had gotten up to check on her.

"Sometimes I like to work at night," she detailed, which was true but not the reason she'd chosen the sofa in the living room over the bed in the master bedroom. "Being downstairs seemed easier."

"I thought you'd left."

Melissa didn't look at her as she spoke.

Liz crossed to her and put her hand on the teenager's shoulders. "I'm not abandoning you or Abby. I know it's going to take a while for you to believe me, but you can trust me."

"Okay."

"I mean it," Liz declared firmly. "We're going to figure this out together. You don't have a cell phone, do you?"

Melissa shook her head.

"We'll get you one after school and program my number in. Then you can always get me. Would that help?"

Melissa brightened. "I'd be able to call my friends, right?"

"Yes."

"And text?"

Liz smiled. "As long as you promise to stop before your thumbs fall off."

"I can do that." The teen pulled a box of breakfast cereal toward her.

"Then we have a deal."

Abby burst into the room and ran over to Liz, then hugged her. "Do I have to go to school?"

"Yes. You have, what? Three days left? You'll survive."

Abby grinned. "I knew you'd say that."

"But you thought you'd ask anyway?"

"Uh-huh."

The girl sat across from her sister and reached for the cereal.

It didn't take either of them long to eat breakfast. After they put their bowls in the sink, Liz reached for her purse. "We didn't get anything for lunch, so do you mind buying?"

The sisters looked at each other, then laughed.

"We can buy lunch," Melissa agreed happily. "That would be, like, totally great."

Liz wondered how long they'd been going without lunch. Couldn't they have gone into a free lunch program? Of course that would have meant someone knowing there was a problem in the first place.

She handed them each ten dollars, then walked them out to the gate. They waved and promised to be home right after school.

"We can bake cookies before dinner," she yelled after them.

When they'd turned the corner, she headed back into the house and made a note of the cell phone errand and started a second grocery list that included ingredients for chocolate chip cookies. Once that was done, she called Peggy to have her overnight Ethan's letter, along with some notes she'd left behind.

When she hung up, there was plenty of thunking from upstairs, telling her Tyler was up and making his way to the shower. She paced nervously until he came downstairs and she was forced to act normal, then she chatted with him through his breakfast.

"I thought we'd make cookies later," she told him, as he finished up his cereal. "When your cousins get home from school."

He grinned. "Sweet."

"Is that about the cookies, or the fact that they still have school and you don't?"

He laughed. "Both."

He got up and carried his bowl to the sink. After rinsing it, he looked for a dishwasher, then frowned when he didn't find one.

"What am I supposed to do with it?" he asked.

"Stack it in the sink," she instructed, thinking if this were a made-for-TV moment, she would be smoking and looking for her morning shot of Jack Daniels. "We're going to be washing dishes the old-fashioned way. By hand."

He looked confused, as if the concept was impossible to imagine. Liz agreed with him, but wasn't willing to buy one for the few weeks they would be in town. At least there was a microwave. A true necessity, she thought. Popcorn was required for movie night.

"What are we going to do today?" he asked, returning to the table.

"I thought we'd take a walk through town," she offered, studying his familiar features and wondering if anyone who saw him would guess the truth. To her he looked exactly like Ethan, but that could just be because she was looking for certain features. "Then you can play Xbox while I work."

His dark eyes crinkled. "I love summer vacation."

"I'm sure you do. But you aren't going to spend three months getting great at your favorite game." Once they were back in San Francisco, there would be classes and a couple of weeks at camp. Maybe there was a day program here she could get him in. And the girls, too, she thought. Although Melissa might be too old.

"How about two months?" Tyler suggested, wiggling his eyebrows. "And twenty-nine days."

"Unlikely." She drew in a breath and wished he was next to her so she could hold him tight. Because as soon as she said the words, everything was going to change. She knew that. The truth would change everything and they would never go back.

"I have to talk to you about something," she said, then added, "It's not bad."

"Okay."

He waited patiently, trusting her. Because she'd never lied to him, had never let him down. She annoyed him because she was the mom and there were rules, but that was different. Expected.

"You've asked me about your dad a lot," she began. "And I would never talk about him."

He wrinkled his nose. "I know."

"I'm ready to talk about him now."

Tyler had been leaning back in the kitchen chair. But then he sat up and stretched his arms toward her, his expression expectant. "My dad?"

She nodded. "He's, um, he's a good guy. A contractor. That's someone who builds things, like houses and—"

Tyler sighed heavily. "I know what a contractor is, Mom."

"Oh. Of course you do. Well, he's a contractor and he also builds windmills. The kind that generate electricity."

"Wind turbines."

"What?"

Tyler looked a little smug. "They're called wind turbines."

"Thank you." She shifted in her seat, wishing she didn't have to tell him and that everything could stay the same. Only that was selfish. Tyler deserved to know his dad and Ethan…well, he deserved to know his son, too.

"He lives here. In Fool's Gold. You're going to be meeting him tonight."

Tyler was out of the chair faster than light. He raced toward her, then threw himself at her and held on tight. "I'm meeting my dad? For real?"

"Yes. I saw him last night and he wants to meet you."

Tyler stared into her eyes. "Tonight?"

"At six."

An awkward time, she thought. They either had to eat really early or really late. Not that she would be in the mood for food and Tyler would probably be too excited, but the girls needed dinner.

She would make them something at five, she thought absently, pulling the shopping list toward her.

"My dad's coming here?"

"Uh-huh."

"You really saw him and everything?"

She hugged him, wishing she could hold on tight forever. "I did." She smoothed back his hair, then stared into his dark eyes. "Stuff with grown-ups gets complicated sometimes. I came back to talk to him about you when you were six. He wasn't here. He was away on business. So I told someone else about you and she promised to tell him, only she didn't."

That much was clear. Ethan had been beyond stunned by the news.

"She lied?" Tyler sounded shocked. He was still young enough that he believed most adults told the truth.

"She kept the truth to herself, which is pretty much the same thing. I thought he didn't want anything to do with us, but I was wrong. He's very excited to see you."

Tyler's eyes widened with hope. "You think he'll like me?"

"I think he'll adore you." She touched his cheek. "You look a lot like him. The dark hair and eyes."

"But I have your smile."

"Yes, you do and I want it back." She leaned in and tickled him.

He laughed at that as much as at the familiar and silly joke.

He leaned against her. "I wish I was still in school so I could tell everyone I have a dad, too."

"You'll tell them in September."

"Do you think Dad will come live with us in San Francisco?"

If she'd been standing she would have fallen on the spot. "Gee, ah, probably not. Your dad's life is here, in Fool's Gold. He has a big family. I don't know who still lives here. Probably his mom and I would guess a few of his sisters."

Tyler stared up at her. "There's more?"

There was an entire herd, she thought grimly. Because Ethan's relatives were also Tyler's. The thought made her a little nervous. How could she compete with an entire family? Not that it was a competition, she reminded herself. But still…

"You have two uncles, three aunts, who are triplets by the way, and a grandmother."

"Cool!"

"I know," she said with false excitement. "You'll have so much family, you won't know what to do with everyone."

"Anyone my age?"

"I don't think so. I don't know for sure. You can ask your dad."

There could be dozens, she reminded herself. Any of his siblings could have married. Ethan might have children from his marriage to Rayanne, although they would be younger.

She shook her head to force out the thought of her encounter with his late wife. There was enough going on without that messing with her mind.

Tyler spun away and pumped his arms. "This is the best, Mom. I have a dad. We're a family."

They were a lot of things, but Liz didn't think *family* qualified. Not with how much Ethan hated her.

"It's going to be interesting," she admitted. Perhaps not in a happy way, but that wasn't Tyler's problem.

"May I use the computer so I can send an e-mail to Jason?"

She nodded.

He ran out of the room. Seconds later, she heard the loud thundering of his steps on the old and creaking stairs.

At eleven, life was simple. A new dad was a great thing. There weren't any complications, no ambivalence, no worries about the future. While she couldn't seem to stop thinking about everything that could go wrong.

"Probably the reason I write what I do," she murmured as she rose and walked to the sink to tackle the morning dishes. Some days murder and mayhem suited her mood. She would work out her frustrations on a deserving victim, then have her character find justice in the end.

But this wasn't fiction—this was real life. And she had a feeling things weren't going to be tidied up quite so easily for her.

CHAPTER FOUR

ETHAN DID HIS BEST TO WORK BUT by ten in the morning he'd given up on the pretense. He wasn't fooling anyone, especially not himself. His sister Nevada had asked him twice if everything was all right. He'd told her that he was fine, but after spending twenty minutes doubling an order for lumber, only to realize it was for a job they'd completed two weeks ago, he knew he had to get out and clear his head.

"I'll be back in an hour," he yelled over his shoulder as he left the office.

"Don't hurry back," Nevada muttered, just loud enough for him to hear.

Normally he would have gone inside and called her on it, but not today. Not when he was still having trouble wrapping his mind around what had happened the night before.

He had a son, he thought, getting in his truck and starting the engine. A child. For eleven years and he'd never once known or imagined or guessed. All because Liz Sutton had kept the truth from him. Deliberately.

The rage that had poured through him the night

before ignited again, burning hot and bright. He forced himself to focus on his driving, to pay attention to little things like stop signs and other traffic, as he steered the truck through town.

Rather than go to his place, he went back to the house where he'd grown up. If anyone could talk him down, it was his mother. Denise Hendrix had raised six kids, surviving the loss of her husband, Ralph, nearly a decade ago. She was the heart of the family, the one everyone turned to when there was a problem. She was rational, thoughtful and would be able to give him a perspective other than his own. Because right now all he wanted was to take his son and bolt.

Not a smart plan, he told himself as he drove through the familiar neighborhood, then turned into the driveway.

He checked the clock on the dashboard of his truck. With all six kids out of the house, his mother had a lot more free time these days. Time she filled with classes and her friends. If he remembered correctly, his mother should be between the gym and whatever lunch date she might have lined up.

He crossed to the front door, but it opened before he could knock.

"I saw you drive up," his mother said with a smile, looking fit in a T-shirt and flared cropped pants. Her feet were bare, her toes painted pink. Although she'd always worn her hair long, a few years ago, she'd cut it off and every time he saw her, it was shorter still. Now it barely came to the bottom of her ears.

"Hey, Mom," he greeted, bending down and kissing her cheek. "You going to get your head shaved next?"

"If that's what I want," she declared, stepping back so he could enter. "I'm working out more and short hair is easier. Today was my yoga class. I seem to be missing the bendy gene. I swear, the positions some of the women get in defy me. I push, but I can't help thinking that at some point, I'll simply snap a bone. I'm at that age, you know. Shrinking and brittle."

"Hardly."

Denise was in her early fifties and could easily pass for ten years younger. Despite the years she'd been alone, she'd never dated. Intellectually he knew it would be nice for her to find someone. But speaking as the oldest son and the one responsible for her, it wasn't anything he wanted to deal with. Beating up some old guy for making moves on his mother wasn't Ethan's idea of a good time.

"Sweet of you to say so." She studied him for a second, her dark eyes seeing more than most people's. "What's wrong?"

"Maybe I came by just to see you."

"This time of the morning, midweek? I don't think so. Besides, I can tell. What is it?"

She moved to the kitchen as she spoke and he followed automatically. Everything big was discussed in the kitchen. All revelations, celebrations, announcements.

She poured them each a cup of coffee, then picked up hers and leaned against the counter.

Her gaze was watchful, her expression neutral. She

would wait as long as it took. As a teenager, he hated her patience. It had made him squirm and writhe until he eventually confessed to whatever it was he'd done wrong. Today he was grateful she didn't try to distract him with small talk.

"I have a son. His name is Tyler and he's eleven."

His mother nearly dropped the mug of coffee. She quickly put it on the counter. Color drained from her face. She inhaled a deep breath, then another.

"Liz Sutton is back in town," he continued. "I noticed her during the race yesterday. I went to see her and she told me." He shoved both hands into his jeans. "I haven't seen him, yet. I will later tonight."

"Liz Sutton? You slept with Liz Sutton?"

"It was a long time ago, Mom."

"I thought I knew about all your girlfriends. When was this?"

Before he could answer, she frowned. "If he's eleven, you were in college. When we let you live in that apartment over the garage during the summer when you were home. You had sex above the garage?"

"Mom, that isn't relevant."

"I think it is. Very relevant. You promised you wouldn't. You said no girls. You lied and you got one pregnant."

"Mom."

She drew in a breath. "Fine. You're right. Liz got pregnant and…" Her eyes widened. "I have a grandson. Oh, Ethan. How did this happen?"

"We just talked about the sex thing."

"No. I mean you having a child all this time. Eleven? You said he was eleven? Why didn't you tell me?"

"I didn't know."

She gasped. "She kept it from you? I can't believe it. How horrible. We have to do something. Are you sure it's even yours?"

Her reaction was a little scattered, but that was to be expected. It wasn't as if he was thinking straight, either.

"I'm not trying to be mean, but are you sure? Eleven years is a long time for her to keep this to herself. And why now? What does she want?"

That was a lot of questions. He went with the easiest one first. "The kid is mine. She wasn't seeing anyone else."

"Everyone knew what her mother was and the things I heard about her. More than heard. She would get drunk, stand in the parking lot of the bar and scream." His mother shook her head. "It was horrible. I always felt so badly for Liz. I used to wonder if I should say something or try to help. I have daughters. I know what it's like. But then she got pregnant."

"Mom, you didn't know she was pregnant."

"You're right." She returned to the table. "I don't even know what to think."

"You and me both."

"Do you think she wants money?"

"No."

"How do you know?"

"She's a successful mystery author. You've read her, remember? She's written five books and they've all done well."

"I guess you're right." Denise made a small sound of defeat and collapsed into a chair by the worn table. "You have a son."

"That's what she said." He settled across from his mom. "I can't get my mind around it all."

"All this time and she didn't say a word?" Denise demanded, her strength obviously returning. "What a total bitch. How dare she keep your son, my grandson, from us. From the family. Who does she think she is?"

His mother was nothing if not loyal, he thought, amused by her easily engaged emotions. Then the humor faded as he remembered she was right. Liz had stolen the one thing that couldn't be recovered: time.

Denise sprang to her feet and paced the length of the kitchen. "Did she even try to get in touch with you? Why now? What's different?"

"She's back because of her brother's kids." She'd said more, but he hadn't been paying attention to much beyond how she'd looked in the moonlight. That was the hell of it—he'd been happy to see her. Had wanted to tell her that she'd grown even more beautiful. He'd apologized for how he'd acted. And she'd let him.

"She didn't come here to tell you about the boy? About Tyler?"

He shook his head. "It's complicated. She says she tried to tell me when she first found out, but when she came back, I was with someone else." He wasn't going to tell his mother he'd been in bed with Pia O'Brian. They'd dated all of two days and honestly, he couldn't remember ever sleeping with her.

"That's it?"

"No. She says she came to town five years ago and spoke with Rayanne. She says she told Rayanne about Tyler and that she wanted to talk to me."

His mother stared at him intently. "And?"

"She claims she got a letter from me, telling her that I didn't want anything to do with her or Tyler. That she was to stay out of town."

Denise folded her arms across her chest. "That's just so typical," she grumbled. "Make up a stupid story and then expect everyone to accept it without a shred of proof."

He would agree, except for one thing. "She says she still has the letter. She's going to have it delivered by tomorrow morning."

"Do you believe her?

"I don't know."

Tears filled his mother's eyes. She sank back into the chair. "All this time a little boy has been out there, a member of our family, and we never knew. He's been lost. Desperate. Alone."

Ethan didn't think Liz would appreciate Denise's assessment of the situation, but his mother had always had a way with words.

"He needs us," she said, touching his arm. "We have

to be there for him. Finding out he has a father is going to be huge."

"I know." He squeezed her hand.

She drew in a breath. "We need a plan. We have to stay calm. You're meeting them tonight?"

"At six."

"Good. You should be friendly with Liz. Don't push her right now. The last thing we want is her running away. I know you're angry and God knows she deserves it. There's no excuse for what she's done. None. It wasn't as if you would have turned her away. You married Rayanne when she got pregnant, and it's not like she was a catch."

"Mom," he began warningly.

She held up her hands. "I know. I'm sorry. You were doing what you'd been taught—taking responsibility and upholding the family name." Then she frowned. "Ethan, this is two girls you've gotten pregnant. I thought your father had the 'safe sex' conversation with you. Did he leave something out?"

Ethan stood and took a step back. "Mom, let's remember the point of the conversation. Liz and Tyler."

"Right. I know you're mad. I'm beyond mad. I just want to squash her like a bug. But we can't. There are things to be worked out. Besides, Tyler is only a boy. He probably loves his mother. You can't get between them. So when you meet him tonight, be friendly to her, as well. Once you know what's going on, then you can come up with a plan."

Hearing her advice helped him to put things in perspective. His relationship with Tyler was his first priority. Punishing Liz could wait.

"Thanks, Mom." He leaned down and kissed her cheek.

"You're welcome." She touched his cheek. "I want to meet him. My grandson."

"You will."

"She's back home now?"

"Yeah." The house had been old and run-down twelve years ago. Now it was worse.

"This will work out," she told him. "You'll see."

"I know."

He would make it work out, one way or another. Liz wasn't going to steal any more time from him.

LIZ AND TYLER SPENT THE morning strolling through town. She'd wanted to familiarize herself with the area, although she quickly found out that she hadn't forgotten anything about living in Fool's Gold. While there were new businesses, and an impressive development of golf course homes, the basic grid of the town hadn't changed at all. If you lived close to the park, you could get anywhere by walking.

A little before twelve, she took Tyler to the Fox and Hound for lunch. She remembered the location being a restaurant while she'd been growing up, although it had been called something else. As they waited for their food, they pored over the visitor brochures she'd picked up on their walk and discussed points of interest they could visit while they were here.

"Do you think my dad will want to take me hiking?" Tyler asked.

"I don't know," she admitted.

She knew that Ethan had been injured in college, shortly after she'd left town. Something about a bike crash. At the time, she hadn't wanted to know the details. From the little she'd seen, he could walk easily enough, so he could probably handle a day hike.

"You said he rode a bike," Tyler repeated. "He raced?"

"Yes. In high school and college. He had a friend name Josh. Josh had hurt his legs and he rode his bike to get his strength back. Like physical therapy."

Tyler nodded, his gaze locked on her. "My dad rode with him?"

"They were friends. They were both really good and started racing together. Then your dad got hurt."

"What happened to Josh?"

Liz pointed to the poster on the wall—the one that showed Josh Golden in racing gear, a helmet under one arm, his free hand holding on to his bike.

"Whoa!" Tyler grinned at her. "My dad knows Josh Golden?"

"I think Josh lives in town."

"Sweet."

Lunch arrived. Between bites Tyler peppered her with questions. Some she could answer, some she couldn't. A few she ducked. By the time they were on their way home, she was exhausted and feeling more than a little frayed around the edges.

"How about giving me some time to work?" she asked as they approached the house.

"Okay. I'll watch a movie." He grabbed her wrist and looked at her watch. "Five more hours."

She forced a smile. No doubt her son would count down the minutes. While she understood and appreciated his excitement, nothing about this was simple for her. Especially Ethan's understandable rage and her own growing sense of having screwed up.

But when the self-doubt threatened, she reminded herself that she *had* come back to tell him about Tyler. Maybe the first effort hadn't been much, but she'd handled the second one the best she could. She even had proof that Ethan had rejected his son. Proof that might not be real.

What kind of woman kept information of a child from her husband?

In high school, Rayanne had traveled with a pack of mean girls and Liz had been one of their favorite victims. Rayanne, Pia O'Brian and a few others had delighted in making Liz's life a nightmare. Liz might have been smart and pretty, but she'd been poor, living in a bad part of town and she'd had a reputation.

It didn't matter that Liz hadn't dated a single guy until Ethan. Not only had he been her first time, he'd been her first kiss. But as far as everyone in high school was concerned, Liz Sutton had been a piece of ass who put out for anyone who asked. Or paid.

There had been plenty of guys who'd claimed to have done her. She'd heard the bragging, the taunts. No one cared that it wasn't true. No one questioned the rumors. After all, her mother was a drunk and a whore—why not her?

She shook off the past, knowing it wouldn't help her now. She had to focus on what was happening today. Wasn't that enough of a problem?

When they reached the house, Tyler raced into the living room to pick a movie. After searching through the collection in the small bookcase by the window, he chose one and brought it to Liz.

"It's kind of a girl movie," he said with a shrug, "but I haven't seen it."

Liz glanced at the Hannah Montana title, then ruffled his hair. "Sometimes girls are fun."

"I guess."

He would find out about girls being fun soon enough, she thought, watching him bolt upstairs. She'd brought the portable DVD player he used when they traveled, along with headphones. So the house would be quiet. She couldn't use noise as an excuse not to work.

After booting up her laptop, she did a quick check of e-mail, then opened her Word document. But despite the half-written sentence and the blinking cursor, she couldn't think of a single thing to say.

Everyone always talked about how great she had it. That being a writer was so wonderful. She could work anywhere, at anytime. Which was, in theory, true. But there was also no one else to do the work when she wasn't in the mood, or when life interfered, like now. No meeting to take her mind off her swirling thoughts. At this point she would happily return to her waitressing days rather than try to come up with a few good pages. But that wasn't an option. She could only type and delete until something finally clicked or there was a miracle.

Today the miracle came in the form of someone ringing the doorbell.

Liz saved her pitiful three sentences and got up from the kitchen table. When she opened the front door, she decided *miracle* wasn't exactly the right word.

Denise Hendrix, Ethan's mother, stood on her doorstep. The woman was well dressed, fit, attractive and based on the fire spitting from her eyes, really, really upset.

"May I come in?" Denise asked, pushing past Liz and entering the shabby living room, then facing her. "We've never met, but I'm Ethan's mother."

"I know who you are."

"And why I'm here?" Denise demanded.

As questions went, it wasn't a difficult one. She nodded.

Denise looked around. "Where is he?"

Liz assumed she meant Tyler. "Upstairs, watching a movie."

Denise's gaze went to the stairs. Longing darkened

her eyes, then faded as the other woman turned back to her. "Probably for the best. You and I need to talk."

"Ethan spoke to you." Liz made the words a statement.

"Yes, he did. He told me you're claiming to have had his child. A child who is now eleven years old. A boy you've kept from his entire family." Denise glared at her. "I told him to be nice and rational. That it would be easier if we all got along."

"Advice you're choosing not to take?" Liz asked, feeling defensive and understanding at the same time. Not exactly a comfortable combination of emotions.

Denise shook her head. "I should, but I can't. You've damaged us all, but your boy most of all."

Liz grabbed hold of her self-control with both hands. She'd never thought to ask Ethan to keep the information to himself. She didn't go around talking about her private life with very many people. It didn't occur to her that he would speak to his mother, and so quickly.

But the Hendrix family had always been close. Something she'd envied when she'd been younger. Now the warm, loving, supportive mother had been replaced by one who perceived one of her own had been wronged.

"I came back to tell Ethan I was pregnant," Liz countered, knowing there wasn't actually any point in defending herself, but unable to stop. "I'd been gone about two months. I found him in bed with someone else."

Denise frowned. "Which I'm sure was very painful,

but not an excuse to keep that kind of information from him. He was a father. He had the right to know."

Liz drew in a breath. "You're right. He did. Which is why I came back five years ago to tell him. He wasn't home and I spoke to his wife. I told Rayanne everything and she promised to tell him. Less than two weeks later, I received a letter from Ethan telling me that he wanted nothing to do with me or Tyler. That I should keep away from him and Fool's Gold. I'm having the letter sent overnight and it will be here tomorrow. I'm happy to give you a copy."

Liz reached for the door and pulled it open. "So if you've only come here to insult me or accuse me of everything from being a whore to tricking your precious son, then I'm done with this conversation."

"I have a lot more to say."

"This may be a crappy little house, Denise, but it belongs to my family, not yours. I'm asking you to leave."

Denise hesitated. She had dark eyes like her son. Like Tyler. Emotions flashed through them.

"He told me about the letter," Denise said grudgingly. "Ethan may not want to believe Rayanne lied to him, but it sounds exactly like her. If there was a problem she didn't want to face, she avoided it. You having Ethan's son would have been a big problem."

Was that a peace offering? Like it or not, this woman was Tyler's grandmother.

Liz crossed to her laptop and hit a few keys, then she turned the computer so the screen faced Denise.

The older woman's mouth dropped open. Color bled away and her eyes widened. She stared greedily at the slide show Liz had started. All the pictures were of Tyler.

"He looks just like Ethan did when he was young. Like all my boys." Her breath caught. "His smile is different."

"It's mine."

Denise glanced at her, then back at the computer. "He's eleven?"

"Yes."

"This changes everything."

Liz didn't know if she meant the fact that they now knew about Tyler, or the fairly obvious proof he was a Hendrix. "I know you don't believe me, but I never wanted to keep Tyler from his father. I did try to tell him. The first time was a poor effort, but the second, I really thought he knew."

"I believe you," Denise said slowly. "But I can't help being angry. We can't get back all the time that was lost."

Liz thought about pointing out that Ethan had been the one to sleep with her, to take her virginity, promise to love her forever, then dump her. That when she'd run, he hadn't bothered to come after her. It was as if she'd never mattered at all.

"Are you going to keep him from us?" Denise asked, sounding both defiant and afraid.

"No. I never wanted that. My life with Tyler wasn't about punishing anyone. He would like to have a big family."

"He could have had one all along," Denise snapped.

"And your son could have been more responsible."

"Don't bring Ethan into this."

"Right. Because I got pregnant all on my own. That whole slut thing, right?"

Denise pressed her lips together. "No. That's not what I meant. I'm sorry."

"I appreciate that, but I have things to do." The door was still open. Liz glanced toward it. "We can continue this another time," she elaborated. "After I talk to Ethan."

Denise hesitated, then nodded and left.

Liz closed the door and leaned against it. Talk about a tough twenty-four hours, and it wasn't over yet.

EXACTLY AT SIX, ETHAN KNOCKED on Liz's front door. Her SUV was still in the driveway. He'd checked on it a couple times during the day. Not that he actually thought she would leave, but he wanted to be sure.

The door opened and Liz stood there, glaring at him. "Right on time," she snapped. "Probably because you're so damn rested, having sent your mother to take care of things for you."

She looked good. All fire and temper, her green eyes flashing. He was caught up in the sight of the freckles he'd remembered. In the dark, he'd been unable to see them, but now he could count them easily. So it took a second for her words to register.

"My mother?"

"She was here earlier. It was great. Because you yelling at me isn't enough of a thrill."

He grimaced. "I didn't tell her to come by."

"You didn't have to. The Hendrixes all stick together. It was that way years ago and nothing has changed. You told her about me and Tyler, and she showed up. Are you really going to stand there and say you're shocked?"

"No," he conceded. "It's totally her style. For what it's worth, she's the one who told me to be rational and reasonable."

"It's not worth very much." She rubbed her temple. "I have to admit in all the years I've been thinking about what it would be like to have you involved in Tyler's life, I never thought of having to deal with your mother."

"She'll do anything for the people she loves."

"Like I'm getting on that list?"

"You know she'll be there for Tyler."

"A small consolation," Liz said. "Right now the only thing I'm grateful for is the fact that she didn't have time to tell me what having your son is going to mean to the Hendrix family name. How we'll have to make sure we act right all the time and do the right thing, so the legacy isn't tarnished." She took a step. "Come on. He's waiting to meet you."

Ethan followed her in. He wanted to ask what she'd told Tyler, what his son was expecting. All day he'd imagined what he was supposed to say or do, how to make it everything Tyler wanted the moment to be. Before he could ask, or even swallow the sudden surge of anger that followed the concern, she stopped and turned to face him.

"He's really excited and a little scared. I told him some about you—what you do, that sort of thing. Please remember however you feel about what happened, he's not to blame."

"I wouldn't do that."

"He's my son," she reiterated, staring into his eyes. "I'll do anything to keep him safe."

A claim Ethan hadn't been able to make until now, he thought, knowing he couldn't dwell on the unfairness of the situation. Tyler was the important one here. The one who had to be protected.

"I'm not going to hurt him," he said gruffly.

She sighed. "Just be careful. The ability to hurt someone is usually in direct proportion to how much that person cares about you."

She moved into the living room, then called up the stairs. "Tyler. Your dad is here."

Ethan braced himself for emotional impact. He heard slow footsteps on the stairs, then his son came into view.

Any doubts he might have had about paternity died the second he saw Tyler. The boy was all Hendrix. From the dark hair and eyes to the shape of his head. He looked like Ethan's younger brothers had when they'd been kids.

An unexpected rise of emotion made it tough to talk.

He was filled with longing and sadness, as well as wonder. His kid. How had this happened without him guessing Tyler was alive?

Liz waited until the boy stepped into the living room, then moved behind him and put her hands on his shoulders.

"Tyler, this is your dad, Ethan Hendrix. Ethan, this is Tyler."

"Hi," Tyler said, sounding uncertain. He stared at Ethan, then glanced away, before looking back.

"I was telling Tyler about how you used to ride bikes when you were younger."

Ethan appreciated the help, even as he resented the need for it. "I was about your age," he said. "My friend Josh had to ride to help his legs get stronger. We had a lot of fun together. In high school, we started racing competitively."

Tyler stared at him, wide-eyed. "You grew up here?"

Ethan nodded. "All my life. I come from a big family. I went away to college, but when I graduated, I moved back home."

"Mom says you have brothers and sisters."

"Two brothers, three sisters. My sisters are identical triplets."

"So you can't tell them apart?"

He smiled. "It was hard when they were younger, but now they're pretty different."

"Do they know about me?"

"Not yet, but when I tell them, they'll want to meet you."

"Sweet."

Liz motioned to the sofa. "Why don't you two sit down and I'll get some lemonade. We have freshly baked cookies, too."

"We made the cookies after my cousins got home from school," Tyler explained, leading the way. "They're still in school until Friday. Melissa and Abby." He wrinkled his nose. "They're okay, you know, for girls."

"Words that will warm their hearts," Liz murmured, before she went into the kitchen. The girls were upstairs, out of earshot, thank goodness.

Tyler launched into a detailed description of his last few days of school, his friends in San Francisco and what movies he wanted to see that summer.

"*Action Boy* looks so cool," he mentioned. "He's starting middle school, like me. He picks up a special rock from outer space and gets super powers."

"Super powers would be a lot of fun," Ethan told him.

"That one starts in three weeks. Mom always takes me on the first day. We go to the early show, except this one time we went at midnight." Tyler laughed. "I was still a kid, so I fell asleep. Mom didn't mind and took me back the next day so I could see what I missed."

Tyler talked on, the conversation growing easier with every passing minute. Apparently he didn't stay shy for long. Ethan watched as well as listened, recognizing a few Hendrix family traits in his son.

The subjects themselves were conventional. School, sports, friends, his family. But the latter gave him trouble, seeing as Tyler's only family was Liz. From what Ethan could tell, she'd been a good mother. Caring, fair and strong when she needed to be. And Tyler had thrived.

He supposed that some part of him should be pleased, but all he felt was deep resentment for what he'd lost. No, he reminded himself. Not lost. What had been stolen from him.

When Tyler ran upstairs to find a favorite video game, Ethan moved into the kitchen. He found Liz there, flipping through a magazine.

"You're not rejoining us?" he asked, leaning against the door frame.

"I thought I'd give you two time together," she said. A faint smile pulled at the corners of her mouth. "Afraid you'll miss the cookies?"

Humor as a peace offering, he thought. While the sexual side of him could appreciate the shape of her face, the appeal of her body, the rest of him wasn't so easily swayed.

"I want more time with him," he said bluntly.

She closed the magazine and rose. "I wasn't trying to keep him from you," she began then shook her head. "Never mind. We'll have that argument when I have evidence on my side. What did you want to suggest?"

"We have a minor league baseball team in town. They're playing tomorrow. I want to take him."

"Sure. What time?"

"The game's at noon."

"Okay."

She was too agreeable, he thought, irritated. He wanted to fight with her, argue. He had too much energy and nowhere to put it. Apparently she could also read his mind.

"I'm not the bad guy," she elaborated softly. "I wish you'd at least try to see that."

"You kept me from my son. There's nothing you can say to make that right. What Tyler and I have lost can never be recovered."

She stared at him for a long time. "I agree I have responsibility for what happened, but so do you. And until you can admit your part of the blame, you're going to be so caught up in the past, that you'll miss the present and what you have now."

"What do I have? A kid who doesn't know me?"

"You have a second chance, Ethan. How often does that happen?"

CHAPTER FIVE

LIZ GOT THROUGH THE REST OF the evening and actually managed to sleep through the night, despite the lumpy sofa. She spent the morning answering e-mail and figuring out when she could see Roy.

Prison visiting hours were on the weekend. At this point she didn't think it was a good idea to leave the girls home by themselves for more than a couple of hours. Not that they weren't capable of handling things—she didn't want them to feel abandoned. But she couldn't take them with her the first time. She needed answers from Roy, and he may not tell her everything with the girls there.

Her last books had used a couple California prisons as a backdrop and she knew some people in the system. After making a few calls, she got through to a contact who thought he might be able to get her in for a midweek visit. Pleased, she opened her Word program and prepared to work.

But the second she saw the blinking cursor on the blank page, she found her thoughts straying from her plot to Ethan. He'd been beyond pissed with her and still was. She'd meant what she'd said—he would have to learn to let it go or he would never have a decent relationship with Tyler. Anger had a way of taking over everything. She should know. It had taken her months to get over what Ethan had done to her. In fact, she didn't think she'd fully let go of her feelings until she'd written that first short story where he'd died a painful death.

Later, when she'd expanded the short story into her first novel, she'd moved beyond the need to punish Ethan. She'd hoped for at least a calm, adult relationship—one that put Tyler first. It was the reason she'd returned five years ago.

She closed the computer and stood. Apparently this wasn't going to be one of those days when the work went quickly and easily. Maybe she'd been trapped inside for too long.

A quick glance at her watch told her that Ethan would arrive any second to take Tyler to the game. She could go for a walk while they were gone. Clear her head.

Fifteen minutes later, she'd gotten through yet another awkward meeting with Ethan, confirmed when he would bring Tyler back, done her best not to notice how great he looked in jeans and a sweatshirt, then watched them drive away.

And then it hit her. She wasn't Tyler's only parent anymore. Suddenly it wasn't just going to be her and her son ever again. There would be someone else involved. Someone else in on the decisions.

A worry for another day, she told herself. After shoving a few dollars, a credit card and her cell phone into her pocket, she locked the front door of the house and started toward town. Three blocks later, she was walking through Fool's Gold, noticing the new businesses and old. Morgan's Books was still there. She remembered the owner from when she'd been growing up. She'd spent hours scanning new titles, writing down which ones she wanted the library to order.

Morgan had been a kind man who'd never minded the time she'd spent, despite the fact that she hadn't bought a single book. Driven by guilt and maybe a little curiosity as to whether or not he stocked her books, she crossed the street. Before she could step into the store, she saw a window display of her latest hardcover. There was a poster of the cover, a good-sized picture of her, a list of several flattering reviews and a banner proclaiming her a "local author."

Liz blinked at the display, not sure what to make of it. She'd never hidden where she'd grown up, but she'd never mentioned it, either. There hadn't been any special events here in town, no book signings. Still, Morgan was treating her like a star.

She pushed open the door and stepped inside. The space was as light and bright as she remembered. There were books everywhere and immediately her fingers itched to hold and open every volume.

She loved books—the weight and smell of them, the feel of the paper against her skin. While an electronic reader took up less room than a stack of books, she had never been able to make the transition. She was a book person.

Morgan's had a big table displaying new books. Hers sat in the middle, the new hardcover and all four of her backlist books. Several customers browsed. No one seemed to notice her.

If this had been any other bookstore, she would have walked to the information desk and introduced herself, then offered to sign any stock. But this was Fool's Gold and somehow the regular rules didn't apply.

Before she could decide what to do, an older woman glanced up and saw her. The woman's eyebrows went up.

"You're Liz Sutton," the woman said in a loud voice. "Oh my God! Morgan! You'll never guess who just walked into your store."

Morgan, a tall older man with dark skin and warm brown eyes, stepped from behind the counter and paused at the sight of Liz. A moment later he winked at her. "I have three new books on horses."

She laughed. The summer she'd turned twelve, she'd been obsessed with horses. Probably because being on one meant the illusion of freedom and being able to ride away. She'd come into his store nearly every day to ask if he had any new books on horses.

"I'll have to check them out," she said and crossed to him.

She'd meant to offer her hand to shake, but somehow she found herself hugging him.

"Welcome back, Liz," he murmured, squeezing her, then holding her at arm's length and smiling. "You've made us all proud. Your books are really good."

She felt both pleased and a little embarrassed. "Thank you."

The older woman reached for Liz's hand. "I'm Sally Banfield. You were in school with my daughter, Michelle. I'm a huge fan. I couldn't believe it five years ago when Morgan told me you'd written a book. I read it and I was hooked. Your detective is one of my favorite characters ever. She's just like the people I know, only a little smarter. But she's real. With problems and everything. I felt so bad her boyfriend got killed in the last book. But he died trying to save her life. It was so romantic. My husband won't even pick up his own socks, let alone die for anyone."

Sally frowned. "I don't think that came out right."

"I know what you meant," Liz offered, knowing any fan was a good fan.

"Have you moved back to Fool's Gold?" Sally asked.

"I, ah, I'm here for a few weeks."

"I can't wait to tell all my friends I really met you." Sally raced toward the door. "You've made my day."

"Thank you."

When she left, Morgan smiled again. "She means well."

"I know. And I really do appreciate the enthusiasm." Liz was willing to overlook the fact that Sally's daughter Michelle had been one of Liz's tormentors.

She pointed at the window display. "Thank you for that."

"You write a great book and everyone wants to hear about a hometown girl doing well. You're famous here."

Something Liz had never considered. Her only concern when she'd found out she had to come back had been avoiding Ethan. Now she had to deal with the reality of interacting with an entire town.

"Famous being relative," she corrected with a laugh.

"We're having our annual book festival in a couple of months. I provide most of the books through the store. If you're still around, we'd love you to sign." He winked again. "Our local authors tend to be self-published, with an emphasis on crafts and legends."

She had no intention of being anywhere near Fool's Gold in two months, but Morgan had always been kind to her, so she didn't want to be rude.

"You're saying you'll make more on my books," she teased.

"You know me. It's all about the bottom line," he joked.

"My plans aren't set, but if I'm here, I'll sign."

"I won't say anything until you're sure. Otherwise Pia O'Brian will have you leading a parade."

"Why would Pia care?"

"She's in charge of all the festivals in town. She co-ordinates the special events and picnics. The book festival is one of her major fundraisers for the town."

Oh, goodie, she thought glumly. Because Pia was exactly the person she wanted to see.

"I appreciate your discretion."

A mother with two teenaged daughters walked into the store. Liz ducked behind them, waved at Morgan and left. She'd barely walked down the three steps to the sidewalk when she had to shift suddenly to avoid running into two women walking together.

"Excuse me," Liz said, her attention still on the bookstore.

"Liz?" a familiar and unwelcome voice asked. "Liz Sutton?"

Liz held in a groan as she turned and met Pia O'Brian's surprised gaze. Pia who had taunted her daily all through high school. Pia who had mocked her clothes, her love of books, her reputation.

The woman next to Pia squealed. "Liz Sutton? I'm such a huge fan!"

Liz glanced at her, then wished she had stayed home. The squealer was one of Ethan's sisters, although she had no idea which one. Not that it mattered. Whatever fanlike feelings his sister might have now would be squashed the second she found out about Tyler.

"Hi," Liz said weakly, doing her best to smile when what she really wanted to do was run. She looked at Ethan's sister. "I'm sorry, I know you're one of Ethan's sisters…"

"Montana."

"I can't believe you're here," Pia commented, still looking as stylish as ever. Her hair was a little shorter and she looked more twenty-something than teen-queen. Otherwise, she was as perfect as she'd been twelve years ago. "When did you get back? And aren't you famous? What are you doing here?"

"She's beyond famous," Montana gushed. "I can't believe it. I work at the library part-time. My boss is going to flip when I tell her you're here."

Montana was pretty and dark-haired with a sensual smile and a curvy body that made Liz feel just a little inadequate. She didn't look anything like the stereotype of a quiet librarian.

"It's a temp job," Montana admitted, at Liz's questioning look. "While I figure out what to do with my life. I actually have a degree in Broadcast Journalism. I went to L.A. to be in the news, but I couldn't find a job beyond making coffee. Plus, it's just too big-city there for me. I also work part-time at the paper. I do some reporting and..."

Montana reached for Pia and clutched her arm. "Oh, God! The book festival. Liz can be our headliner." She turned her wide, dark eyes on Liz. "You *have* to say yes. I swear if I have to put out another display of easy crafts with twigs and branches, I'll die. Or at the very least lose my sense of humor. You would be a huge draw. Everyone knows you locally, and we could get some real press. Don't you think Liz would be great?"

"Sure," Pia responded, studying Liz. "Assuming Liz wants to participate."

"Of course she does." Montana glanced at her. "Don't you?"

"Liz is a big-time author," Pia acknowledged, her expression unreadable. "*New York Times* bestsellers in hardcover. A little out of our league."

Liz couldn't tell if Pia was helping her or not.

Montana glanced at her watch and groaned. "Well, you can convince her because I have to be at the library in five minutes." She grinned at Liz. "Welcome back. I love your books. We should get together and talk."

And then Montana was hurrying away, leaving Liz alone with Pia.

Pia smiled. "Montana is the most enthusiastic person I know, and that's saying something. While we'd love to have you sign at the festival, you were looking a little trapped. How about if I schedule time to give you my best pitch but I promise not to be offended if you refuse? Not that I won't call your publicist and beg."

Liz didn't understand. Pia was being…nice. Pia was never nice. "I don't know if I'll still be in town," Liz said slowly. "I'm not sure how long I'm staying."

"You could come back for the signing. Make a weekend of it." She laughed. "No pressure, I swear. So how are you? I haven't seen you in forever. It's been what? Eleven or twelve years since you were last here?"

"Something like that. You're still in the neighborhood?" Liz did her best to make sure the question sounded as if she were interested rather than judging.

"They can't get rid of me, although they keep trying." Pia grinned. "Actually, except for college, I never left. Like Montana, I'm a small-town girl. Unlike her, I've found what I want to do."

"I heard you plan all the festivals."

"I'm Fool's Gold's party girl, and I mean that in the nicest way possible."

It wasn't anything Liz could have imagined the other woman doing. Pia had seemed more like someone who would marry well and join the ladies-who-lunch crowd.

"You look great," Pia told her. "I've seen your pictures on the books, but they're different. More, what? Formal?"

"Stern," Liz admitted. "What I write requires me to look serious in my pictures."

"You probably wouldn't sell as many books if you appeared in taffeta and a pink boa."

"Exactly." Liz found herself relaxing a little. A lot of time had passed. Maybe they'd both changed and grown up. "Are you married?"

"No. I've never been very good at taking care of things. Although I'm looking after a cat for a friend and that seems to be going well." Pia frowned. "At least I think it is. He hasn't tried to kill me in my sleep and just last week he let me pet him. Well, it was more an accidental brush of my hand against his back, but we're making progress. You?"

"I don't have a cat." Liz smiled. "Never married, either."

"Really? But you've always been so beautiful. Back in high school, the guys practically killed themselves trying to get you to notice them. You left the rest of us semi-normal girls feeling like trolls. It was very depressing."

Liz felt her smile fade as she stared at the other woman. "Is that what you thought? The guys wanted my attention?"

"Sure."

Liz thought about the horrible comments, the gross come-ons, the snickers. How someone had spray-painted *whore* on her locker and one of the football players had claimed to have naked pictures of her that were for sale. The drunk carload of guys who had pulled up next to her while she'd been walking home from work late one Saturday night and had said between them they had twenty bucks. That should be enough for all of them to do her.

Pia laughed again. "You probably have to have extra security at your book signings to keep the love-crazed fans away. I think I would have liked being famous. Oh, well. In my next life."

It was as if they were having completely different conversations, Liz thought, confused by Pia's friendliness and seeming inability to remember the past with accuracy.

"There's a group of us girls who get together," Pia continued. "Sort of a girls' night out. Or *in*, because we meet at someone's house and drink a lot. It's fun. I think you'd know a few people who come. We'd love to have you." She pulled a business card out of her purse and turned it over, then grabbed a pen. "Give me your cell."

Liz recited the numbers, still feeling as if she were having an out-of-body experience.

"It's great you're back," Pia told her. "Let's go to lunch or something and catch up. And think about that signing."

The two women parted. Liz continued to walk toward the park by the lake. She was sure she looked completely normal on the outside, while on the inside, she was more than a little confused.

Pia O'Brian friendly? How was that possible? Liz did believe in a person's ability to change, but she wasn't sure she was ready to accept a full-blown miracle.

"I'VE NEVER HEARD OF THE Fool's Gold Mountaineers," Tyler told Ethan as they found their seats.

They were both carrying hotdogs and drinks. Ethan kept his eye on the boy to make sure Tyler didn't trip, but the eleven-year-old didn't seem to have any trouble navigating through the sparse crowd. They settled three rows up from the field, about a third of the way from home plate to first base.

"They're a short season A league team," Ethan said, then tugged on the brim of Tyler's new scarlet baseball cap. "You know what that means?"

"They don't play a long season?" Tyler asked with a grin.

"Very good. You've heard of Triple A and Double A minor league baseball, right?"

The boy took a bite out of his hotdog and nodded.

"This is another kind of minor league team. Their season runs from early June to early September. The opener was last week."

"You go to a lot of games?"

"I get here when I can."

"Mom and me went to see the Giants play a few times. That was real fun. There were a lot more people than here."

"Fool's Gold is a lot smaller than San Francisco."

Tyler picked up his drink. "Mom takes me to lots of stuff. Museums, which sound really bad, but sometimes are fun. We go to the children's theater and we saw the *Lion King* musical twice." He swallowed some of his soda. "I'm kinda old for Disney, but it was still pretty sweet."

Ethan stared at his son and tried not to let himself think about all the years that had been lost. There was no win in that. He told himself to focus on this moment, and let the rest take care of itself.

At least Tyler seemed ready to accept him. Liz hadn't turned her son against him—which he probably should appreciate. Of course if she hadn't kept Tyler from him, it wouldn't be an issue.

"Do you like school?" he asked.

"Uh-huh. I really like math. I'm good at it. Mom says I get that from you." The boy frowned. "That's so weird. I never knew who she meant when she said that. But now, I'll know she means you."

Tyler grinned, then took another bite of his hotdog.

"I'm good at sports, too," he added, when he'd chewed and swallowed. "Mom says she's a klutz." He hesitated. "That means she's not really coordinated."

"Thanks."

Tyler beamed. "I didn't know about you riding bikes and stuff. Now I'm going to ride my bike more."

"Maybe we can ride together sometime."

Tyler's eyes widened. "Could we? Sweet! But you'll go really fast and beat me. That's okay. I'll get better as I grow. That's what Mom always tells me. That I'm good now and I'm going to get better."

That was the pattern, Ethan thought grimly. Whatever they were talking about, Tyler had a story about his mother. A positive, supportive example of what a great mother she'd been. Their closeness was a good thing, or so he tried to convince himself.

"Mom says you build windmills. The kind they use for electricity. Can I come see?"

"Sure. We have a wind farm outside of town. We can go there, and you can see where I build them."

"They're really big, right?"

"Bigger than you can imagine."

The game started, distracting Tyler. After they'd stood for the national anthem, they settled back in their seats. Tyler asked about Ethan's family and the construction business. Ethan told a couple stories from when he'd been younger. The afternoon sped by and when the game ended Ethan had the sense that he knew his son better, along with a certainty that knowing Tyler was going to change his life forever.

They walked back to Liz's old house.

"If the Mountaineers win this season, they don't get to go to the World Series," Tyler said.

"No, but the good players will be moved up in the league and maybe get to play in the majors."

"I can hit pretty far," his son told him. "I don't catch so good."

"We could practice," Ethan suggested.

"Yeah?" Tyler grinned. "Mom tries, but she throws like a girl." His eyes twinkled. "Although I'm not 'posed to say that. She gets mad. One time she told me this whole long story about girls having different hips and how they walk differently and it makes it harder for them to throw like a guy. I sort of understood what she was saying, but then I asked what her hips had to do with her throwing and she got mad."

Ethan chuckled. "I'm sure she did."

"Sometimes moms are complicated."

"It's not just moms. It's all women. Just when you think you've got them figured out, they surprise you."

Tyler continued to look up at him. The smile faded. "Do you have other kids?"

Ethan felt a tightness in his chest. Without thinking, he put his hand on Tyler's shoulder. "No. I don't."

"So it's just me?"

Ethan nodded.

"I wouldn't mind a brother, but I sure don't want a sister."

Liz was sitting on the front porch when they got back to her place. Tyler raced toward her and threw himself in her arms.

"We had the best time," he said. "The Mountaineers won and the manager got mad at the umpire and got thrown out of the game."

"That can't be good," she replied, releasing her son. She looked over his head toward Ethan. "Sounds like everything went well."

He nodded, determined not to react to her in a T-shirt and shorts. Nothing about the clothes was special—it was the woman inside the clothes that made him take notice.

Her legs were long and toned, the skin smooth. Her bare feet made her look vulnerable. His instinctive reaction was to protect. Then he had to remind himself that Liz was the bad guy here, which made him uncomfortable.

"I'm gonna tell Melissa and Abby about the game," Tyler announced and ran inside. The screen door slammed behind him.

"I'm glad you had a good time," she said.

Ethan let his anger take over. "There shouldn't be anything to be glad about. I shouldn't have to get to know my son. I should be a part of his life. You didn't have the right, Liz. You didn't just screw with my life, you screwed with Tyler's."

She didn't say anything for a long moment, then she

reached behind her and picked up a letter. The envelope was smudged and had the look of paper that had been handled a thousand times. She held it out to him.

He didn't want to take it. Because in that second, looking into her eyes, he knew she'd been telling the truth. That five years ago she *had* tried to tell him about Tyler.

His fingers closed over the envelope. The date on the postmark confirmed her story, as did the handwritten address. The writing wasn't his—he could see that immediately. But it was close enough that someone else could be fooled. After all, it wouldn't have occurred to Liz that someone was trying to mislead her.

He pulled out the single sheet of paper. The message was brutally clear. "I know about the kid you claim is mine. What we had ended years ago. I have my own family now. My own responsibilities. I don't want anything to do with him or you. Stay away from me and from Fool's Gold."

The letter didn't excuse her running away and not telling him about her pregnancy, but it explained a lot. Suddenly his anger wasn't as hot or bright as it had been. He was the one left feeling played by a woman who had claimed to love him.

Rayanne had known, he thought, shaking his head. She'd known for months, had gone into labor knowing he had another child out there and hadn't said a word. She'd kept the truth to herself, even as she died in his arms.

While theirs might not have been a love match, he'd thought he'd known her. Had understood her. But he'd been wrong. She hadn't been willing to take a chance that he might want Liz's child more than he wanted hers. He knew Rayanne well enough to believe that.

The deception changed everything, he thought grimly, although he couldn't say how. It wasn't just the act of omission—she'd deliberately lied to Liz. What if Tyler had needed him? Liz would never have contacted him. Not after reading those words.

"I'm sorry," Liz murmured.

He returned his attention to her, saw the sympathy in her green eyes. "What have you got to be sorry about?"

"You were married to her. She's gone. You can't ask her why she did it or know if she ever regretted what she did."

He already knew the answer to both. The only real question was how he could have been so wrong about the woman he'd married.

He put the letter back in the envelope and handed both to her. "I guess I owe you an apology."

"I'll remind you of that the next time you're mad at me. I expect that to be in about fifteen seconds." She gave him a slow smile. "You've become emotionally volatile in my absence. It's a little surprising."

"Maybe I'm exploring my feminine side."

"Maybe you need medication."

He leaned against the railing. "You really did try to tell me about Tyler."

She nodded.

There were still the first six years of Tyler's life to deal with, but that was for another time. A few words on a page had changed everything.

"Can we start over?" he asked.

Her expression turned wary. "While I appreciate the offer and don't mean to sound ungracious, it's really just a matter of time until you're pissed at me again."

"Don't you want to take advantage of my good mood?"

She grimaced. "No, thanks."

"You should. Have dinner with me. We can talk logistics."

She shook her head. "Thanks, but I'm not ready to be exposed to the questionable society of this town. Eating out, with you, in a restaurant, isn't my idea of a good time."

"At my place. Tomorrow night."

"You cook?"

"I have many talents."

A light wash of color stained her cheeks. "Yes, well, I have three minors I have to worry about. Melissa is fourteen and plenty old enough to be left on her own, but under the circumstances, I'm not sure I want to leave her in charge. She's had enough responsibility for a while."

"My mom can come over and watch them."

Liz winced. "I'm sure she's a lovely woman, but I'm not up to another encounter with the soul that is your mother."

"Then I'll ask one of my sisters."

Liz considered that. "If Montana will stay with the

kids, I'll go. I ran into her today and she doesn't hate me. In your family, that's practically a miracle. Of course she doesn't know about Tyler and it's possible finding out will change everything, but a girl can dream."

"Montana it is," he agreed. "She'll be here at six to-morrow."

"How do you know she doesn't have plans?"

"I don't, but she owes me."

"Typical male."

He grinned. "Is that a yes?" he asked, although he already knew the answer.

She sighed. "Yes."

LIZ HAD ALMOST TWENTY-FOUR hours to regret her decision and she did her best to make use of the time.

Dinner with Ethan? What had she been thinking? More alone time so he could yell at her again? Not her smartest move. But now, as she got ready to walk over to his place, she knew she wasn't going to back out. She and Ethan had too much they had to talk about—mostly practicalities when it came to him getting to know Tyler. With a little luck, and proof that she had tried to contact him five years before, they might be able to have a normal, regular conversation. Like adults.

Maybe.

Montana arrived right on time, as bubbly and gushing as she had been the day before.

"I brought books for you to sign," Ethan's sister

spoke as she entered the house. "Not tonight. I'll just leave them and you can get to them when it's convenient. And Pia told me I'm not supposed to bug you about the book festival, but offering my babysitting services in exchange for you coming to the festival isn't exactly the same as bugging, right?"

Liz couldn't help laughing. "Do you drink a lot of coffee?"

Montana grinned. "I get that question all the time." She glanced around, as if checking to see if they were alone, then lowered her voice. "I heard about Tyler and that you tried to tell Ethan before. That Rayanne kept it from him. I know we're not supposed to say anything bad about someone who's dead, but I'm not even surprised she did that."

Liz wanted to ask her why, but the three kids came down the stairs just then.

Introductions were made, the pizza ordered and rules for the evening established. Liz made sure her cell number was written down. She'd already talked to Melissa about Montana coming over to watch the younger kids and the teen had agreed she was happy not to have to take on more responsibility. Just before she left, Liz checked to make sure the pizza money was on the dining room table.

But the two twenties she'd left were gone.

"Did somebody take the pizza money?" she yelled toward the living room.

The kids and Montana were already engrossed in

picking out their movies for the evening. A mumbled "I didn't see it" drifted back to her.

Liz checked under the table, to see if the money had fallen. But there weren't any bills tucked behind chair legs. Maybe she'd only planned to put out the money.

She removed two more twenties from her wallet and handed them to Montana.

"Have fun," she called. "I should be back by ten, but if I'm not, everyone goes to bed then. Bye."

"Bye, Aunt Liz."

"Bye, Mom."

"Have a good time," Montana told her. "Get Ethan to tell you about the book festival."

"You're relentless," Liz said as she walked to the door.

"One of my best qualities. It marks me as a Hendrix."

CHAPTER SIX

ETHAN'S HOUSE WAS ON THE OTHER side of town, which meant it was a fifteen-minute walk. With the longer days, the sun was still out, the sky blue. She distracted herself by naming the flowers she passed. As she knew little more than the basic rose/carnation/daisy types, it wasn't a totally successful diversion.

Instead she questioned her choice of clothing for the evening. She'd wanted to be casual but not too casual, settling on a cap-sleeve T-shirt in light green and a white denim skirt that showed off her spray-tanned legs. With her red hair, real tanning was impossible and only promoted sunburn and freckles.

Maybe she should have simply worn jeans. Did a skirt imply a date? She didn't want him thinking she thought this was more than it was.

Before she could make herself totally insane, she turned on Ethan's street and paused to admire the house. It was relatively new, craftsman style with a wide porch and plenty of wood. Cream shutters contrasted with the deep green of the main house.

There was plenty more to appreciate, but she had a

feeling that if she stood in front too long, she wouldn't have the courage to go inside. Eventually the neighbors would notice her frozen on the sidewalk, assume she was crazy and call the police. From there it would all be downhill, proving that going inside was probably the safest and best plan.

She made her way to the front door, which opened before she could knock. Ethan stood there, looking tall and masculine and sexy in jeans, boots and a soft white shirt with the sleeves rolled to the elbows. His hair was slightly mussed, his expression both welcoming and expectant. For a second she felt a very different kind of tension—one that began low in her belly and worked itself all over her body. While it was better than nerves or annoyance, it wasn't any safer.

She'd loved Ethan once, she reminded herself. That made her vulnerable. Just because they'd worked through a few things didn't mean she could relax now. Noticing that he was a good-looking guy who made her insides sigh with appreciation wasn't anything she had time for.

"You made it," he noted.

"Amazing but true." She stepped inside. "Great house. Did you build it?"

"A few years ago."

"With Rayanne?" she asked before she could stop herself.

"No. I sold that house."

Because of the memories? Probably, she thought,

telling herself not to ask questions if she didn't want to hear the answers.

"Come on in," he said, motioning her to the left.

The entryway was large and open, with a two-story ceiling and dark wood floors. She crossed the space and entered a huge living room with a fireplace at one end and a view of the mountains through big windows.

The furniture was masculine but comfortable, the artwork conservative. Rugs covered enough of the hardwood floor that sound didn't echo. On the far side was an opening to a dining room.

He led the way into the kitchen which was filled with cherry cabinets, miles of granite and large south-facing windows. Two bar stools had been pulled up to the counter. There was a bottle of red wine and two glasses, along with a plate of appetizers. Delicious scents of garlic and spices drifted from one of the two stainless steel ovens.

"I'm impressed," she said.

"Don't be. I know a great caterer. I call, food arrives, I heat it."

He waited until she took one of the seats before reaching for the wine.

"The perfect bachelor lifestyle?" she asked.

"Some days." He opened the bottle with an easy, practiced motion. "You're not married, either. Want to talk about it?"

She took the glass of wine he offered and shook her head. "Not really."

"Because of the guy or because we should stick to safer topics?"

"I think safer topics are a better idea," she answered cautiously.

"You sound wary."

"I'm prepared to practice my duck-and-cover skills."

He gave her a smile. "Because I may start using you as target practice again?"

"Absolutely."

The bar was high enough that with her sitting and him standing, they were practically at eye level. She could see all the shades of brown that made up his irises, the long, thick lashes that took her three coats of mascara to achieve. If she inhaled deeply, she would catch the scent of soap and man. A scent she remembered, even now.

"Tonight we've called a truce," he declared, touching his glass to hers. "Remember?"

"And I can trust you?"

The smile turned into the slow, sexy grin she remembered. The one that made her think about how long it had been since she'd had a man in her bed. No, not a man, she corrected herself. *This* man.

They might have been young, but he'd still been a whole lot more than her first time. He'd been her best time. He'd made love with a combination of affection and tenderness no one else had matched. He'd made her believe that anything was possible.

And then he'd broken her heart.

"A truce," she agreed, knowing that having loved Ethan once, she would always be vulnerable to him. She had to stay strong to protect herself and Tyler.

He moved to the other side of the counter and pushed the plate of food toward her.

"How's it going with Roy's kids?" he asked.

"So far, so good. I've got them fed and feeling safe, so that's half the battle." She leaned toward him. "They survived on their own for nearly three months. Roy's wife left them one hundred dollars and took off. I want to report her to the police, but I need to talk to Roy first. Find out what he wants."

Ethan looked stunned. "She abandoned two kids?"

"Walked out and never came back. The money ran out, the utilities got turned off. Melissa's been stealing what they needed to survive."

"No one noticed?" he asked. "No one called social services?"

Liz thought about her own childhood. "You'd be amazed at how many kids slip through the cracks. I'm going to see Roy tomorrow. I wanted to go there while the girls are still in school." She glanced at him. "Would you mind taking Tyler? I don't think he's ready to see Folsom Prison."

"Sure. Bring him by the office."

"Thanks."

"What's going to happen to the girls?"

"I don't know," she admitted. "I'm hoping Roy has a plan. If he doesn't, my family just got bigger."

"You'd take them?"

She nodded slowly, thinking if there wasn't anyone else, she didn't have much choice. She knew nothing about teenage girls, except she'd once been one. She hoped that was going to be enough.

"That's a lot to take on," he said.

"You'd do the same for one of your brothers or sisters."

"Probably. If Mom didn't take them first."

"She is a tiger." Liz did her best to keep her tone light.

"You'll like her a lot more when you get to know her."

"Something else to look forward to," Liz murmured, hoping she wouldn't be in town long enough for any of Ethan's family to be an issue.

"Having Roy's kids in your life would change everything," he told her.

"I know. I'm still kind of in denial. Better to wait and see what happens than start any planning now. If the arrangement *is* permanent, then we'll all figure it out together."

She looked up and saw him staring at her. "What?"

"Just waiting for you to admit you were killing me over and over again in your books."

She shrugged, trying not to smile. Or be happy that he'd obviously read her books. "You should be flattered. You're a recurring character in a successful series of books."

"I'm a dead body. Not much to be flattered about."

"You always get a name and a history."

"Along with a very graphic description of my death."

This time she did smile. "You're a tough guy. You can handle it."

He smiled back. "I'm hoping to persuade you to move on to another victim."

"The writing muse is a tricky thing."

He leaned against the counter. "You don't believe in muses."

"How do you know?"

"You wouldn't give up that much power to a force you couldn't control."

He was right, but it startled her that he had figured it out. No doubt their pesky past was to blame. Before she could figure out what to say, the oven timer dinged.

Saved by the bell had never sounded so good.

THEY MADE IT THROUGH DINNER talking about safer topics. The catered food was excellent, the wine good enough that she didn't protest when he refilled her glass twice. The result was a pleasantly full feeling combined with a slight buzz. Liz wasn't drunk, but she was glad she was walking rather than driving home.

"Does the town look different to you?" Ethan asked when they'd finished eating. It had grown dark outside. A cool breeze drifted in through the open windows.

"There's been a lot of growth," she said, turning her glass slowly. "Those new houses out by the golf course. When I left, I'm not sure they'd even broken ground on the lots. There are a few new businesses. Daisy's place is now the Fox and Hound."

"Daisy's place has been five different restaurants in the past ten years. No one knows why—it's a good location. Lots of foot traffic."

"There are new people, too," she added, glancing at him. "And some old. I ran into Pia yesterday, along with your sister."

Although she was watching carefully, nothing about his expression changed.

He seemed to sense her scrutiny and frowned. "What?"

"I thought you'd have something to say about her."

"Pia? Why?"

"Because she's here. Because when I first found out I was pregnant, I came back to tell you only to find you in bed with her." She held up her hand. "Sorry. That's not truce material. You'll tell me that I left and you could see whoever you wanted. That will hurt my feelings, then I'll yell and we'll fight and I'm tired of fighting. At least for tonight."

"You don't need me here for this conversation, do you?"

"Apparently not." She sighed. "I do have a question about her, though."

"Pia?"

She nodded. "In high school, she was really horrible, right? Mean and bitchy and not someone you'd leave a small child with?"

"She wasn't the nicest person."

"Good. Then it's not my imagination. Because she was totally different yesterday. Friendly and nice. It was so unexpected, I felt like I was having an alternate-universe experience. I started to wonder if I was remembering the past wrong or something."

"You're not." He hesitated. "I didn't sleep with Pia."

Liz was sorry she'd brought it up. Apparently Pia wasn't the only one to have bitchy moments. "It doesn't matter."

"It does. We were at a party, I was missing you and lonely and mad. I'd been out with her a couple of times, I took her home, but I was too drunk. Nothing happened."

All this time later, she found herself wanting to believe him. "Ethan, it was a long time ago."

"I didn't sleep with her," he repeated.

Information that shouldn't make a difference, but still loosened a knot inside of her.

"Thanks," she said.

"You're welcome." He picked up his wine. "I know why you left, but I wish you'd stayed to talk to me."

She shrugged. There was no way that would have happened. "You went back to college and forgot about me."

"I never forgot."

There was something about the way he said the words. Something about his dark gaze. She felt herself drawn to him, or maybe she was drawn to their past.

Ever since she'd gotten the e-mail from her niece, her life had been crazy and confusing and she hadn't had a chance to catch her breath.

"You swore you'd never stay here," she remembered, to distract them both. "After college, you were going to see the world."

"It didn't work out that way."

"The injury?"

He stared at her. "You know about that?"

Ethan had entered college on an athletic scholarship. He and Josh had always planned to take the racing world by storm. They would compete together, sharing the victories. They'd planned back-to-back Tour de France wins, arguing about who would be victorious that first year.

In college Ethan had been hurt enough that he never had the chance to race competitively.

"I wasn't reading the paper searching for your name, if that's what you're asking," she corrected. "But I heard what happened. I'm sorry."

He shrugged. "That was a long time ago. I finished college and came home to sulk." One corner of his mouth turned up. "Not that I would have admitted it at the time. Then my dad died unexpectedly. My mom fell apart. Everyone looked to me and I had to make it right."

Which sounded like him. Even in high school he'd been a steady kind of guy. Not that rejecting her had made him hero material.

She told herself to let that go, at least for now.

Tonight was about getting to know each other again so they could be friends and deal with Tyler.

"You took over the business?" she asked.

He nodded. "Learned it from the bottom up. Took me a while to figure out I liked building things. Then I started with the windmills."

"And the rest is history?"

"Something like that."

"You could have walked away," she said. "But the thought didn't cross your mind, did it?"

"No. You know me—it's all about family. The Hendrixes' place in our town's history." His tone was filled with both humor and pride.

He'd been like that before, she remembered. Proud of his heritage and amused by it at the same time. Back in school, he'd claimed he was different from his father, but he was wrong. When push came to shove, he worried more about the family reputation than doing the right thing.

She probably should have resented him for that, but she couldn't. It was who he was. It was like resenting feathers on a bird—a waste of time. He was who he had always been—a basically good guy with a few faults.

Their eyes met. Something crackled between them. Awareness, she thought, feeling a sense of yearning she hadn't felt for years. A wanting that was based on both what she knew had been possible once, and a sense of loss. She'd carried emptiness around for so long now. A dark hole where her love for Ethan had once lived.

There had been other men who had tried to claim her heart, or at least her body and her attention. Occasionally she'd had relationships. With Ryan, she'd done her best to convince herself she was in love—but she'd been wrong. There had only ever been Ethan.

He'd been the one who had made her believe, both in herself and in possibilities. With him, she'd been able to imagine a place that wasn't Fool's Gold. They'd talked about going away together, about a future. He'd told her that he wanted to marry her.

She felt a sudden unsteadiness, even though she was sitting. As if past and present had somehow become entwined. She knew that wasn't possible, that she and Ethan were incredibly different people. That any feelings she had were the result of the wine and the stress and maybe how good he looked sitting across from her.

He swore under his breath. "Don't," he breathed. "Don't look at me like that."

"Like what?"

Instead of answering, he rose and circled the bar. She came to her feet without being prompted. They were standing so close, she could feel the heat of him.

They stared at each other, a sense of the inevitable growing. Of being unable to escape, and knowing she didn't want to. Then his hands were cupping her face, drawing her to him. She went willingly, pressing herself against him even as his mouth claimed hers.

The kiss was hot, insistent, erotic. His mouth was firm and tender, better than she remembered and she had thought she'd remembered it all. Her arms went around him as she held on.

They pressed together, hard to soft, male to female. He was thicker, broader. A man now. A man who pulled her close and tempted her with a kiss that tore at her soul.

Their tongues tangled in rediscovered erotic yearning. He tasted of the wine and of himself—flavors that were impossible to resist. She tilted her head to deepen the kiss, leaned into him, wishing she could crawl inside. He dropped his hands to her hips, his fingertips lightly touching the curve of her butt. Without thinking, she pushed her hips toward him in an age-old invitation. Her belly came in contact with something hard and thick and dangerous.

Sexual need exploded. It crashed into her with no warning and left her breathless and hungry. Desire poured through her, liquid heat that stole her strength, her will and her common sense. Knowing he wanted her, knowing what he would feel like inside of her, was too much.

Maybe it was the past she couldn't seem to escape, or everything that had happened in the last couple days. The emotional ups and downs that left her unable to think things through. All she knew was that she wanted Ethan with a passion she hadn't experienced in a long time and if she didn't have him that second, she would probably die.

He must have read her mind, or felt the shift in her

body because the hands on her hips tightened. He moved his mouth from hers, only to trace an arousing line down her jaw to her neck. He nipped on her earlobe, before licking the sensitive spot right below it.

He pulled up her T-shirt, then reached behind her and unfastened her bra. His mouth closed on her tight, aching nipples, licking and sucking until she shivered with arousal. Each tug, each stroke, sent fire racing through her. She burned everywhere. The frantic need grew until it was more powerful than her heartbeat, more necessary than air.

Her legs were weak, her core swollen and damp. She touched his arms, his chest, then dropped her hand to his erection, cupping him through the thick fabric of his jeans.

Still sucking on her breasts, he shoved up her skirt and slipped his fingers between her thighs. He found the promised land on the first try, easing his fingers against the hypersensitive, swollen flesh. She pulled back long enough to rip off her cotton bikini panties, then returned to his welcoming embrace.

He thrust two fingers inside her, using his thumb to rub her very center. In a matter of seconds, she could barely breathe. Tension and pleasure competed. Her legs wobbled.

Ethan eased her back a step. She felt the kitchen island behind her. As he slid her onto it, she heard flatware hit the floor, followed by the crash of a dinner plate. His gaze locked with hers, as if the sound didn't matter. As if there was only this moment and the two of them.

He was still rubbing her, moving his fingers in and out. Her muscles tightened around him, drawing him in deeper. He stroked with a sureness that allowed her to surrender. The steady rhythm of his thumb matched the pounding of her heart. She could see the fire burning in his dark eyes and knew there was no turning back. Maybe that chance had never existed.

She unfastened his belt, then the button on his jeans. She eased down the zipper, mindful of how big and hard he was, and how good he would feel inside her.

She shoved his jeans down his hips, then did the same with his boxers. The second she freed him, he stepped forward, replaced his fingers with his erection and pushed into her.

The force of the thrust pushed her back a good six inches. She braced herself on the countertop, her hands jarring loose a glass and more flatware. She didn't care. Nothing mattered but how he filled her, stretching her, satisfying her, going deeper and harder, the heat building between them.

He had hold of her hips. She wrapped her legs around him. They were joined so completely, she had the feeling they could never be separate again. More and more until all she could think about was the pleasure spilling over and around and then she was coming.

She cried out her release. His low groan accompanied her sounds of satisfaction. They strained toward each other, making it last as long as possible, the contractions slowing and finally stilling.

The kitchen was silent except for the low hum of the refrigerator and the sound of their breathing. Reality returned as Liz slowly lowered her legs and Ethan stepped back.

She'd just had sex with Tyler's father—on a kitchen bar. She'd been back in town less than a week and she'd already surrendered to a man who had rejected her years ago, accused her of lying and keeping his son from him. A man who was nothing but trouble, with a huge family and ties to a town she couldn't wait to leave.

"Crap," she muttered as she carefully slid to her feet, then stood and steadied herself. "Crap, crap, crap."

"Liz," he began.

She held up a hand to stop him. "Don't," she ordered as she pulled down her skirt. Her panties were somewhere on the floor, but she didn't bother looking for them. "Just don't. This was really stupid. On the stupid scale, it gets a ten."

He pulled up his boxers and jeans. "It's not like I planned this. It was just one of those things."

Typical man, she thought, picking her way through the broken glass. It was a whole lot more than that. It was trouble. No matter what happened between them, the sex would be lurking. She'd given in when she'd meant to be strong.

"What the hell were you thinking?" she demanded. "Don't you ever use a condom?"

He stiffened.

She sucked in a breath. "I'm on the pill, you idiot, but haven't you learned anything since high school? This was a huge mistake. It never happened. Am I clear? Never."

"You can't pretend it away."

"Watch me," she declared as she made her way to the front door.

Her purse was where she'd left it, on the small table in the entryway. She grabbed it and left, walking briskly to the sidewalk, ignoring the slightly squishy feeling that was the lingering proof of what they'd just done.

Ethan didn't come after her and she was grateful. By the end of the block, she was willing to admit she might have overreacted. By the second block, she knew the person she was really angry with was herself, not him. By the time she got home, she didn't feel any better about what had happened and she didn't have a clue how she was ever going to face him again.

Whoever said you couldn't go home again had been dead wrong, she thought as she climbed the steps to the house where she'd grown up. You could and being there was nothing but a disaster.

CHAPTER SEVEN

PASSING THROUGH A METAL detector, then being patted down before going into prison had a way of putting one's life in perspective, Liz thought the next morning as she waited while the guard searched her purse. When she'd been cleared to proceed, she followed yet another guard into a small room with a table, half a dozen chairs and a small window looking out onto a courtyard.

Since it wasn't a regular visiting day or a normal visiting room, they would have an element of privacy. She pulled out a metal chair and sat down. The room was cool and despite the small size, she felt oddly exposed. Although that could have more to do with what had happened the previous evening than her meeting with Roy.

She hadn't slept at all. Telling herself she'd acted irresponsibly and impulsively didn't make for a restful night. Nor did the waves of sense memory that shuddered through her from time to time. Physical reminders of the music Ethan had played on her skin.

The last thing they needed were more complications, but here they were. And she had no one to blame but herself.

Sucking in a deep breath, she pushed the memories and recriminations to the back of her mind. She would beat herself up some more on the drive back to Fool's Gold. Right now she had to concentrate on seeing her brother for the first time in nearly eighteen years.

As if on cue, the door—opposite the one she'd used—opened and a man entered. He was a few inches taller than her, with thin gray hair and weary green eyes. She knew Roy was in his forties, but he could have easily passed for a man in his sixties. For a second he stared, confused, then he smiled.

"Damn. Look at you," he greeted as he approached. "They said I had a visitor. I couldn't figure out who. It's not the regular day and no one comes to see me. I thought it was a mistake. How you doing, Liz?"

"Hi, Roy. It's been a long time."

She'd been twelve when he'd taken off without warning, leaving her in the hands of an indifferent parent. Still a child. She'd grown up a lot that summer.

"You look good," he told her, pulling out one of the chairs and sitting down. "I've read your books. You're famous now, aren't you?"

"Not exactly." She settled in a chair across the table. "But I know a guy who got me in to see you on a non-visiting day."

"That's something."

He looked tired—as if the road of life had been too long.

"I'm real proud of you, Lizzy," he continued. "Real proud."

"Thanks." She glanced around the bleak room. "What happened? How'd you end up here?"

He shrugged. "There was a fight in a bar. I defended myself, but the D.A. didn't see it that way. It wasn't my fault."

The words were familiar. It had been like this before, she thought sadly. When she'd been younger. Nothing had ever been his fault.

"How long are you in?" she asked.

"Fifteen to twenty. I'll get out sooner. For good behavior." He leaned toward her. "You seen my girls?"

"I have. They're great. They miss you."

"I miss 'em, too. I should write more, I know. Time has a way of slipping by. I'm a busy man."

He was in prison—how busy could he be? But she knew there was no point in having that conversation.

"I was surprised you'd moved back to Fool's Gold," she said. "When did that happen?"

"After Mom died." He frowned. "I thought you knew. I always stayed in touch with her. I came back when she got sick. It was fast. She went into the hospital and a week later she was gone. I'd just married Bettina and we didn't have a place, so when I found out Mom had left me the house, I moved us there."

She shook her head. "You stayed in touch with Mom? You wrote and called?"

"Sure. I wrote you, too. After I left. You never answered. I thought you were irritated or something."

"I never got the letters," she said softly, trying to breathe through the pain. Roy had written? She'd thought he'd simply disappeared, abandoning her without a second thought.

"You know what Mom was like," Roy reminded her. "She had her weird rules."

Liz remembered. Her last contact with her mother had been the older woman's request that Liz not bother her again. Someone in the hospital had contacted her through her publisher to tell Liz that her mother was sick. Before she could finalize her travel arrangements, she'd received another call saying her mother had died. At that point, returning to Fool's Gold for the funeral had seemed pointless. Now she knew that Roy had been there.

"Relationships are complicated," she murmured, not sure what she should have done differently. There was no real sense of loss, just an absence of connection, and sadness. Roy was her brother—they should have been a family, but they weren't. They were only relatives.

"I came to see you because of your girls," Liz informed him. "Melissa e-mailed me a few days ago." She hesitated. "I'm sorry, Roy, but Bettina is gone."

He turned away. "I wondered," he muttered, return-ing his attention to her, looking more resigned than surprised. "I haven't heard from her in a while. She took the girls with her?"

"Um, not exactly. Bettina took off a couple months ago. Melissa and Abby have been on their own ever since."

The color drained from his tired, wrinkled face. "That bitch. She never said a word. Are they all right?"

"They're fine. Melissa's been taking care of both of them. When it got to be too much for her, she found me through my Web site. I came right away. Some arrangements have to be made…."

Roy rose and crossed to the window. He stood there, his shoulders bent. "I got no one, Lizzy. Those girls? They're all I have. Can you take 'em?"

She wanted to say no. She barely knew her nieces and looking after them for a few days was very different than taking responsibility permanently. But even as she tried to refuse, she knew she couldn't. If the girls didn't stay with her, they would go into foster care, probably be separated. Who knew what would happen to them.

"I'll sign whatever papers you want," he added quickly. "To make it easy on you."

"Of course I'll take them," she replied, smiling when he turned to face her. "But I can't stay in Fool's Gold. My life is in San Francisco, as is Tyler's."

"He your husband?"

"My son. He's eleven."

Roy grinned. "You got a boy? I didn't know."

Their mother had known, but obviously she hadn't

felt the need to pass on the information. "He's great." She pulled a picture out of her purse and carried it over to Roy.

Her brother stared at the photo. "He's a good-looking kid."

"I think so."

He swallowed. "Maybe San Francisco would be better for my girls. A chance to start over where no one knows about me. I tried to settle in town, but it didn't go well. People couldn't get past the family name, you know? You could sell the house and put the money away for them. For college or a wedding or something."

She thought about the battered old structure that was as tired-looking as Roy. "It would need some work," she began.

"Not much. I got most of the projects started."

"I noticed that."

He smiled sheepishly. "I'm not one for finishing." The smile faded. "I need you to take care of my girls, Lizzy."

Perhaps it had always been inevitable that things would end up this way, she thought. "They'll be safe with me."

"I know they will. You've gone and gotten all fancy, with your books and everything. They'll like that."

"They'd like to see you."

"No. Not here. I don't want them thinking of me here."

"You're their father. They need to know you're all right."

He sucked in a breath. "Visiting day is bad, Lizzy. Everybody crying. There's no being together."

"Their stepmother abandoned them, they don't know me at all. You're the one person in their life they know loves them."

"Fine. But give me a couple of weeks. I'll write 'em and let 'em know I'm thinking about 'em."

"Sure. I'll be in Fool's Gold a bit longer." Figuring out what to do with the house would take some time. She had a feeling that neither girl would be especially excited about the thought of moving. Melissa had certainly been clear about that already.

"Thanks, Lizzy," Roy said, hugging her.

She held on, trying to reconcile the man she hung on to with the brother she had adored. But it was impossible. Too much time, she thought sadly. Too many miles.

"I'll be in touch," she promised and walked toward the door that would lead to the outside world, while Roy stepped through the one that took him back to prison.

"SO IT'S A CAMP?" TYLER ASKED. "Mom sends me to a day camp in the summer. I went overnight a couple of times, up in the mountains."

Ethan glanced at his son, then returned his attention to the road. "This is both," he explained. "Kids come from all over and they stay for a couple weeks. Local kids can come up daily, if they want. There's a bus that takes them."

Liz had dropped off Tyler about an hour ago,

hovering by the front door until the kid had reached Ethan's office. As if she was avoiding him. Who was he kidding—of course she was avoiding him. Why wouldn't she?

Ethan had planned for Tyler to stay in his office for the morning, maybe head over to the turbine manufacturing facility. But Raoul had called and asked to meet him at the camp and Ethan had figured that was as good a way to spend a morning as any. Maybe going to the camp would be a better distraction. He needed something to stop him from thinking about what he and Liz had done the previous night.

Ethan hadn't meant for anything to happen. It had been so far off his radar, he hadn't even thought about coming up with a plan to avoid having sex with Liz. He'd been so damned angry—he still was.

Although he had to admit seeing the letter had shifted things. And being alone with Liz had been better than he'd remembered. She'd always been beautiful and smart and funny. Now she was those things plus she had a maturity that appealed to him. He'd wanted her years ago and he still wanted her, even though being with her meant nothing but trouble.

He turned off the main highway, onto a private road marked by a red sign pointing to "End Zone for Kids."

"The guy who started the camp used to play football," Ethan said. "Raoul Moreno. He was a quarterback for the Dallas Cowboys."

Tyler looked at him, his eyes wide. "I know who

he is. Does he ever come to the camp? Do you think I can meet him?"

"Remember I told you I had a meeting with a guy? He's that guy."

"Sweet!" Tyler bounced in his seat. "That's so awesome. I can't wait to tell my friends."

"I'll take a picture with my cell," Ethan told him. "You can e-mail it to them."

"All right!" Tyler stared out of the front of the truck. "Are we there yet?"

Ethan laughed, then turned into the mostly empty parking lot. The camp would officially open on Saturday when the first inner-city kids arrived. The day camp for locals began on Monday.

Initially, Ethan had wondered at the wisdom of mixing the overnighters with kids from town. His sister Dakota who ran the camp for Raoul, had explained that it was a good learning experience for both groups. Usually small-town kids and inner-city kids had almost no contact, except possibly during regional and state-wide play-offs. Getting them involved with each other now meant expanding their world view before they made up their minds about what the world was like.

Ethan parked between a Ferrari and his sister's beat-up Jeep. Tyler was out of the truck before the engine was off, jumping impatiently as he waited for Ethan.

"Is that his car? It's really cool. I like the color."

They walked into the main building, where there

was a big living area and the dining room. The offices were in back.

As they made their way down the hall, Ethan studied the walls, the fit of the windows and looked for anything that needed touch-ups before the camp opened. He'd already walked the property with the job foreman, creating a punch list of things that needed to be finished. From what he could tell, it was all done.

Raoul's office door stood open. Ethan walked in and found the other man sitting on the corner of his desk, rather than behind it. Josh Golden was there, too. They both looked up when he and Tyler entered.

"Hey, Ethan," Raoul greeted, standing and holding out his hand. "Thanks for making the drive."

"No problem."

The two men shook hands. Ethan turned to Josh and did the same, then put his hands on Tyler's thin shoulders.

"This is Tyler," he introduced, pausing before adding, "my son."

Raoul greeted the boy, while Josh looked as stunned as a cartoon character going off a cliff.

"Your son?" Josh repeated. He mouthed "Who?" over Tyler's head.

"His mom is Liz Sutton."

Tyler shook hands with both men, then stared adoringly between Raoul and Josh. "You're both really famous."

"I'm better looking," Josh said easily. "And smarter. Raoul's kind of homely."

Raoul grinned. "I could snap you like a twig. If it wouldn't make a mess, I'd do it right now."

Tyler stood as if mesmerized by the thrill of the moment.

"What are you doing here?" Ethan asked Josh.

"Talking to Raoul about a pro-am golf tournament. Pia's been on my ass about it." Josh hesitated, glanced at Tyler, then cleared his throat. "I mean butt. She's been on my butt about getting him to sign up. She seems to think people will care that we have some ex-quarterback playing. I think they'll find it boring."

"He's threatened," Raoul said, settling back on the corner of the desk.

Ethan grinned. "He sure is. Probably scared he won't be Fool's Gold's favorite son."

Josh frowned at Tyler. "Do you hear a buzzing sound? Not conversation. Something more annoying."

Tyler laughed.

"I'm playing in the tournament," Raoul told Josh. "Want to put your money where your mouth is?"

Ethan shook his head. "You might not want to bet against Josh. He's pretty good at golf."

"So am I." Raoul sounded confident. "How about five thousand a stroke? The winner donates the money to the charity of his choice."

"Done," Josh said easily. He turned to Ethan. "You playing?"

"No, but now I'll be watching." He glanced at Tyler. "We'll have to talk about who we're willing to bet on."

Tyler looked between the two competitors. They were both tall and muscular. Josh was what his name implied—golden. Blond hair, hazel eyes. Raoul was dark. Ethan had worked out with them enough to know they were well matched physically. Each could bench press about three hundred pounds. As could he. But he worked out because he liked it. Sometimes it seemed like Josh and Raoul were in the gym because they had something to prove.

"You'll pick me," Josh declared easily and winked at Tyler. "They're going to talk business for a while. Want me to give you a tour of the place?"

"Sure," Tyler said eagerly. "You've been here before?"

"A few times. You think a guy like Raoul could do this all on his own?"

Tyler laughed.

Raoul sighed. "You're overcompensating again. Should I feel sorry for your fiancée?"

Josh's grin turned cocky. "Ask her yourself. She'll tell you how satisfied she is."

Josh and Tyler left. Ethan and Raoul settled at the small conference table in the corner, a stack of folders between them.

"Is Josh always like that?" Raoul asked, obviously amused.

"Since he was a kid. Underneath the cocky exterior, Josh is a great guy."

Raoul nodded. "He's been a big help with the camp. I've never set up anything like this, but his work on the cycling school gave him a lot of good ideas. Not that you need to tell him that I said that."

"I won't." Ethan flipped open the first folder. "We've worked through the punch list. I'll take a look around, but from what my foreman told me, we're done with the refurbishing."

"You promised me a camp I'd be proud of," Raoul told him. "You were right."

They went through the various projects. The next phase was more bunkhouses and clearing an area for an ice skating rink. Raoul wanted the camp to go year-round. Ethan made notes of what he wanted to double check, including housing for the overnight staff.

"You still thinking of putting in a house for the camp director?" he asked.

Raoul shrugged. "I would, but Dakota said she's not interested in living on-site. She prefers her place back in town."

Ethan studied the detailed map of the camp. "There's plenty of room for a couple of houses, if you decide you want to stay here all year."

"I'm with your sister. I'd rather be in town."

Ethan chuckled. "Don't want to give the kids that much access?"

"No. They'd never leave me alone." Raoul leaned back in his chair. "If I decide I want to build a place instead of buy, would you give me a bid?"

"Sure. Got anywhere in mind?"

"I'm looking at a few lots. There are a couple of old

houses that have potential, but they'd need gutting or close."

"I can do either." Ethan closed the folder. "You sure you want to settle in a small town? Fool's Gold is pretty different from Dallas."

"I like it here," Raoul admitted. "I've traveled a lot, seen most of the world. I'm looking for a home base. Something permanent."

Ethan would guess Raoul was in his early thirties. His football career had been a stunning success, so money wouldn't be a problem. "I have three sisters," he said lightly. "Stay away from them."

Raoul laughed. "Spoken like an older brother."

"You got that right. Besides, there are plenty of other women in town. A lot more women than men, in fact."

"I've noticed that. Lots of pretty ones, too. Anyone else you want to warn me about?"

Ethan thought of Liz, her shiny red hair, the scent of her skin, the way she tasted when he kissed her. He remembered her passion, her cries as she came, the flash of anger in her green eyes as she'd pointed out that what they'd done was fifty kinds of stupid.

The memories were enough to heat his blood. He found himself wanting to see her again. No. Not see. Make love. Slowly, this time. In a bed, with plenty of time to remember and even more to explore.

A wanting complicated by their past, Tyler and anger.

"There's no one," he said.

Raoul's gaze seemed to see more than it should. "You sure?"

"Positive."

LIZ CHECKED HER LIST, BEFORE turning her cart toward the checkout line. Pia had called a couple hours ago about the girls' night in. When Liz had tried to beg off, saying she didn't want to leave the kids by themselves, Pia had offered to move the party to Liz's place. Liz had been so unprepared for that suggestion, she hadn't figured out a way to say no. In a matter of seconds, she'd gone from unwilling participant to hostess. It was a move that would make any four-star general proud.

At least it was a distraction, Liz thought. There was no way she could panic about what to serve *and* think about Roy while worrying about Ethan. Her brain simply wasn't that big.

She got in line behind an older woman and wondered if she should buy another bag of ice. Pia had said everyone would bring plenty of liquor. Liz only had to provide snacks. Someone named Jo would bring the blender. But blender drinks required a lot of ice.

She eased out of line and started to turn toward the freezer case, when a woman in her fifties, someone Liz had never met, stopped her.

"Are you Liz Sutton?" she asked, looking more annoyed than friendly.

Liz hesitated. "Yes."

"I thought I recognized you. I'm friends with Denise

Hendrix and I wanted to tell you that I think what you did is just awful. What kind of mother keeps her child from his father? There's no excuse for that. You hurt a wonderful family with your selfishness. I hope you're happy now."

"Not so much," Liz murmured as the other woman stomped away.

Still astounded by the encounter, she grabbed a second bag of ice, and returned to the checkout line. As she stood there, she felt as if everyone was staring at her, judging her.

"Hateful old cow," she muttered quietly, wishing the name-calling would make her feel better. It didn't.

When the clerk announced the total, Liz picked up her wallet and pulled out the bills.

There should have been over one hundred dollars, but instead there were only three twenties and a single five. She frowned, sure she'd checked her cash before she'd left the house, but obviously not. She shoved the money back into her wallet and zipped a credit card through the machine.

The girls were home by the time she arrived at the house and Tyler had returned, as well. They competed for her attention as they talked about their day. She listened and nodded, doing her best to keep smiling, to forget the woman at the grocery store and not get lost in thinking about Ethan, either. Which was tough with Tyler starting every sentence with, "And then my dad…"

She got the food put away, chicken breasts in the

oven for the kids and explained about the women coming over that evening.

"I thought the three of you could go to the video store and rent movies for tonight," she suggested.

Abby and Tyler agreed. Melissa tilted her head.

"Maybe I could stay with you," she said. "You know, not with the kids."

Abby and Tyler rolled their eyes. "We're not kids," Abby chided. "And you're not all that grown-up. You're only fourteen."

"I'm a teenager," Melissa reminded her.

Liz didn't know what exactly happened at girls' night in, but she knew there was a lot of drinking.

"How about if you stay for the first half hour," she suggested. "While everyone is getting here. Then you can go upstairs."

"Fine," Melissa conceded with a sigh. "But I'm very mature."

"I know, honey. You did a great job while you were alone." She hesitated, then asked the girls to sit at the table. "I want to talk about your dad."

Tyler hovered by Liz. "Should I go upstairs?" he asked in a loud whisper.

She nodded. "I'll explain all of this later."

"Okay," he said, and ducked out of the room.

She settled across from the girls who were huddled together, shoulders touching, identical fearful expressions in their eyes.

"I saw your dad today," she began. "He really misses both of you and said to tell you how much he loves you."

"Did you tell him about Bettina?" Melissa asked.

"I did. He was angry and hurt, but so proud of you for taking care of your sister. I explained how you got in touch with me and he was really impressed."

Melissa looked both pleased and afraid. "He's not coming home, is he?"

Liz reached across the table and took their hands in hers. "No, honey, he's not. He's going to be at Folsom for a while longer." She drew in a breath. "I'm going to be taking care of you."

Abby and Melissa exchanged another glance.

"I want to see my dad," Abby said.

"In a couple weeks we'll go for a visit. And your dad said he'd write you."

They both nodded. Abby's eyes filled with tears. Before Liz could go to her, she pushed back her chair and ran up the stairs.

"I'll talk to her," Melissa declared, sounding far older than fourteen.

Liz wanted to ask who would take care of Melissa, but knew this wasn't the time. Damn Bettina, whoever she was, and Roy for getting in trouble in the first place. He'd been impulsive when he'd been younger and it didn't sound like that had changed. Unfortunately, now his daughters had to pay the price.

She checked on the chicken, then went through the list of snack foods she'd bought. There were different cheeses, some frozen bruschetta she would heat after the chicken was done, chips, salsa, avocados for guacamole. She'd bought boxes of crackers, various cookies, the ingredients for a quick seven-layer bean dip and a presliced veggie plate. If Pia and her friends wanted something fancier, they were going to have to give Liz more than four hours' notice.

She climbed the stairs and went into the master bedroom. She kept her clothes here and shared the master bath with her son. After going through the few items of clothing she'd brought with her, she picked a dark green wrap shirt made out of one of those amazing fabrics that never wrinkled. She changed her shirt, decided her jeans were fine, and replaced her Ryka walking shoes with cute flat sandals.

Tyler and Abby walked into the bedroom. The young girl looked a little puffy around the eyes, but otherwise fine.

"We're going to get the movies," Tyler announced. "Is that okay, Mom?"

"Sure." She gave him a twenty and smiled at Abby. "You'd probably like something funny for tonight."

Her niece nodded, then barreled toward Liz and threw herself into her embrace. Liz hugged her tightly.

"I know it's scary right now," she whispered. "But I'm going to take care of you."

Abby nodded and stepped back.

"We'll be right back," Tyler called as they headed for the stairs.

"Get something funny," Liz yelled after him from the doorway.

"Oh, Mom."

Liz grinned and returned to the bedroom.

She pinned back her hair, then washed her face before smoothing on moisturizer. Melissa inched into the bedroom.

"Abby's better," she said. "This is hard on her."

"On you, too."

Melissa shrugged.

Liz opened her zipped cosmetic bag. She pulled out concealer and smoothed the cream under her eyes, then blended with her ring finger. The mineral base she used went on next. When she'd covered her freckles and blended the color, she dug in the bag for her eye shadow.

"How do you know what to do?" Melissa asked. "I bought some makeup at the drugstore. You know, before. I couldn't get it right. Plus, I didn't like how that liquid stuff felt on my skin."

Liz glanced at her niece. At fourteen Melissa was old enough to wear some makeup. At least mascara and a little lip gloss. The girl's skin was smooth and had that glow older women spent a fortune trying to duplicate.

"A base is for smoothing out the color of your skin and hiding imperfections," Liz told her. "Your skin is practically perfect."

"Unless I get a zit."

"They happen. As for the rest of it, I learned by doing, mostly. We can practice together this weekend. The basics aren't hard."

"Really?" Melissa looked both hopeful and almost afraid. As if anticipating anything good was a mistake.

"Sure."

"Okay. Thanks."

Liz dug around in her bag again and pulled out a tube of gloss. "In the meantime, try this. It's one of my favorites."

Melissa took the container and turned it over in her hand. "Sugar cookie?"

"Oh, yeah. It looks good and tastes better. Sometimes it's very cool to be a girl."

CHAPTER EIGHT

LIZ GOT THE KIDS FED, THE movie started and the frozen bruschetta in the oven. The schedule was tight enough that she didn't have time to let her nerves get out of control, which was good. Well before she was ready, her doorbell rang and it didn't stop for about twenty minutes.

Nearly a dozen women piled into the cramped living room. She already knew Pia. Jo Torelli was new. Jo owned the local bar and was a relatively recent transplant to town. The Hendrix triplets arrived together and Liz was relieved they seemed relatively friendly. Before she could do more than say hello, Pia walked in with Crystal Danes.

Liz remembered the pretty blonde from high school. "It's so great to see you," she said with a laugh.

Crystal smiled and hugged Liz. "Hmm, I thought you'd be sending me a cut of your royalties. Who do I talk to about that?"

Pia glanced between them. "I didn't know the two of you were friends. Crystal was three years ahead of me in high school, so she was what? Two years ahead of you, Liz?"

Crystal linked arms with Liz and grinned. "I met Liz in our senior creative writing class. Even though she was a lowly sophomore, our teacher thought she had talent and invited her."

Crystal had been the only student who would speak to Liz. All the others had resented her presence and basically ignored her. A few of the girls had made mean comments about Liz's clothes, while two of the guys had hounded her about her reputation.

But in the creative writing class, Liz had done her best to ignore all that. She'd found she could forget everything in the writing process.

Each of the students had to write a short story every three weeks, then read it aloud. The first time, Liz had been terrified. While the teacher had offered glowing praise, the class had been silent when she'd finished. Feeling embarrassed and exposed, Liz had slunk back to her seat.

But at lunch that day, Crystal had sought her out and told her the story was amazing. That the other students had been silent out of shock, or maybe jealousy. Crystal had encouraged her to keep writing.

Four years later, when she was alone with a baby and terrified in San Francisco, she'd remembered Crystal's words and had signed up for a writing class. While she'd begun with another short story, eventually it had become a novel which had turned into her first published book and the beginning of her professional writing career.

"Crystal told me I had talent," Liz admitted. "No one had believed in me before."

Crystal squeezed her arm and laughed. "I'm an angel in disguise. Now if only I could perform a miracle or two on myself, right?"

Liz didn't know what she was talking about, but she saw pain flash through Pia's eyes and Jo turned away, as if uncomfortable with the words.

Crystal didn't seem to notice. Instead she released Liz and smiled at Melissa. "Hello. Do you have any idea where the snacks are? I'm starving."

"Right in here," Melissa said shyly. "I can show you."

"That would be great."

They walked away. Before Liz could ask what Crystal's comment had meant, Jo held up a very industrial-looking blender.

"I need a plug and some counter space," she announced. "I'm saying upfront that while I disapprove of fruit drinks on principle, I'm making an exception tonight. I've come up with a mango-strawberry margarita that is going to make you all worship me."

"I'm glad I bought extra ice," Liz told her as she led the way into the kitchen. "I'll get glasses. Will everyone have margaritas?"

"Not me," Crystal declined as she walked into the kitchen behind Jo.

"I'll make yours without tequila," Jo said easily.

"You're very good to me."

"Don't let word get out."

Crystal laughed, then picked up a tray of veggies. "Should I take these out to everyone?"

As she turned, the light caught her full in the face. Liz was shocked to see dark shadows under her eyes and a gray cast to her skin. It hadn't been noticeable in the kinder light of the living room, but under the glaring fluorescents, she looked drawn and sick.

Liz did her best to keep her shock from showing. "That would be great," she responded. "Thanks."

"You're welcome. Oh, and Melissa went upstairs. I think we scared her, which makes me feel bad."

When Crystal had returned to the living room, Jo glanced at Liz, obviously reading her expression. "Crystal's sick. Cancer. She's been fighting awhile, but she's not winning."

Liz felt as if someone had hit her in the gut. "Oh my God. No. She's too young."

"Cancer doesn't seem to care about that. You okay?"

Liz nodded, although her stomach churned, as if she was going to be sick.

Jo picked up a pitcher of mix and dumped it over the ice in the blender, then poured in a generous amount of tequila. "Prepare to watch the lights dim," she called and turned on the blender.

Less than a minute later, Liz was pouring the slushy concoction into glasses. She took them into the living room where the other women had claimed seats on the worn sofa and the floor. Someone had pulled in battered chairs from the dining room. She did her best to smile and keep things normal. Everyone else was. Apparently that's how Crystal wanted things.

Dakota and Nevada sat together; but Montana jumped up the second Liz entered.

"I was telling everyone about the signing."

Pia rolled her eyes. "Montana, I swear. You're as subtle as an elephant. We agreed not to bug Liz about the signing."

Crystal looked up from her place nestled in the corner of the couch. "Don't you like signings?" she asked.

"I'm not sure how long I'm going to be here," Liz admitted.

Conversation shifted to events in town. There was talk of the new hospital being built and rumors about ex-football star Raoul Moreno moving to town.

"He's very good-looking," Montana said with a sigh.

"Interested?" her sister Dakota asked.

"Not for me, but maybe we could fix him up with Liz and she would be so grateful, she'd do the signing."

Pia groaned and leaned back against the wall. "You have a one-track mind."

Dakota laughed. "She's the stubborn one. And before any of the rumors get out of hand, yes, Raoul is thinking of settling here in Fool's Gold. He likes the small-town feel."

Topics shifted to other people, the general lack of men and what was being done about bringing more of them to town. Charity Jones, the new city planner, was teased about capturing the heart of Josh Golden, the last great eligible bachelor. Although everyone seemed comfortable with Raoul Moreno claiming the title. Liz thought about pointing out that Ethan was single, but was afraid it would stir up memories of their very public breakup all those years ago.

The talk was comfortable, if not exactly familiar, Liz thought. Growing up, she'd never felt as if she were part of the community, but maybe some of that was her fault. Sitting in the living room where she'd lived, getting slightly buzzed on margaritas, hanging out with women she hadn't seen in years, she felt a sense of loss. That maybe the friends she'd been looking for all those years ago had been right in front of her. If only she'd bothered to look.

Not Pia, she thought, watching the now charming woman laugh at something Crystal said. Their relationship had been a little too "mean girl" for her liking. But what about Crystal or even Ethan's sisters?

Her experiences in high school had made her cautious about making friends with other women. But maybe she'd been too quick to walk away from something important. Something she'd realized she was missing.

Her gaze slipped to Crystal who, despite her illness, appeared happy and content. Talk about having character. Liz had a feeling she was more the curl-up-and-whimper type.

"Am I allowed to ask how you started writing?" Montana inquired, interrupting Liz's thoughts. "That's not the same as talking about the signing."

Liz laughed. "You're right. It's not even close."

"Tell her it's because of me you're famous," Crystal called out.

"It's true," Liz agreed. "Crystal told me I had talent and to never forget that."

Pia was next to her friend and grabbed her hand. "You're such a good person. It's intimidating. Tell me again, why do I like you?"

Everyone laughed.

"Seriously," Montana pressed. "How did you start?"

"I wrote a short story about a man who was murdered and found I couldn't let the idea go," Liz explained. "It kept getting bigger in my mind."

She left out the part about the cathartic nature of killing Ethan over and over again. At least in fiction. It was kind of a writer thing and she doubted anyone else would understand that it didn't mean she was dangerous or creepy.

"I was alone with a baby and I couldn't afford cable," she continued. "Writing felt like a way to escape the pressure."

Crystal turned to her. "Where did you go when you left here?"

"San Francisco."

Liz had the feeling there were going to be more questions but just then Jo appeared with another pitcher of margaritas and the conversation shifted to the various summer festivals. Montana grinned at Liz.

"If you would just agree to sign," she began, "we would have the best festival ever."

It was one book signing, Liz thought. She did them all the time. So what if it was here? She could handle a couple of hours at a table, talking to her fans. And Liz appreciated that Montana was the only Hendrix still speaking to her.

"Sure," she said.

Montana straightened. "Seriously?"

"Why not? I'd love to."

Even if she wasn't still living in Fool's Gold, she could drive in for the day. Tyler could hang out with his dad, her nieces could see their friends and then they would all go back to San Francisco, where life was normal and people standing in the grocery store didn't know anything about you.

An hour later, Liz went to check on the kids. As she stood, she had to steady herself for a second. Her balance felt off—apparently she'd been drinking more than she'd realized. At the bottom of the stairs, she paused as a burst of loud laughter filled the room. She grinned. She wasn't the only one who was feeling the alcohol. Good thing everyone was walking home.

After confirming all three of her charges were totally engrossed in their movie, she returned to the kitchen, opened the last few packages of cookies and dumped them on two plates. Normally she would arrange them neatly, but right now that seemed impossible.

Pia walked into the kitchen. "I don't know how Crystal stands us. She's the only one not drinking."

Liz looked up, her sense of contentment fading. "Jo mentioned she was sick."

"She's dying," Pia said flatly. "Today she doesn't look like it, but she is. They've given her less than six months. She's working with hospice. This is the first time she's been out of her apartment in a week. She's living on painkillers."

"I'm sorry," Liz whispered, the gut-clenching returning.

"Me, too. She's a good friend." Pia drew in a breath. "I don't want to talk about it. Knowing I'm losing her is impossible and makes me cry. As drunk as I am, I probably won't stop for hours and no one wants that. Least of all Crystal."

Liz nodded and had to swallow before she could speak. "Are you up to carrying in a plate of cookies?"

Pia eyed the plate doubtfully. "What happens if I drop them?"

"They fall?"

She smiled. "I can make an effort." But instead of reaching for the plate, she leaned against a counter. "Why didn't you come back? When you found out you were pregnant?"

Not a question Liz wanted to answer. "It wasn't an option."

"Of course it was. Even if your mom wouldn't have taken you in, there was still Ethan and his family. You shouldn't have kept his kid from him. It wasn't very nice."

It was one thing to be yelled at by an older woman she didn't know, but it was quite another to have Pia O'Brian passing judgments on her.

"And that's the whole story?" Liz asked, trying to stay calm and keep her voice low.

Pia rolled her eyes. "Oh, please. It's not as if you tried to tell him."

"You're wrong," Liz told her, planting her hands on her hips. "I did come back. Pretty much as soon as I found out I was pregnant. I'd been gone all of three weeks. You'd think after how in love he claimed to be he would have waited to replace me, but no. He was in his little apartment over the garage. Naked. In bed with someone." She narrowed her gaze. "He was in bed with you, Pia."

Pia slipped and had to grab onto the counter to stay upright. Her mouth dropped open. "No," she breathed.

"Am I wrong?"

Pia winced. "I did get him into bed, but it's not what you think."

"You weren't trying to have sex with him?"

"Okay, yes. It was that, but I…" Pia shook her head, then swore. "I'm sorry. I didn't mean…"

Liz waited. "Didn't mean what? To take him?"

"You were gone. Plus, I wasn't completely sure the two of you were actually dating. Josh said something that one time and Ethan denied everything."

Not an afternoon Liz cared to remember. It had been difficult enough working as a waitress in the one place the popular kids liked to hang out, but it had been sheer torture being there when Ethan came home from college and they started seeing each other. They'd both agreed it was better if no one knew about them. He had his family's reputation to think about. After all, he was a Hendrix.

Liz had been young enough and foolish enough to think that was a good reason to slink around behind everyone's back. Today she wouldn't bother. Either a man wanted to be with her or he didn't. But back then she'd been so grateful to have someone care about her. Especially Ethan.

Ethan who was accepted everywhere he went. Ethan who had a family that was always sober and kind and respectable. Ethan's mother didn't show up at the grocery store drunk and talk about being with other women's husbands.

Liz had never actually met Ethan's father, but she heard him speak once, at a fundraiser to refurbish the city park. He'd been stern, but eloquent as he talked about duty and responsibility and how as citizens of the town, everyone had to participate and give of themselves. She'd been drawn to the man and intimidated. After seeing him, she knew why Ethan didn't want anyone to know they were involved. Ralph Hendrix wouldn't have approved.

Then Josh had mentioned seeing the two of them

together and another friend had called her a whore. Ethan had not only denied they were dating, he'd said he wasn't so desperate as to need to be with someone like her.

Pouring a milk shake over his head and walking out hadn't healed the wound in her heart.

She didn't want to remember any of this, Liz thought grimly. She didn't want to be here, dealing with her past. The people, the memories, her complete inability to feel as if she'd made progress emotionally were just a few of the reasons she'd never wanted to come back.

"Your relationship with Ethan doesn't matter," she stated, turning away from Pia. "My point is, you don't know what the hell you're talking about when it comes to my son, and you need to remember that."

"I'm sorry."

Liz nodded.

"I mean that. I'm really sorry. I shouldn't have said anything."

"No, you shouldn't," Liz declared facing her again, trying not to see the regret in Pia's eyes.

Pia opened her mouth, then closed it. "I really am sorry," she whispered, then walked out of the kitchen, leaving Liz alone.

If the buzzing in Liz's head wasn't enough to tell her that she wasn't going to have a good time come morning, the tightness in her chest hinted that a hangover might very well be the least of her problems.

Damn this town, she thought as she grabbed the cookies and braced herself to return to the party.

LIZ WOKE UP WITH A MILDER headache than she deserved and a determination to put together a plan to get out of Fool's Gold as quickly as possible. The house was the biggest problem. What to do with it. Keeping it for the girls was a possibility. As a rental, it could provide income and the value would increase over time. Although that would require fixing up the place. Selling it presented the same fix-up dilemma. Maybe the best place to start was to speak with a Realtor. Get some actual numbers and see what made the most sense.

As much as she wanted to pack her car and run, she knew she couldn't. There were Roy's girls to think of. Melissa and Abby wouldn't want to move. They'd already lost their dad and stepmom. Their home was all they had.

But she couldn't stay here, she thought, feeling desperate. It was a twisted kind of hell for her. Which meant what? Endure the town as long as she could and give the girls more time to adjust to her and moving?

Not a decision she could make without a second cup of coffee.

She made her way to the kitchen. Melissa was on the phone with one of her friends and Abby had gone next door to play. Tyler was with his father. She got out the phone book and called a couple real estate offices from her cell.

An hour later, she'd confirmed what she'd already

guessed. No one would commit without seeing the house in person, but the consensus was for rental property and fixing up was required. A sale could be "as is" but that seriously cut down on the number of interested buyers as well as the price.

Liz had a feeling the house was all the girls could expect to get from their father. Her gut said that fixing it up and then renting it made the most sense. Let the property value increase while Melissa and Abby were growing. If they wanted to sell it later, they could. She could even pay for the renovations herself.

She got out a pad of paper and started making a list. She would have to get an attorney to draw up a title transfer. Roy had said he wanted to put the house in the girls' names. Fortunately, Bettina wasn't on the title, so she wasn't going to be a complication.

Liz wandered back into the kitchen for more coffee, then headed for her computer. Maybe she could get in a couple of pages before Abby and Tyler returned.

Her timing was off. She'd barely clicked on her word processing program when her son flew into the house. He bounced onto the sofa next to her, then threw his arms around her.

"How are you?" she asked, hugging him back and kissing his forehead.

"Good. Dad had doughnuts and he only let me eat two. And I saw the new designs for a windmill. Dad says it's going to be more energy efficient. And he really liked the card I gave him."

Tyler continued to relive his morning in real time. Nearly every other sentence began with "Dad says." Liz told herself this was all good news, even as she felt a little less important in her son's life.

A fleeting emotion, she told herself. One that would pass.

"Then Dad said it was your fault that I don't know him because you kept me from him. Dad says you were wrong not to let us be together."

Liz nearly fell out of her chair. "Excuse me?" she asked.

Tyler's eyes got big and he looked worried. "He wasn't mad when he said it, Mom. Don't be mad."

Don't be mad? Don't be mad when she was doing everything she could to bring father and son together and Ethan was going behind her back, trying to make her look guilty? Had he bothered to mention how badly he'd treated her twelve years ago? Or the fact that she'd come back to tell him about his kid and his wife had been the one to keep them apart? Of course not.

"It's fine, I was just surprised," she said, forcing a smile. She glanced at her watch. "I thought we'd go to the pool later. And Montana wants me to bring you by the library to look at some new books they got in."

His face brightened. "Can we go now?"

"Sure. Why don't you tell Melissa, so she knows. And I want to make a quick call."

"Okay."

He raced upstairs. When she heard his feet thundering overhead, she picked up her cell and Ethan's business card. She was put through to him immediately.

"We have to talk," she said by way of greeting. "Now."

He hesitated. "I have an appointment."

"I don't give a damn."

"Okay. Starbucks in fifteen minutes?"

"Fine." She hung up.

SHE LEFT TYLER WITH MONTANA at the library and promised to be back in half an hour. What she had to say wouldn't take more than a few minutes.

Ethan was already sitting outside when she got there. An umbrella shaded him from the bright sun.

"What's up?" he asked, looking tall and handsome and annoyingly confused. "You sounded upset."

She ignored the way her body reacted to the sight of him, not wanting to remember what being with him had been like. Better that she remembered all the ways she'd killed him in her books. And the even more painful way she would kill him in the next one. It was what he deserved, the bastard.

"What were you thinking?" she began. "We're supposed to be working together. At least that's what you said. I'll accept that you're mad at me. Fine. But don't you dare talk about me with my son. You had no right to tell him it was my fault that you and Tyler don't know each other and that I was wrong to keep him from you. Do you think you're helping your cause? Not only does it make me regret ever coming back, it makes me know I can't trust you at all."

His body tensed. "He told you."

"Of course he told me. I'm his mother. He tells me everything." She was fighting blinding fury. "Did it make you feel all manly to crap all over me in front of my kid?"

"No. I'm sorry. I shouldn't have said that. We were talking about what he usually does in the summer and on his birthday and all I could think was how much I'd missed. I lost it."

"Not much of an excuse," she said, doing her best to keep her voice low. "Do you think you can come between Tyler and me?"

"No. That's not what I was trying to do." He stared into her eyes. "I swear, Liz, I'm sorry. I reacted. It was stupid."

"You say that to me, but did you bother saying it to Tyler?" She waited. He shook his head. "Figures. You're playing us, Ethan. And that's a huge mistake. No one will win that game."

"I'm not trying to come between you."

She held his gaze. "You expect me to believe that?"

"Probably not." He sucked in a breath. "I was mad."

"You're mad all the time."

"I have a good reason."

She leaned toward him. "Yes, you do. And you also know I'm not as much the devil as you first thought."

"I'm sorry, Liz. I was an idiot," he apologized, sounding as if he meant it.

It was easier to believe that rather than think he was deliberately trying to undermine her, but easier didn't necessarily mean right.

"You want me punished," she said, her voice quieter. "You need to get over that."

He drew in a breath. "I know."

ETHAN *DID* KNOW, BUT SOMETIMES it was damn hard not to react. He'd lost so much and even though it wasn't all Liz's fault, it was tough not to blame her.

She stared at him, her green eyes flashing with anger, her mouth set with determination. She would take him on, if necessary. He wanted to say she couldn't win, but he wasn't sure that was true. She had eleven years' worth of a relationship with Tyler. He'd known his kid all of two weeks.

Bitterness threatened, but he pushed it away. She was right—he had to think before he spoke.

"I'm sorry," he repeated.

She sighed. "I guess I have to at least pretend to believe you."

"You could try actually believing me."

"Don't push it."

"I was wrong."

"Yes, you were." She shook her head. "Okay. I'll do my best to let it go. Just don't do that again. We have to work together. If we don't, the person who gets hurt the most is Tyler. You're everything he's ever wanted. You don't have to destroy me in order to make him love you."

Ethan stiffened. "That's not what I was doing."

"Wasn't it?"

He hesitated. "Maybe. This is really new for me. I'm reacting, rather than thinking."

"I'm doing my best to understand that."

She sounded as if she didn't want to, which irritated him. Then he told himself it was time to stop being angry. Liz was right—they did have to work together.

"I'd better get back to the library," she said. "I don't want your sister thinking I've abandoned Tyler."

He pushed to his feet, then grabbed her hand.

Her fingers were warm. Touching her reminded him of the last time they'd been together. Of how, despite everything, the passion was still there, lurking. Heating. Making him want in a way he hadn't in a long time. There had been other women. He'd even gotten married. But there had been no one like Liz.

Something hot flared in her eyes. She gave him a brief smile. "You're trouble. You know that, right?"

He grinned. "One of my best qualities."

"A debate for another time."

He thought about kissing her, about leaning in and tasting her again.

A complication neither of them needed, he told himself as she squeezed his fingers then walked away. There were still too many other issues to work through. But he wouldn't say no to more alone time with her, he thought, watching her walk away.

"What was that all about?"

He turned and saw his mother walking toward him. She had a shopping bag in each hand.

He took the bags from her and set them on a chair. "Liz and I were talking about Tyler."

His mother's gaze sharpened as she studied his face. "Is that all? It looked like more to me. You're not starting something with her, are you, Ethan? After what she did to you? To all of us?"

His reaction was instinctive. "Don't worry. Liz doesn't matter to me at all. There's nothing between us."

"It's good to know that some things never change."

But the words weren't spoken by his mother. He turned to his right and saw Liz standing just behind him. Her expression was unreadable, but he saw a flash of pain in her eyes.

"In case I was wondering," she added, picking up the keys she'd left on the table.

She turned on her heel and was gone.

CHAPTER NINE

LIZ WAS STILL SHAKING AS SHE climbed the three steps to the library. She told herself it didn't matter. That Ethan had to say that to Denise. It wasn't as if his mother was a fan. Besides, there wasn't anything else to tell the woman. But in her gut, Liz felt just as dismissed and hurt as she had twelve years before—when Ethan had denied their relationship to all his friends.

She might have had a child with him, and slept with him and still be fighting feelings from the past, but the bottom line was, she couldn't trust him. Not ever. He couldn't escape his family name and reputation anymore than she could.

She reached for the front door and pulled it open. A woman with a stroller smiled. "Thanks for the help," she said.

"You're welcome."

The twenty-something woman pushed the stroller through the door, then turned back.

"Are you Liz Sutton? I thought I recognized your picture from your books."

Liz nodded cautiously.

The woman's warm smile faded. "My sister went to high school with you. When she told me that you were the class slut, I didn't want to believe her. But now that I've heard what you did to poor Ethan Hendrix, I know every word is true. I'll never read your books again."

Hit number three, Liz thought, standing in the sunlight, determined not to go inside until she was sure she wasn't going to cry.

She told herself the young mother didn't know her. That other people's opinions had no meaning. That the truth was much less clear than most people realized. All of which was bullshit, she thought, finally stepping into the cool darkness of the library.

As soon as they got back to the house, she was getting out the phone book, she promised herself. She would get bids on fixing up the house and pay whatever premium was required to get the work done quickly. When the house was finished, she would take the girls and Tyler, return to San Francisco and never, ever come back to this hellhole.

THE ONLY BRIGHT SPOT IN AN otherwise hideous morning had been Montana's enthusiasm over the book signing. Ethan's sister had insisted on showing Liz the initial design for the posters and all the Internet postings. Montana swore people would drive into town from hundreds of miles away, just to meet Liz and have her sign books. Liz was less sure of her popularity, but it beat being verbally spit at by the locals.

She helped Tyler carry his armload of books into the house. He'd picked out several he thought Abby might like, which Liz appreciated. After sending him to his room to play computer games for an hour, she called Melissa and Abby into the living room.

The two girls sat on the sofa. They looked impossibly young, she thought, wishing things had been different for them. However much she might currently hate her own life, what Abby and Melissa were feeling was ten times worse. They were just kids who didn't deserve what had happened to them.

She sat on the coffee table in front of the couch and leaned toward the girls.

"I'm going to fix up the house," she began. "Your dad started a lot of projects, but I don't know how to finish them. So unless one of you is holding out some secret contractor knowledge, I'll be hiring a team to finish the work."

Melissa looked wary, but Abby smiled. "I can help."

"I'm sure you can."

"What happens after the house is finished?" Melissa asked.

Not the question Liz wanted to answer. "We're going back to San Francisco."

Melissa and Abby exchanged a look. Tears filled Abby's eyes while Melissa started shaking her head.

"No, we're not," she announced. "We're staying here. We live here."

"I know it will be hard," Liz began.

"It doesn't have to be." Melissa stood up. Her face

was red, her eyes bright with tears she blinked away. "We'll run away. We don't need you."

Abby stood, too, then leaned into Liz who hugged her close.

"I'm sorry," Liz murmured into her hair, hanging on tight. "I'm sorry."

"W-what does Dad say?" Abby asked in a whisper.

"That you're going to stay with me."

Abby raised her head. "He doesn't want us, does he? No one wants us."

"I want you," Liz assured, wishing she had the power to take away their pain and make them feel safe. "No matter what, we'll be together. Your dad being in prison isn't about you. It's about him. If he wasn't there, he'd still be here."

"With us. Where we belong," Melissa snapped. "In our house. You're going to sell it, aren't you? And take all the money."

Liz continued to hold Abby, but turned her attention to the teenager. "I'm going to fix it up. Then the three of us will sit down with a real estate agent and discuss the benefits of renting it versus selling outright. Either way the money will go into trust for both of you. For when you're older. This isn't about taking anything from you and I think you know that."

"You're taking away everything," Melissa said, losing her battle with the tears. They spilled down her cheeks. She brushed them away and glared at Liz. "You can't do this to us."

"Tyler and I can't stay here. San Francisco isn't so far away. You'll be able to visit your friends."

"How?" Melissa asked.

"Tyler will be coming back to see his dad. You can come with him. I'm not trying to make this worse. We need to settle in to being a family. I want that. You girls are important to me."

"I'm not going," Melissa said, crossing her arms over her chest. "You can't make me."

Abby stared at Liz. "I want to be with you."

Liz kissed her forehead. "I'm glad. I want you to keep in touch with your friends. We'll work on that. Okay?"

Abby nodded.

"She's lying," Melissa told her sister. "She doesn't care about us at all."

"If she didn't care, she'd just leave," Abby noted, still holding on to Liz. "Like Bettina did. We don't have a choice. There's no one else."

The simple words spoken with the wisdom of a child, broke Liz's heart. No eleven-year-old should have to be so keenly aware of life's unpleasant realities. Tyler was the same age and he didn't know anything about how the dark side of the world operated.

"I want to make it work," Liz reiterated to Melissa.

"I'm not leaving," Melissa told her and walked out.

"She'll get over it," Abby said, stepping back. "It'll take a while, but she will. She was scared when we were alone before."

"Weren't you?"

"Yeah, but I had someone taking care of me. She didn't have anyone."

"I'm sorry," Liz apologized. "I wish I'd known about you before."

"Me, too."

AFTER LUNCH, THE FOUR OF THEM went to the community pool. They found a cool spot in the shade. Liz leaned against a tree, opened her laptop and prayed for inspiration. Technically her deadline was generous enough that she wasn't exactly behind. Not yet. But give it another few weeks and she would feel the panic.

While her computer booted up, she gazed around the pool, taking in the other mothers and kids. Most of them seemed to know each other. One of the blessings—and curses—of small-town life.

She turned her attention to Tyler, spotting him easily from years of practice, then finding Melissa and Abby. Their red hair made them stand out in the crowd. A good thing, she told herself. After the morning she'd had, she was due for a break or two.

The streak didn't last. Five seconds later, someone spoke her name.

"Liz."

She didn't have to look up to recognize Ethan, who was very possibly the last person she wanted to see right now. Or ever.

"Tyler told me that you'd be here after lunch."

She kept her gaze firmly on her screen. With practiced ease, she opened her word processing program, then loaded the book in progress.

He dropped to the grass next to her. "Did I mention that I'm sorry?"

Grateful for the big hat she'd pulled on and the sunglasses shielding her eyes, she turned toward him. At least she didn't have to worry about him seeing she was more hurt than angry. He wouldn't know about the bitter taste of betrayal on her tongue or the lingering sense of having been hit in the gut.

"I didn't mean for you to hear that," he explained.

"Right. So you're apologizing for me hearing it but not for saying it. Thanks for the clarification."

His gaze sharpened. "That's not what I meant."

"Isn't it? It's what you said."

"Dammit, Liz, give me a break."

"Why? You spent the first part of the morning telling Tyler that it's my fault you and he don't know each other and the hour before noon telling your mother that I don't mean anything to you. I wasn't expecting you to declare I was the love of your life, but a little respect would have been nice."

"You're right."

"But that was too much. Instead you threw me under the bus. I'm not even surprised. You've done it before."

His gaze never left her face. "Why is it you get to tell me to stop bringing up the past, but you get to do it as much as you want?"

She opened her mouth, then closed it. She was angry and hurt and didn't want to admit he had a point. One she was going to ignore.

"We slept together, Ethan. We didn't plan it, but it happened. We have a child together. You can't say we're on the same team to my face, then undermine me every chance you get."

He drew in a breath. "I know. I'm sorry. I keep saying that and I mean it. Everything is different. Complicated. I'm trying to figure out what happens next."

"What happens next is we come up with a plan. A way for you to spend time with Tyler."

"I am spending time with him."

Despite the fact that he couldn't see her eyes, she looked away. "For later," she clarified. "When I go back to San Francisco."

His jaw tightened and his eyes darkened. "You're leaving? When?"

"I'm not sure. I want to fix up the house. I'm hiring a contractor to do the work. Then we're leaving." She turned back to him and pulled off her sunglasses. "This isn't about keeping you from Tyler, I swear. We'll do alternating weekends, share holidays."

"I don't want you to leave."

"That's not an option. I can't live here. I have a life I need to get back to. A job."

"You can write anywhere."

"You speak from experience?" she asked, her voice sharp with annoyance. "I hate it here. Everyone is very comfortable getting in my face about my past and they don't know what they're talking about. I don't see anyone blaming you. I want you to know your son. I want you to be a part of things, but whatever plan we come up with isn't going to include me staying here. When the house is finished, we're all leaving."

Ethan stared at her for a long time. She tried to read his expression but couldn't tell what he was thinking. He wasn't happy, but it hardly took insight to figure that out.

Finally he stood. "Thanks for the update," he said at last.

"You're pissed."

"You're stealing him from me. Again."

"What do I have to do to convince you that's not what I'm doing? You keep forgetting I'm the one who tried to get you into his life five years ago. I want this to work. But it's going to have to happen with him living in San Francisco."

He nodded once and left. Liz checked on all three kids, then leaned against the tree and drew in a breath.

There would be consequences, she thought grimly. With Ethan there were always consequences. He would probably try to convince her to stay. Which was fine. Let him try. But there was nothing he could say or do to keep her in town. And the sooner he figured that out, the better for all of them.

LIZ STILL WASN'T SLEEPING, so morning came early. With the kids out of school, she didn't have to worry about getting them up and ready, but there were other consid-erations. Mostly that today the construction team would arrive to start the remodeling. Jeff, the burly fifty-something contractor she'd hired, had promised his team would be at her place no later than seven. The fact that they would be done by four each day was minimal comfort.

She had set her travel alarm for six, showered, dressed and made coffee. She was on her second cup when someone knocked on her front door.

She crossed the living room to open it and smiled at the three women and one guy she saw on her porch.

"Right on time," she began, then blinked several times when she noticed the identical beige T-shirts they wore.

Instead of the ladder and truck logo she'd seen in the phone book, the name "Hendrix Construction" was spelled out in a sturdy font.

"You're not Jeff's crew, are you?" she asked already knowing the answer.

The woman closest to the door handed her a cell phone. "Boss said you'd want to talk to him."

She did her best not to shriek. "How thoughtful of him. If you'll excuse me?"

She closed the front door, looked at the number already punched into the cell phone, and pushed the send button. He answered on the first ring.

"Don't take it out on the team," Ethan said.

"Take what out on the charming construction crew on my front porch?"

"You know. And it's not Jeff's fault, either. He owed me."

"You seem very determined to make sure I blame you," she countered, her voice low, but still thick with anger. "Don't worry. I have every intention of making sure you pay for this."

"Look, you wanted your house fixed up. My team will do a great job."

She stepped away from the door and clutched the phone tighter. Outrage churned the coffee in her stomach. "Dammit, Ethan. What is wrong with you?"

"I bought out Jeff's contract. At a premium."

"I hope he totally screwed you."

"He made a profit."

"At least one of us is happy." She glanced around the run-down house and knew fixing it up wasn't optional. "Why are you doing this? Is it the thrill of constantly bugging me?"

"I want to know what you're doing. You're taking my kid away from me, Liz. I don't want any surprises."

"How is any of this a surprise? I told you my plan and made it very clear I want to work things out. I want you to have a relationship with Tyler. Why can't you believe that?"

"I do. I'm covering my bases. You ran once. You can do it again."

The unfairness of the accusation made her catch her breath. "I ran after you told all your friends I was some cheap whore you'd never bother with. The night before you'd promised to love me forever." She grabbed the back of the sofa. "Never mind, Ethan. I totally get it. You can't be trusted and you assume the world is just like you. Watch me all you want, if it gives you a thrill. I don't care. I've got nothing to hide. But here's the thing. Some of us do the right thing because it's what we've been taught, while others do it because it's who they are. I know which side I'm on in that discussion. If you're worried about how someone is playing this game while hiding his true character, you should look in the mirror."

She hung up, then crossed to the front door and pulled it open. After handing back the cell phone, she motioned for the crew to come in.

"You might as well get started," she told them.

It didn't matter who did the work, she thought as she walked upstairs. The sooner everything was finished, the sooner she could get the hell out of Fool's Gold.

But the morning surprises weren't quite over. As she walked into the master bedroom where Tyler was sleeping, she found Melissa standing by her dresser. The teen had Liz's wallet in her left hand and three twenties in her right.

Their eyes met. Liz had a feeling she looked shocked and more than a little stupid. The mystery of the lost pizza money and the missing bills from her wallet the previous week was suddenly solved. A sense of betrayal battled with the realization that the few months of abandonment had affected Melissa more than she'd let on.

The teen dropped the wallet back into Liz's purse, let the twenties flutter to the floor as she pushed past Liz and raced out of the room. Liz followed, reaching Melissa's bedroom door just before the girl could push it closed.

Melissa sat on her bed, her arms folded across her chest, her gaze locked on the floor. Liz pulled over the chair at the desk, then sat down.

"I guess we should talk about this," she said slowly. "I'm sorry. I should have thought the situation through. You were left with nothing, forced to steal to feed yourself and your sister. I can tell you that you're safe over and over again, but why should you believe me? You don't know me from a rock, I'm threatening to take you from your home and your friends. What if I leave like Bettina did? You'd have nothing. Nowhere to go. And there's Abby. You love her, but she's a big responsibility. You're only fourteen. It's way too much."

Melissa didn't speak. Her hair covered most of her face, but Liz saw the tears dropping onto her folded hands.

Liz ached for her. While she knew there had to be consequences for stealing, these were extraordinary circumstances. She wanted to be fair but also supportive.

"How much do you have?" she asked, trying to remember exactly how much was missing.

Melissa swallowed and raised her head. There were

tears in her eyes, and a look of both defiance and shame. "One hundred and twenty dollars."

"Did you have a goal in mind? An amount that would make you feel safe?"

The girl shrugged. "I don't know. Maybe two hundred dollars."

From a fourteen-year-old's perspective, that probably was enough. Reality was very different.

"I should be giving you and Abby an allowance," Liz told her. "I didn't even think of it. Let's talk later, when your sister is up. You'll get it weekly. That will be for spending money." She hesitated, not sure how to handle the stealing, but determined to do what felt right.

"I'll give you the rest of the money you need so that you have two hundred dollars. We'll put it in a safe place that only you and I know about. It will be there to make you feel safe. In return, you'll stop stealing from me. Agreed?"

The defiance faded. "You're not mad?"

"I'm disappointed, which is different. I understand why you took the money, but that doesn't make it right."

"So I'm still going to be punished."

Liz hid a smile. "I think it's important to be consistent."

"There are always consequences," Melissa grumbled with a sigh. Her gaze drifted to her nightstand. "Probably my cell phone would be the worst. For..." She sucked in a breath. "A week."

Her voice was barely a whisper and more tears filled

her eyes. Liz felt relief at the words. From what she could tell, Melissa was going to grow up to be an amazing person. She would try to remember that the next time her niece went off on her about the whole moving thing.

"I think two days is plenty," Liz said. "On one condition."

"Which is?" Melissa sounded relieved and a little wary.

"We're going to be staying in town for a few weeks while the work is done on the house. I've signed up all three of you for the new day camp. End Zone for Kids. I want you to help me convince Abby and Tyler this will be fun for them."

Defiance won over relief. "I'm too old for camp. I'm practically in high school."

"I know," Liz agreed. "When I called to register Abby and Tyler, I learned they have a program for older kids. It's sponsored by the university film school. Students are supposed to be in high school to get in, but I convinced them you were mature and more than ready for the experience. I don't know exactly what's involved. I think you learn about making movies. Everything from writing scripts to acting. Unless you think that would be too boring."

Melissa jumped to her feet, her face bright with excitement. "Really? I get to do that? Learn all about it and maybe be in a movie?"

"That's what they said."

"I would love that."

"Good. Then you'll help with convincing Abby and Tyler?"

"Sure." Melissa picked up her cell. "I have to call Tiffany and…" The light faded. "I guess I'll tell them in a couple of days," she corrected as she handed over the phone.

Liz took it and put it in her pocket. "Thanks. Want to wake up your sister while I tackle Tyler?"

Melissa nodded. "What time do we leave?"

"Eight-thirty. Abby and Tyler are in a computer animation class. I hope they like it."

"They'll love it."

Melissa turned to leave, then came back and hugged Liz. "I'm sorry," she whispered. "About taking the money."

"Me, too, but I understand why you did it." She put her hands on the girl's shoulders. "I'm not going to walk away from you and Abby. I know it's going to take time, but it would nice if you started to believe me."

Melissa nodded. "Okay." Then she left.

Liz watched her go, appreciating the temporary truce. It was just a matter of time until they were fighting about the move. Melissa wasn't going to give in on that easily. Regardless, it wasn't a battle the teen was going to win. There was absolutely nothing anyone could say or do to convince Liz that she was staying in Fool's Gold. She might have to return for the signing and to deliver Tyler to his father every other weekend, but she would do everything in her power to never again call this place home.

LIZ PICKED OUT HER CHOICE FOR lunch in a matter of minutes. The barbecue chicken salad looked great. It was what to have with it that had her stumped.

"You look determined," Pia noted from across the table. "Should I be worried?"

Liz forced a smile. With everything going on in her life these days, the last thing she'd wanted to do was have lunch with Pia. But the other woman had insisted and Liz hadn't been able to say no.

"I'm fine," she replied, trying to unclench her teeth. "Just a little stressed."

"How's it going with Roy's daughters? Are they having trouble adjusting to you?"

"Among other things."

Pia looked sympathetic. "I can't believe you're going to be taking care of them. They're young girls. You don't even know them."

"They're family."

Pia's blue eyes darkened with an emotion Liz couldn't read. "Yes, that is important, isn't it? The whole family connection. I hope they know they're lucky to have you."

"I'm planning on moving them to San Francisco. They're not happy about it—especially Melissa. Right now things are fine, but we'll be fighting again later."

The waitress appeared to take their drink orders.

"White wine," Liz decided firmly. "Chardonnay."

"Me, too," Pia said, then grinned when their server left. "I don't usually indulge in the middle of the day."

"Me, either. But I'm walking home from here, the kids are taking the bus and I've earned it."

"They're up at the new camp?"

"Yes. Even Melissa was excited." Liz told her about the film class.

"Sounds like fun," Pia commented as their wine was delivered. "Keeps them from getting bored."

Liz sipped her wine gratefully. "There's going to be construction in the house. My brother was great at starting projects, but didn't feel enthused about finishing them. The house needs to be fixed up so we can sell it or rent it out. I haven't decided."

"You haven't been back in years and now you're dealing with all this," Pia described, sounding sympathetic. "That can't be easy."

"It's not," Liz admitted. "Between the unexpected responsibility of my nieces, Tyler getting to know his dad, me having to deal with Ethan and being back in Fool's Gold, it's been an active couple of weeks." She took another sip. "Ethan's mother hates me."

"Denise? I doubt that. She likes everyone."

If only that were true, Liz thought. "She doesn't like me. She's angry about me keeping Tyler from Ethan and the family."

"Well, sure."

Liz looked at the woman sitting across from her. "Let me pause and bask in your sympathy."

"Sorry. I didn't mean for it to come out like that. But from her point of view, she's lost time. Nothing can make up for that." Pia held up her hand. "And before you go off on me about sleeping with Ethan right after you left—first, I didn't know you were actually dating him. Second, nothing happened. He was too drunk that night and we didn't make a second attempt."

"You're saying lack of penetration means it doesn't count?"

"Something like that."

Liz was too tired to fight, even with Pia. "I'll accept the blame for the first six years that were lost, but not after that. I came back again."

She briefly told Pia about her meeting with Rayanne and the subsequent letter.

Pia's blue eyes widened. "I can't believe she did that. I know Rayanne had her problems, but to keep Tyler from Ethan? And then she died without telling him."

"Why are you surprised? She was never very nice. To me the question is more about why Ethan ever got involved with her."

"She was pregnant when they got married," Pia informed, then paused as their salads were delivered.

Pregnant as in they *had* to get married? Liz waited until the server had left to lean forward. "That's why they got married?"

"Uh-huh. I think Rayanne had picked out Ethan a while before, but he wasn't that interested. Then she got pregnant and he wasn't the kind of guy to walk away."

Liz ignored the stab of pain at hearing that and refused to wonder if he would have been willing to marry her if he'd found out about Tyler. She knew the answer. After all, Ethan was a Hendrix.

"Then I showed up," Liz said. "Threatening her happy world."

"She must have been terrified. Especially if she knew that you and Ethan had been involved before. She would have thought she could lose everything." Pia looked at her. "You probably think she deserved it. She wasn't exactly nice to you in high school."

Neither were you. Liz thought the words, but didn't say them. Pia was different. Not the same mean girl she'd been back then.

"No one deserves to lose everything," Liz said at last.

"But it happens." Pia sipped her wine. "It did to me."

"What are you talking about."

"You don't know? Oh, right. You were gone by then." Pia shrugged. "My senior year of high school it all fell apart. My dad lost his job."

"He owned the company, didn't he?"

"He was president, which isn't exactly the same thing. It seems sales weren't as good as he had led the board of directors to believe. He'd also been stealing money for years. Not telling the employees was one thing, but not telling the IRS is another. He was charged with tax evasion, fraud, theft. I can't remember everything. My mom took off for Florida. I wanted to stay here and finish high school. She agreed. When I graduated, she said, after what she'd been through, it would be better if I learned to stand on my own."

Liz didn't know what to say. "I'm sorry." Her own mother hadn't been a prize, but at least she'd grown up used to it. Pia's mother had done an about-face at the worst time in a young girl's life. That made things worse. "What about your dad?"

"He killed himself the day before the trial started."

Liz dropped her fork onto the table. "Pia. I'm so sorry."

"It was a long time ago."

"That can't make it any easier to deal with."

The other woman looked at her and smiled slightly. "It makes it easier to forget. Besides, I was a real bitch in high school. Maybe I earned it."

"No. You didn't. I really am sorry."

"Sorry enough to let the whole naked-with-Ethan thing go?"

Liz nodded. "I was never really angry at you."

"I'm a safer target than Ethan. Right?"

Liz shrugged. "And you're also insightful. That's annoying."

Pia's smile turned genuine. "This is probably where we say we're going to start over and really be friends."

Liz thought about everything going on in her life. How there wasn't anyone she could talk to. How nice it would be to have someone on her side.

"I'd like that," she admitted.

"Me, too."

Pia sighed. "You need to give the town a chance. I

know things have been rough, but the people here will support you, if you give it time."

"No, thanks. I'm not buying into the theory of small-town bliss."

"Maybe we'll change your mind."

"Maybe hell will freeze over."

Pia laughed. "You never know."

CHAPTER TEN

AFTER A FEW DAYS, LIZ SETTLED into a routine. The construction crew showed up every morning and made impressive progress on the house—a fact that surprised her. She had wondered if Ethan had told his people to go slow, but he obviously hadn't. The kids settled into the rhythm of day camp, taking the bus up the mountain every morning and riding it back down every afternoon.

They all loved their programs, especially Melissa, who had already spent two evenings online checking out the USC Film School. Ethan had seen Tyler twice, which she encouraged. He'd also tried to talk to her, which she'd resisted. Despite his apology, she was still hurt by what he'd said to his mother. The honest assessment that she didn't matter shouldn't have been a surprise, but knowing that didn't take away the sting of the words.

He was a weakness. Here, in town, on a sunny morning as she walked by the lake, she could admit the truth. There was something about Ethan. Maybe because he was the first man she'd ever loved, ever been with. Maybe because they had a child together. Whatever the reason, he could get to her in a way no one else could. Around him, she was vulnerable. Which made him dangerous.

Avoiding him might not be the most mature response, but it was the safest.

Liz glanced at her watch. She'd had a productive writing morning and had rewarded herself with this walk. But now it was time to head back to her computer and review the pages she'd written. To make them better, sharper.

She took the path leading back to town, thinking that she could stop for a latte. The caffeine would perk her up and give her the energy she needed to push through the pages. She'd barely made it to the corner when someone called her name. She turned and saw Montana waving.

While Ethan might not be one of her favorite people at the moment, Liz found herself smiling as Montana approached. Ethan's sister was unfailingly cheerful and enthused. There were days when a little enthusiasm was the best gift possible.

"Taking a break?" Montana asked as she approached. "I'm desperate for coffee. I was up all night reading. It's so hard when a book is great, you know? So great you can't stop reading even though it's late and your eyes are burning."

"It's the best compliment any writer can ask for," Liz told her. "Come on. I'll buy you a latte."

They got their coffee, then sat in the shade on the small patio outside Starbucks.

"My mother hates you," Montana stated cheerfully. "Okay—maybe *hate* is too strong, but she's still going off on rants about you."

Liz held in a groan. "Thanks for the update."

"Don't worry about it. She starts out feeling sad about how everyone said really bad things about you in high school. She has three daughters and knows if anyone had talked about us that way, it would have broken her heart. Then she admits it would have been tough to raise a kid on her own and how you did such a great job. Then she starts in on the fact that you would have been welcome in her house and all she missed and then she's throwing pots and we're ducking for cover."

Liz winced. "You have a gift for making things come alive."

Montana laughed. "The outbursts have a little less energy every time. In another month or so, she'll be calm." Her humor faded. "It's not you she's mad at. It's circumstances. I think she understands more than she's letting on."

"I hope so," Liz said, thinking that Denise would always come down on Ethan's side. After all, he was her son and Liz was just the woman who had kept Tyler from the Hendrix family.

"Dakota and Nevada are pretty much staying out of it," Montana continued. "And my other brothers barely know what's going on. Mom will come around. It's worth the wait. Once you're part of the family, she'll do anything to protect you."

"She might make an exception for me," Liz murmured.

"No," Montana corrected, briefly touching her arm. "I'm saying this all wrong, aren't I? She'll be there for you, Liz. I promise."

"Thanks. How's the book fair coming?"

"Great."

Montana launched into details about the project. Liz pretended to listen, but instead thought about the other woman's words. Liz's track record with Ethan wasn't exactly impressive and while the idea of Denise being on her side was tempting, she knew better than to hope for too much.

"If you have anyone you want to invite," Montana was saying, "let me know and I'll put them on the list. We're going to have a VIP reception and everything. A chance for lesser mortals to mingle."

Liz laughed. "Lesser mortals? I don't think so."

"It's how we see ourselves. We have a club with bylaws and everything. So anyone from San Francisco?"

"No, thanks. My friends there have all been to plenty of signings. I think my assistant would like to come, though. Every time I talk to her, she wants to know about small-town life." Obviously Peggy had been watching too much TV, Liz thought grimly. If she knew the reality of Fool's Gold, she would run in the opposite direction.

Montana's eyes brightened with interest. "No one of the male variety longing for your return?"

"Sorry, but no."

Montana sighed. "Damn. I was hoping one of us had a decent love life. Mine sucks." She sipped her coffee. "I can't believe you're not married. You're successful, beautiful, totally together."

If Liz had been drinking, she would have choked. "Is that how you see me?"

"Well, yeah. It's who you are."

"Not exactly. I'm more the scrambling-to-keep-up kind of person," Liz told her. Beautiful? Not even with perfect lighting. "The book success is great, but it's what I do, not who I am. And there are downsides."

"Crazed fans?"

"I'm sure I have a few. But the bigger problem is more how people think about me. The assumptions."

Montana leaned toward her. "By people you mean guys."

Liz laughed. "Did you have to choose this moment to be perceptive?"

"It's a gift. Who is he?"

Liz hesitated, then decided she didn't mind telling the story—even if it made her look stupid. "His name is Ryan. He's a writer, too, which should have been a clue. When we met, he'd published two classic coming-of-age novels. Sort of a poor man's Nick Hornby, without being even close to that good. But he'd had some modest success. We met at a launch party for another author. He was charming and I was…" She drew in a breath. "I was lonely."

"How long ago was this?"

"About four years ago. I'd been raising Tyler on my own, I'd managed to get my first book published, and while it had done well, it was a first book. I didn't know if I had a career or a single lucky break. I was still working as a waitress to support us, writing at night and getting by on about four hours of sleep."

Liz shrugged. "We talked at the party, exchanged numbers. I didn't think anything of it. And I didn't hear from him for about three months. At the time he said it was because he'd been on the road, looking for inspiration for his next book." She wrinkled her nose. "I figured out later, it was because he was waiting to see how my second book did."

Montana's eyes widened. "No way."

"Uh-huh. I suppose if it hadn't been successful, I never would have heard from him."

"What a jerk."

"A very smooth, good-looking jerk," Liz told her, remembering how dazzled she'd been on their first date. Ryan couldn't have been more attentive and interesting. Not to mention funny, charming and kind. He'd been great with Tyler, too. He'd played her and her kid, and she hadn't known at all.

"He was everything I could have wished for. I was crazy about him. We got engaged."

"You were married?" Montana's voice was a squeak.

"No. Somehow the wedding never got planned. Which turned out to be a good thing. He went to New York to meet with his publisher about his new book. He wouldn't tell me what it was about, which was fine. That was his process. While he was gone, I watered his plants."

Liz rested her forearms on the table. "Okay—let me just admit I was really curious about the book he was writing. He'd been so excited about it and his previous book had bombed. I wanted him to do well."

Montana's mouth twitched. "You went snooping."

"Not my finest moment, but yes. There were some notes on his desk and I read them."

"It wasn't very good?" Montana asked sympathetically.

"Worse. It wasn't his. He'd stolen my idea. Unlike him, I do talk about my stories. I can be tedious and annoying about it. It's how I work through problems before I start the actual writing. So he knew everything I was going to do. He had taken the entire story, changed the names and written it. Without saying a word."

Liz still remembered standing in Ryan's office, hearing nothing but a rushing sound. She'd wondered if there was something wrong with her brain—a stroke or something. Because what she'd been reading hadn't made sense. It couldn't. The man she'd said she would love forever, the man she'd promised to marry couldn't possibly have taken her work for his own. There had to be a mistake.

Montana swore softly. "What did you do?"

"I tried to convince myself I was crazy. Then I got mad. I waited until he was home and I confronted him."

"Did he deny it?"

"No. Apparently having a good idea isn't enough. His editor had hated the book and told Ryan they wouldn't be publishing him anymore. Ryan was furious. He blamed me. He said I'd known what he was doing and had tricked him into writing a story that didn't work. He said it wasn't fair. That he had the actual talent. I was nothing but a hack, yet I had all the success."

She still remembered the fury in his eyes, the loathing.

"He'd never been interested in me beyond what I could do for his career. He'd lied about nearly everything, especially how he felt about me." Liz managed a smile. "The good news is he moved away after that and my recovery was fairly quick. Apparently I wasn't as in love with him as I'd thought."

But it had been one more illustration of the lesson that men shouldn't be trusted. Not with something as delicate as a woman's heart.

"How did Tyler take it?" Montana asked.

"It turns out my son had never much liked Ryan but he hadn't told me because he wanted me to be happy. Which makes me about the luckiest mother ever."

Montana sniffed. "Now I just want to hug him and never let go."

"I know how you feel."

"And kill that Ryan jerk. Want me to give Ethan his name so he can beat him up?"

Liz shook her head. "Probably best if Ethan doesn't hear the story at all." She didn't need him to know how stupid she'd been.

"You're right. But still. I hope he's punished in some way."

"I suspect Ryan will be unhappy for most of his life. That's punishment enough for me. I'm just happy to have escaped. He gives writers a bad name."

"You should tell the college to start giving your scholarship to students who want to be writers. That would be very cool."

"What are you talking about?"

"Your scholarship. Okay, it's not yours, but it's named after you. Here. At Fool's Gold Community College."

If they'd been drinking alcohol, Liz would have thought Montana was drunk. But it was the middle of the day and they'd only had lattes. "I don't have a scholarship at the college."

"Sure you do. It was set up a while ago. I don't know all the details, but it was started with the scholarship you didn't use."

Liz stared at her blankly. "The scholarship?" Nothing about this made sense.

"You had a scholarship out of high school. Remember?"

"Sure. But I left."

"Exactly. Someone had the idea to use that as seed money to fund a scholarship every year. They're given to women who have faced hardship—financial or personal. I know because I looked into applying. You really don't know about this?"

"No."

"You should talk to the college. They can explain the details."

"I will," Liz assured, thinking that Montana had to be wrong. Who would have started a scholarship in her name?

An hour later, she had the information package in her hand and was smiling at a very excited clerk in the admissions office.

"We're all huge fans," the older woman told her. "I can't believe you're really here. We read all your books."

"Thanks," Liz said. "Can you tell me about the origin of the scholarship?"

The woman, her tag read Betty Higgins, frowned. "I would have thought someone would have been in touch with you about it. Very strange. Anyway, when you left town without using your scholarship money, someone suggested giving it to another student. But then several people came in with anonymous donations, increasing the amount and we realized we could make this an annual scholarship instead of a onetime gift."

Betty glanced around as if to make sure they were alone and lowered her voice. "I moved here a few years ago, but heard all about your sad story. How your mama, God rest her soul, wasn't exactly maternal and a lot of boys said hateful things about you. Apparently many people knew you were having a rough time of it and they felt badly. So they put this all together. Your scholarship is one of our most popular. Not only for people funding it, but for the women who apply. Most of the recipients are returning students. Women with families, trying to give themselves a better future. It's so inspiring."

Talk about too much information in too short a time, Liz thought, her head spinning.

She remembered the scholarship she'd been offered and how she'd planned to use the money to go away to college. She and Ethan had spent the summer talking about being together on a university campus. How perfect it would be.

Then he'd denied even knowing her and she'd taken off. She'd never given the money a second thought. She'd left because staying was impossible.

That much she could handle, but Betty's claim that people had known about her circumstances astonished her. Part of her appreciated the gesture of donating while the rest of her wondered where they'd been when she'd been young and alone. A kind word back then would have meant the world to her.

It was too much, she thought.

"Thanks for the information," she said.

"You're welcome." Betty smiled. "This is such a

thrill. I can't wait to tell everyone I met you. Oh. We're having our reception in a few weeks. For the recipients. Can you come?"

"I, ah…"

"It's only for an hour or so. I know those women would appreciate the chance to thank you in person."

"I didn't do anything," Liz countered. "I'm not the one they should be thanking."

"You're an inspiration. In fact, two of the women wrote about you for their essays. How you started with nothing and made yourself a success. Why don't I send you an invitation and you can think about it?"

"Um, sure." Liz cleared her throat. "Thank you."

"It was my pleasure."

Liz left the college and walked to her car. But instead of driving home, she made her way back into town and parked outside of the Hendrix Construction office. Before she could change her mind, she turned off the engine and went into the building.

After giving her name to the receptionist, she paced the small waiting area. Seconds later, Ethan appeared, looking tall and strong and pleased to see her.

Inside her belly, something fluttered. Something hot and bright and dangerous. She ignored the sensation.

"Is this a good time?" she asked. "Can you talk?"

"Sure."

He led the way to his office. "Everything all right?" he inquired as he closed the door behind her.

"No. Nothing's all right. I'm still mad at you, by the

way, so don't think everything is fine between us. I hate this town. I hate everyone knowing everything about me. Your mother is still angry at me, and I hate that part of me understands why. I blame you for most of this, in case you were wondering. But just when I think I know exactly where all the pieces fit, I get surprised."

"A good surprise or a bad one?"

"Good." She paced the length of his office. "There's a scholarship in my name."

"At the community college."

"You knew?" She spun to face him.

He leaned against his desk. "Sure. It's been around awhile."

"You never thought to tell me?"

"Why would I?"

Right. "I don't know why, but I feel like it changes everything. But where were these caring people when I was growing up? Why didn't someone tell protective services that my mother was slapping me around? Why didn't someone notice that she supported herself with casual prostitution with her underaged daughter in the house? Probably because they didn't want to get involved. So they ignored the problem until it went away, and then they started a scholarship in my name. Does that make sense to you?"

She crossed to the window and turned back. Moving seemed required. She wasn't sure what would happen if she stood still. Scream maybe. Or fall apart.

As she passed Ethan, he grabbed her and pulled her close. At first she resisted, but then she collapsed into his arms, wanting to feel his strength surround her.

"It's okay," he murmured.

"You think?"

"It will be."

She sucked in a breath, letting her hands rest on his shoulders. "This town is making me crazy."

"If it makes you feel any better, old Mrs. Egger cornered me yesterday. Slapped me with that big purse of hers and accused me of not respecting you. Not only did she give me *what for* because I'd, and this is a direct quote, 'ruined the reputation of a perfectly respectable girl,' she pointed out that if I was going to let my sperm loose on society, I should keep track of them." He shuddered. "I never want to hear a woman in her eighties talking about my sperm."

Liz leaned her forehead against his shoulder and smiled. "I always liked Mrs. Egger."

"I thought you'd say that." He put his hand on her chin, pressing until she looked at him. "I know this is hard."

"You really don't."

"I'm trying to understand. I want you to like it here."

Meaning he wanted her to stay. Which wasn't going to happen, but there was no reason to go over that material again, she thought, wanting to stay in his arms forever.

Her gaze dropped to his mouth. Wanting burned. Not just for how kissing him would make her feel, but because when she was with him, nothing else could touch her. There was only the man and what they could do to each other.

"I thought I was only going to have to deal with Roy's kids," she admitted. "You weren't supposed to be a part of this."

"Too late to get rid of me now."

"I don't want to," she said.

"What do you want?"

An impossible question, she thought. One without an answer.

No. That wasn't true. She had plenty of answers, just none she wanted to share with him.

"I want us to be friends," she told him. "I want to be able to trust you."

"You can."

"I don't think so."

He kissed her. "Come on, Liz. You know me. I'm a good guy."

"Are you saying there aren't any more surprises?"

Before he could answer, his phone buzzed.

"Sorry to bother you, Ethan, but it's that call from China."

Liz stepped out of his arms. "When did you go international?"

"Not me. The windmills." He frowned. "I need to take this call, but then I want to talk to you."

"I'm fine. Go be successful. I have to get home."

"Liz, I—"

She cut him off with the shake of her head. "International calls shouldn't be kept waiting. I'll see you later."

She stepped out of his office and made her way to her car. Thoughts spun in her head. That there were multiple versions of the past. While she resented the fact that no one had bothered to step forward when she was growing up, she hadn't been as ignored and forgotten as she'd thought.

Which meant what? That Fool's Gold wasn't evil? She'd never thought of it that way—at least not in general.

The information about a scholarship in her name shouldn't have made a difference, yet she found herself feeling better about nearly everything and wasn't exactly sure why.

LIZ WOKE EARLY THE NEXT morning with a growing sense of the inevitable. After showering and dressing, she went downstairs and started coffee. The kids would sleep until the construction crew arrived, which gave her a half hour or so of perfect quiet.

She took her coffee out onto the front porch to enjoy the stillness of the morning. The air was cool, the sky clear. The sound of birds greeted her as she settled on the top step with her mug.

Maybe she needed more time before making her decision, she thought cautiously. Yes, there were things she really hated about this town, but there were other parts she liked. Melissa and Abby were desperate to stay and after all they'd been through, shouldn't she consider their feelings? Tyler would enjoy living close to his dad and Liz knew it was what Ethan wanted, too. Ethan's mother was a problem, but better a rabid grandmother than one who wasn't interested at all. Given time, maybe she and Liz could come to terms.

Of course Liz could be completely fooling herself. There was the possibility she was blinded by a scholarship, a few kind words and the feel of Ethan's arms around her. Clarity would come with time, she told herself. She didn't have to tell anyone she was having second thoughts about leaving.

An unfamiliar sedan pulled up to the curb and an older man in a suit got out. He stared at her a moment, shrugged, then reached for something in his car.

"Morning," he said as he approached, an envelope in his hand. "You're up early."

She smiled. "It's the only time it's quiet."

"I hear you." He hesitated. "My workday starts in a couple hours. I was on my way to Starbucks. They've got me hooked on their lattes. Can't get going in the morning without one."

She rose and moved to the gate. While the conversation was pleasant enough, she felt uneasy with the man's presence.

"Can I help you with something?"

The old man nodded slowly. "I would have come back later, but seeing as you're already up... Elizabeth Marie Sutton?"

How did he know her name?

She felt a prickling sensation on the back of her neck.

He held out the envelope, then waited until she took it. "You've been served."

CHAPTER ELEVEN

"You slimy, weaselly, disgusting bastard," Liz yelled the second Ethan stepped into his office building.

Ethan came to a stop and stared at her cautiously. Liz looked ferocious, which wasn't good, but he had a feeling he knew why.

She stood by the reception desk. It was still early enough that most of the staff hadn't arrived. Nevada's truck was in the parking lot, but his sister was nowhere to be seen. She normally arrived around six-thirty. Today hadn't been an exception. The only difference appeared to be that she'd let Liz in to wait for him.

"I should have known," Liz continued, her green eyes flashing a level of rage powerful enough to melt steel. "You say one thing to my face and go behind my back. And here I stand. Surprised. Which makes me an idiot. Well, I'm done being stupid where you're concerned. Know this—I will never trust you again. Ever. Do you hear me? I hope you rot in hell. I hope there's a special place there just for you."

She picked up the message pad from the reception desk and threw it at him. He sidestepped the missile easily. When she reached for the computer flat screen, he grabbed her arm.

"Stop."

"I won't." She wrenched free and glared at him. "There's no excuse for what you did."

The envelope was in her hand.

He wrestled with regret, then reminded himself that she hadn't given him a choice. "They weren't supposed to serve you until this afternoon. I was going to come tell you myself. This morning."

"Oh, please. Let's not even pretend that's true. You've always been a coward and a liar. That hasn't changed."

He grabbed her arm again and this time didn't let go. "I was going to tell you. I started to explain yesterday."

If her gaze had had laser power, he would be a small stain on the rug right now.

"That's so much bullshit," she snapped. "And here I am wearing sandals."

She tried to pull free, but he didn't let her go. "Liz, calm down. We have to talk."

She continued to tug. Afraid he would bruise her, he finally let her go. She staggered back a step.

"I was going to tell you," he repeated.

He read the betrayal in her eyes, the hint of pain. "Liar," she echoed, then waved the envelope. "If this is how you want to play it, then fine. Because I know some damn good lawyers."

"I'd hoped we could work it out ourselves."

"You're the one who went to court, Ethan."

He had. He'd seen a family court judge and asked for an injunction. One that forbade Liz from leaving Fool's Gold with Tyler.

"I didn't know how else to stop you from taking Tyler away," he explained.

"I have a right to a life," she said, rubbing her arm. "That life is in San Francisco."

"You can explain that to the judge next week."

"I will. I also plan to tell her that I made two efforts to tell you about Tyler and that the only reason you don't already have a relationship with him is your late wife kept the information from you. So don't think you'll make me the bad guy in all this."

"You were going to leave," he reminded her, doing his best to hold his temper. It wouldn't help anyone if they both got mad. "You didn't give me a choice in the matter. You just said that I could have alternating weekends. As if that was enough."

She stared at him. "Is that what this is about? You want more time? Then why didn't you come to me and say that? Why involve a judge?"

"Because I've already lost too much time as it is. I'm not losing any more. You could walk away tomorrow and I couldn't stop you. Now I can."

"There were a lot of ways to guarantee my cooperation. This isn't one of them."

"The person I care about here is Tyler."

"And you think I don't?" she demanded. "You think I haven't spent the last eleven years lying awake at night, worrying about him, doing what I think is best? Do you think it was easy to come back here five years ago to tell you about him? Do you think it was pleasant talking to Rayanne, listening to her judge me for having had your baby? Do you think I liked her calling me a whore?"

His gut clenched. He wanted to say that Rayanne wouldn't have done that, only he knew better. She would have said that and more. Liz would have represented everything she'd both hated and wanted. Beauty, brains, determination.

He wanted the past to be different but the truth is his relationship with Rayanne had been a mistake. He'd been bored, she'd been pursuing him and if she hadn't gotten pregnant—probably on purpose—he would have broken things off sooner rather than later.

But she had gotten pregnant and he'd accepted the responsibility. The way he would have done with Liz.

"I would have married you," he said softly.

Words he'd expected to make things better. Instead the fury returned. "Yes, I know. Despite having denied even knowing me, let alone swearing you were in love with me, you would have been noble and married the slut you'd knocked up. Lucky me. I could have been your wife. What a thrill to spend my life wondering what horrible things you were saying about me. We could have had T-shirts made. 'I didn't want to marry her. I don't even like her.' That would have been great."

"Dammit, Liz, I said I was sorry. I was young and

stupid. Or does the absolution only go one way? I'm supposed to get over your halfhearted attempt to tell me about Tyler when you were first pregnant. That's fine, because hey, you tried. But my screw up is unforgivable? Want to test your theory in the general public? Or before the judge?"

She raised her hand, as if to hit him. He grabbed her wrist.

They were both breathing hard, glaring fiercely at each other. There was no softness in her expression. No affection, no passion. He'd paid a high price to keep her from leaving. He knew that.

"Tyler is my son," he said, releasing her. "I've already lost most of his childhood. I'm not willing to lose any more. I protect what's mine."

"Selectively," she corrected, lowering her arm and walking to the door. "You'll protect what's yours selectively. Let's not forget that."

She walked out. The door slammed behind her.

Ethan stood in the foyer, his fists clenching and unclenching. Helplessness washed through him, which only infuriated him more.

Liz made him crazy—more than any other woman he knew. She had the ability to make him see the worst in himself—and to want to fix it. She was maddening and difficult and, he had to admit, maybe she was right.

An office door opened and Nevada stepped out into the main room. His sister, dressed in jeans and a work shirt, as always, her boots worn and practical, stared at him.

"You're beyond stupid," she said. "You know that, right?"

"I had to stop her from leaving."

"I understand, but jeez, Ethan. There were a lot better ways to go about it. You should have at least warned her."

"I was going to."

"Famous last words." She walked over to him. "I was younger than both you and Liz, but even I heard talk about her. People said ugly things about her mom and assumed they were true about her, too. She grew up with that, every single day."

He didn't want to hear this, didn't want to know he might have gone too far. "She would have taken Tyler from me."

"So you'd rather be right than win?" Nevada asked. "You're smarter than that. There's too much at stake here. You've just made Liz your enemy. Is that what you want?"

"I didn't know what else to do."

"What happened to sitting down and talking?"

"Not something Liz and I can do." The one evening they'd tried, they'd ended up making love in the kitchen. While he would enjoy repeating the experience, it didn't accomplish anything. "This solves the problem."

"If you believe that, you're even more stupid than I thought. Do you get what Liz is going through? Being back in town can't be easy. You know how people speak their minds. She's at the receiving end of a lot of criti-cism. Liz doesn't have anyone on her side. Okay—Montana likes her, but is one friend enough? You're her son's father. She should be able to trust you and she can't. No wonder she wants to leave. You're lucky she didn't kick you in the balls first. I would have."

"I love you, too, sis," he said sarcastically.

She gave him that pitying look that always made him uncomfortable. "You don't get it and because of that, you're going to lose."

"What don't I get?"

"I know what Dad used to tell you. We all heard the lectures about what it meant to be a Hendrix. How we had to protect the family name. You got it more than all the rest of us put together. You're the oldest. You would have done anything for him. You gave up your life to take over the family business when he died." She touched his arm.

"Dad was wrong, Ethan. There are more important things than the family name and reputation. There are the people we love. There's doing what your heart tells you is right."

"I'm not in love with Liz."

"No, but back then, you were supposed to be. Doing what's right isn't supposed to hurt someone you care about."

LIZ SPENT THE MORNING WEEDING. The alternative was breaking every plate in the house, as a way to vent her temper. While the theory was great, she wasn't sure it was especially smart, considering not only would she have to replace all the dishes, she would also be the one cleaning up the mess.

As she dug and hacked in the garden, she did her best to look at the situation from Ethan's point of view. An attempt that still made her want to punch him really hard.

What she would agree on—not that she was going to tell *him* anytime soon—was that if she expected him to let the past go, she would have to do the same. Yes, he'd been horrible to her nearly twelve years before, but she'd been worse. She'd made a halfhearted attempt to tell him about her pregnancy, then had disappeared for six years. Not exactly a mature decision.

But an injunction?

By eleven she was hot and sweaty and ready to let go of her fury, if only to get into the cool house. She waited until the construction crew left for lunch, then showered quickly and worked until about three. Then she gathered the ingredients for cookies, cranked up the CD player and danced along to the Black Eyed Peas until the kids got home.

"Mo-om!" Tyler said when he walked into the kitchen with Melissa and Abby. He sounded both horrified and confused. "What are you doing?"

"Making cookies. I've already made some oatmeal raisin. Now I'm moving on to peanut butter."

Tyler wrinkled his nose. "I meant the other part."

"The dancing?" she asked with a laugh and turned the player up even louder. "It's fun."

She reached for Abby who took her hand and began to move her hips. Melissa surprised her by spinning around, then waving her arms in time with the music. Soon even Tyler joined in and they were all dancing around the kitchen.

Liz showed them how to form a conga line and they were weaving through the downstairs, bumping into the sofa and yelling the words to the song.

She broke free of the line and spun in a circle as the song ended. Abby and Tyler flopped onto the sofa, both giggling. But Melissa stood still, her face etched with sadness.

"What's wrong?" Liz asked.

"My mom used to dance with me," the teen said. "My real mom. Not Bettina." She gave a smile that faded quickly. "I don't remember very much about her."

"You remember her in your heart," Liz said. "That's what's important."

"I guess."

Abby stood and sighed. "I don't remember her at all."

Liz moved to her and touched her cheek. "That's okay. I'm sure she understands and loves you very much."

"From heaven?"

Liz nodded. Now wasn't the time to get involved in a "life after death" discussion.

"You promise?"

"Yes," Liz told her. "I promise. No matter what, your mom loves you."

She wanted to look at Tyler, to see if he got the message as well, but kept her attention on Abby.

"Dad never wrote us," Melissa pointed out.

Liz didn't know what to say. Roy had promised he would. These were his daughters. Families could be complicated, she thought sadly.

"Does he still love us?" Abby asked.

"Yes." Liz pulled her close, then held out her free arm to Melissa. "He does. Right now he's dealing with a lot." What had he said? That he was a busy man? She didn't understand how he could ignore his children, but this wasn't about him. It was about making the girls feel better.

"Can we go see him?" Melissa asked, then cleared her throat. "I want to go see him."

"I'll take you," Liz said hesitantly. "But you have to be prepared. Your dad is in prison. It's not like the movies. It's a lot less clean and it's a little intimidating." There was also a smell, but some details were better left blurry. They would find out soon enough. "I'm not saying that to change your mind, but to warn you what it's going to be like."

"I want to see him," Melissa repeated. "Abby, if you're scared, you don't have to come."

"I want to see Dad, too," she whispered.

Liz hugged them both. "Then we'll go."

She glanced at Tyler, who was watching her wide-eyed. Theirs had always been a quiet life, she thought. With routines and predictability. Sure, she'd pulled him out of school once or twice a year for a fun day in the city, but that had been a good kind of surprise. Not every unexpected event fell into that category.

Reality came in all shapes and sizes. In the end, he had two parents who cared about him, even if they couldn't care about each other. She would die for her child. While Ethan might not be there yet, he was determined to be a part of Tyler's life, which was an excellent start.

As for her nieces, they would have to take things slow. Seeing Roy would make his prison sentence real. Whether or not it made leaving harder or easier, she couldn't say. But however things turned out, they would find their way to becoming a family.

In the kitchen, the timer dinged.

"We have cookies," she announced, releasing the girls. "I'm going to need some help sampling. Any volunteers?"

All three of them yelled out they were willing and together they walked into the kitchen.

ETHAN WANTED TO IGNORE his mother's voice-mail request that he stop by on his way home that evening, but knew it wasn't a good idea. Denise didn't make many demands of her children, so when she asked for something, they mostly paid attention.

He had a feeling he knew the topic she would want to discuss. He would rather chew glass than talk about his relationship with Liz, but he didn't see how he could avoid it. Sometimes having close relationships was a giant pain in the ass. If he and his mother were estranged, he could cheerfully ignore her. But they weren't, and the affection between them demanded he be forthcoming.

He parked in front of the house and walked to the front door.

"It's me," he called.

"I'm in the kitchen."

He moved to the rear of the house, then stepped into the bright, open kitchen. His mother stood at the counter, pouring sun tea into tall glasses filled with ice. She wore cropped pants and a pink T-shirt, was barefoot and had a country station playing on the radio.

Everything about this was familiar, he thought as he took his usual seat at the large table in the center of the room.

"How's it going?" he asked.

"Good. Great." She approached him with the glass and set it in front of him. "I met someone. His name is Roger. He owns a shipping company. We're going to Las Vegas together on Friday."

He stared at her, the words sinking into his consciousness. "What?"

Her dark eyes were alive with excitement. "It's wonderful. To think I could fall in love again, and at my age.

The sex...well, I won't get into that, but trust me. It rocks my world."

He could have choked. As it was, he could barely speak. "You met a guy? Just like that and you're running off?"

"Of course not," she snapped and cuffed him on the back of his head. "That would be stupid and irresponsible. I'm a firm believer there should only be one idiot in the family at a time and right now that's you."

His mind reeled with the shift, as he struggled to figure out what she was saying. She collected her glass and sat across from him.

"There's no Roger?" he asked, wanting confirmation.

"There's no Roger. Just my son, who is doing his damnedest to screw up. You must get that from your father."

The world seemed to steady itself. He drew in a breath. "You heard about the injunction."

"Yes, and if I was closer, I'd hit you again. Talk about stupid. Are you trying to drive Liz away?"

He rubbed the back of his head, doing his best not to wince when he passed over the place where she'd hit him. "I thought you didn't like her."

"I'm ambivalent. I'm angry about the time we've lost with Tyler, but I can see her side of things. She didn't have it easy when she was growing up. As the mother of three daughters, I ache for her. Where was *her* mother? Talk about a difficult situation. Which you've made worse. What were you thinking?"

"That I didn't want her to run. She's leaving. She told me flat out that she was fixing up the house, then going back to San Francisco. I couldn't lose him again."

Denise frowned. "I don't understand. Why would Liz allow you to see Tyler, why would she be so cooperative, then threaten to take her son away?"

Ethan shifted in his seat. "She didn't say she was taking him away, exactly. She said that we would work something out. Custody. Visitation. Whatever."

His mother stared at him, disbelief widening her eyes. "You're telling me that Liz was willing to come up with a plan, and you served her with an injunction? To what end?"

"What if she disappeared? I'd have no way to find her. No way to see Tyler."

"Is there anything about her past behavior that would make you think even for a second that she would disappear? She's been perfectly up-front with you. Okay, not the first few years, and I'm still angry and hurt about that. But we'll put that aside for now."

She picked up her iced tea, then set it down. "Since she's been back, she's been cooperative, hasn't she? She really did try to tell you about Tyler five years ago. You have written proof of it. What more did you need?"

Control, he thought, knowing he couldn't explain that to his mother. She wouldn't understand and if she did, she wouldn't approve.

"We'll work it out," he said instead.

"In front of a judge? That will be friendly and

pleasant." Denise shook her head. "I don't get it. What did you hope to accomplish by acting like that? Getting her attention?"

His head snapped up. "I'm not looking for Liz's attention."

"Aren't you?" She seemed to consider the idea. "You were in love with her once, weren't you?"

"I was a kid. We both were."

"I was nineteen when I met your father. Being young doesn't make the love any less real."

"Fine. I loved her." He'd loved her but he'd been too much of a jerk to admit it. To stand up to the town and his friends. To admit his feelings out loud.

It wasn't behavior he'd been proud of. Looking back, with the wisdom of hindsight, he knew he hadn't been ready for Liz. Hadn't deserved her.

He'd been blessed with a happy, normal childhood. He hadn't realized that little had been asked of him, so he hadn't had to prove himself. On the surface, he'd seemed like one of the good guys, but underneath, he'd been immature and selfish.

It had taken the accident that had ended his racing career to start the process of maturing him. But even that hadn't been enough. Because he'd come home to sulk, to complain. It was only after the death of his father, when he'd been forced to take over the family business, that he'd finally started to grow up.

"I wasn't ready," he said slowly. "Not to be what Liz needed. If I'd known she was pregnant, I would have done the right thing and married her. But I don't think we would have made it."

"You might have surprised yourself."

"You're my mom. You have to believe the best of me." Even when it wasn't true.

She and Nevada were right, he thought. Serving Liz had accomplished nothing but alienating her. Maybe he had wanted to get her attention. If so, he'd picked a lousy way to do it.

"She needs someone on her side," Denise told him. "You have your family and the town."

"Not everyone in town," he assured, remembering the old lady who'd gone after him with her purse.

"You're still coming out ahead. If we're not careful, Liz will feel overwhelmed and take off. Honestly, I'm not sure I would blame her for that." His mother paused, then scrunched her face. "I could have been a lot more supportive and understanding. I should have been. I want to know my grandson, and Liz is the key to making that happen."

He thought about pointing out that if push came to shove, they could go to court. Force Liz to let Tyler spend time with the family. But in the end, no one would win. Certainly not Tyler. And as Liz had pointed out several times, the kid was the most important part of the equation.

"I can't take the injunction back," he said, not completely sure he would if he could. Although he still wasn't sure why. His mother was right—he was trying to prove something.

"You may not be able to take it back, but I can make an effort, and I'm going to. Liz has been in this by herself for too long. I'm still angry about missing the first eleven years of Tyler's life, but if I don't let that go, my emotions will affect everything else. And not in a good way. Besides, Rayanne is to blame for the last five years. This is so complicated." She looked at him. "I suppose you're going to be an idiot for a while longer."

"Apparently."

She surprised him by smiling. "Sometimes you remind me so much of your father. He was an idiot, too."

"And you still loved him."

Her smile broadened. "Yes, but Liz might not be as smart as me."

CHAPTER TWELVE

LIZ HAD NEVER BEEN TO A CITY event-planning meeting before. When Pia had called to invite her, she thought the afternoon might be interesting. Her stay in Fool's Gold was temporary but she might as well get a feel for the good as well as the bad. If nothing else, she may be able to put the experience in a book.

A little before two, she walked to the City Hall building and found her way to the meeting room. When she opened the door, she was surprised to find herself in a good-size open space, with about three dozen chairs facing a long table and a podium. Most of the chairs were full, and three women chatted by the head table. Montana and Pia were among them and smiled at her.

Liz smiled back, then went to find an empty seat.

Her choices were limited. There was one next to a young mother with a baby. Liz didn't recognize her, so they hadn't gone to school together. Odds were the woman wouldn't care about Liz or her past. There were several older women sitting together, but after the recent comments on her character by strangers, she wasn't sure she wanted to risk the wrath of a potential mob.

Unable to find a place that felt safe, she settled for a seat in the back corner. With any luck, she would be ignored.

A woman in the row in front of her turned to face her. "Hi," she said. "I'm Marti and I just love your books."

"Thanks."

"Your main character is wonderful. She feels so real. And thank God you're not putting too much gore in your books. I know violence is part of the genre, but some authors go too far."

"I enjoy writing my stories," Liz acknowledged, knowing a neutral response was usually best. The truth was she always liked hearing her readers opinions, even when she didn't agree with them. Readers probably thought she ignored what they said, but that wasn't true. Liz had made not a few changes in story lines based on reader input.

"I love reading them," Marti repeated, before smiling and facing front.

Pia moved to the podium and called the meeting to order.

"We're planning the book festival," she began. "Thank you all for coming out this afternoon. This is going to be our biggest and best program ever, which means lots of opportunity for volunteering. We'll get to that later. First, let me go over the program."

A screen rolled down behind her. She pushed a few buttons on her laptop and a big poster appeared. It was bright and inviting, giving the dates of the Fool's Gold annual book festival. The border was filled with pictures of both authors and books. Liz was relieved to see that she was just one of the many on this poster. The one Montana had shown her a few days before had featured her prominently. Not something to endear her to the other local authors.

"We're going to set up in the park," Pia continued. "Given that we have a few better-known authors this year, we're expecting a larger crowd than usual."

"That's right," someone in the front called. "There's that mystery writer everyone's been talking about. What's her name?"

A ripple of laughter flowed through the room. Liz chuckled. "I can't remember," she said loudly. "But I've heard she has an attitude, so watch out."

An older woman stood up and waved at Liz. "I have a new quilting book out this year. Chances are my fans are going to be flooding the park. Just so you're prepared."

"I look forward to meeting them," Liz told her.

Pia looked at Liz with a teasing expression. "I think our local *New York Times* bestselling author can handle the competition."

Pia went through the list of authors. As promised, most of them were local, self-published and their books dealt with unusual or dying crafts. Using sticks for art and furniture. Making meals from what one can find on the forest floor. There was mention of an author who wrote about the Indian legends. The book sounded interesting, but when Liz asked Marti about the author, the other woman told her no one ever saw him in town. He lived in the mountains and kept to himself.

"There are tons of rumors," Marti admitted. "Seeing him is like seeing Bigfoot. I've heard everything from him being one-hundred-and-eight, English and a former explorer to him being young, gorgeous and really rich." She lowered her voice. "Personally I like the second story best."

Liz thought the old British explorer sounded more intriguing. She would have to look up the mysterious author at the signing.

Despite everything going on, she found herself looking forward to the event. Her usual signings were in big stores or at industry events. Very organized and predictable, with crowd control and readers kept at a respectful distance. This sounded more fun. She liked the idea of being part of a writing community. There were days when figuring out a new way to serve chicken for Tyler seemed impossible. Feeding someone what could be found on a forest floor was impressive.

Pia went through the rest of the programs, the various opportunities for volunteering, then opened the meeting for questions.

Two people wanted to know about taking sign-up sheets around town. The only man at the meeting pointed out that just because there were more women than men in town didn't mean it was right to take over all the men's restrooms every time there was a festival. Men had needs, too. Pia promised to look into the problem.

"Anything else?" she asked.

The young mother with the baby rose slowly. "I'm sure a lot of you aren't going to agree with me, but I have to say, I'm just sick about having that woman here." She pointed at Liz. "What she did to Ethan is shameful. Keeping his little boy from him all those years. It's worse because of him losing Rayanne and their baby." The woman's eyes filled with tears. "Rayanne was a sweet girl and now people are saying terrible things about her." She glared at Liz. "I don't believe any of them."

The room went silent as everyone turned to stare at Liz. Her warm fuzzies about the signing, the town and ever thinking it was smart to come back, disappeared. She sat in her seat, embarrassed, angry and determined not to blush. Speaking any words seemed impossible, let alone the right ones. What was she supposed to say?

"Let's stay on topic, everyone," Pia reminded from the front of the room. "We're here to talk about the book festival." She glanced at the young mother. "Melody, I know Rayanne was your friend, but this isn't the time or the place to have this conversation. Can we please finish up here."

Both her voice and her gaze were sympathetic. Liz appreciated the support, although she still felt sick to her stomach. Then the woman next to Marti rose.

"Melody, you need to get your head out of your butt. Liz didn't do anything wrong. She was a kid, dealing with a lot of crap." The older woman cleared her throat, then faced Liz. "I knew your mother and I had a bad feeling about what was going on at your house every night. I knew she drank and I knew there were men in and out of that place. A lot of us knew and we didn't do anything to protect you. We should have. You were just a little girl."

The woman drew in a breath. "I'm sorry for my part in that. I've given money to the scholarship and I've acted differently since then. But that doesn't make up for me turning away when you were growing up."

Several other women nodded. Melody looked furious.

"That doesn't excuse what she did to Ethan."

"Maybe if you spent more time looking after your own family, you wouldn't have time to worry about something that happened all those years ago," the older woman snapped. "After all, your husband spends plenty of nights up at the lodge, flirting with a certain cocktail waitress."

Several people gasped. Melody went red. Pia grabbed the microphone.

"People, *please.* This is getting out of hand. Obviously we need to finish this another time. We—"

The door by the front of the room opened. An older woman walked in. It took Liz a moment to recognize the mayor. Marsha Tilson looked pale and it was obvious something bad had happened.

Pia stared at her. "It's Crystal, isn't it?" she asked softly, her voice picked up by the microphone.

The mayor nodded and held out her arms. Pia went into them and started to cry.

Liz stared at them both, unable to believe what she'd just heard. Crystal couldn't be dead. Sure she was sick, but Liz had seen her only a few weeks before. She'd been walking and talking and...

Her eyes burned with unshed tears. Liz remembered the pretty, friendly girl from high school who had taken the time to give her hope.

"Oh, Crystal," she whispered. "Not so soon."

Nearly everyone in the room began talking. A few were crying. Liz got up and slipped out before anyone noticed.

As she walked home, she thought about Crystal, the town and how coming back had changed her life forever. She could leave and swear she would never return, but Fool's Gold had made a mark on her. One that nothing could erase.

There were horrible people here, but there were also good ones. People like Crystal, who took the time to change a life with a few words.

FAMILY COURT WAS IN THE county courthouse—away from the center of town. A fact that made the experience slightly more bearable, Liz thought as she walked into the old building. There were murals in the massive entryway—the kind painted in the 1940s and depicting farmworkers and loggers. The subjects stood ten or fifteen feet high, the sure brushstrokes and colors still vivid after all these years.

Liz saw Ethan waiting by a bank of elevators. He wore a dark suit and white shirt, very different from his usual jeans and boots. Professional looked good on him. Not that a man with his height and muscled body ever looked bad, she thought, trying not to notice.

They moved toward each other. She squared her shoulders, grateful her three-inch heels meant she didn't have to look up very far to meet his gaze.

"No lawyer?" he asked.

"We're meeting the judge in her chamber," Liz stated. "It's an informal meeting. The lawyer I contacted suggested trying to keep it friendly for as long as possible."

"With the judge," he noted, his gaze unreadable. "Not with me."

"I'm not the one who started this."

He shoved his hands into his front pockets. "I didn't want you to leave."

Something she could understand. Despite her claims that he could see Tyler whenever he wanted, she understood the fear of losing the one thing that mattered.

"You should have talked to me before doing this," she told him evenly. "This is where you went and now we're stuck."

"You owe me, Liz," he said quietly.

"Maybe, but this is the wrong kind of payback."

"I need to know I'm not going to lose my son."

"What did I ever do to make you not trust me?"

"You didn't tell me right away."

So they were back to that, she thought, both annoyed and sad. The same road, the same words, the same feelings. They were trapped and she didn't know how to make things different.

They walked to the waiting room, and then were called into the judge's chambers.

Judge Powers was a small woman, with dark hair and a petite build. She sat behind a large desk and leaned back in her leather chair as Ethan and Liz walked into the room.

She motioned for them to sit across from her, then drew in a breath.

"This sort of action makes me tired," she began, her voice thick with irritation. "You're wasting my time and the court's time. You are two reasonably intelligent people who went to all the trouble to create a child together. Now, when your son is eleven, suddenly I have to deal with this?"

Liz had to consciously press her lips together to keep her mouth from falling open. She hadn't known what to expect, but it sure hadn't been a beginning like that.

"Your Honor," Ethan responded, "there are some extraordinary circumstances."

"There always are," she said, reaching for her reading glasses and opening a file. "Dazzle me with them."

Ethan briefly explained about how Tyler had come

to be in his life. Liz gave him points for being fair about her attempts to tell him. He was a little dismissive of her first effort, but detailed the second accurately.

Judge Powers frowned. "Your wife kept the information about your son from you?"

Ethan nodded.

"There's a prize," the judge commented. "Where is she now?"

"She died a few years ago."

The judge drew in a breath. "I'm sorry for your loss. So now you're back in town, Ms. Sutton. I understand you're caring for your brother's two daughters while your brother is incarcerated. Is that correct?"

Liz nodded, shocked for the second time in the very short meeting. "Yes, Your Honor."

"Don't look so surprised," the judge said. "I do my homework. What you're doing with them is admirable. I've heard you plan on taking them to San Francisco with you. How do they feel about that?"

"They're not happy about the decision."

"They're teenage girls. They're not going to be happy about anything." She picked up the folder and looked at Ethan over her glasses. "This wasn't the smartest thing you've ever done."

"I'm beginning to see that."

"It's done now. You're going to have to deal with it. Both of you. School starts the Tuesday after Labor Day. You have between now and the Friday before Labor Day to come up with a reasonable plan. You will present it to me at nine that morning. If I like it, then everything will be fine. If I don't…"

She smiled tightly. "Trust me. You're going to want me to like it." The smile faded. "However, if you don't come up with a plan, then I will put both of you in jail and charge you five hundred dollars a day until you do. Each. That should cover the cost of three additional children being put in our already overcrowded foster care system. Have I made myself clear?"

Liz nodded. She had no idea if Ethan did the same, but then they were being shown out.

She stood in the corridor feeling as if she'd just escaped a war zone.

"Jesus." Ethan shoved his hand through his hair. "I wasn't expecting that."

"We're going to have to figure something out," Liz insisted, glancing back at the door. "While I'm sure you're not excited about paying five hundred dollars a day, either, I can at least work from jail. You made this happen, Ethan. Now we're both stuck."

"I did what I had to do."

"You'd rather be right than anything?" What happened to the gentle, funny man she'd fallen in love with? Was he gone forever? Or had the person she'd cared about been little more than an illusion?

"I can't lose Tyler again."

"You won't," she said, frustration boiling inside of her. "How many times do I have to tell you before you'll believe…"

She stared at him as understanding dawned. "Of course," she whispered. "You can't believe me. Because if I'm reasonable, if I *really* want you to get to know your son, then I'm not the bad guy. And just maybe part of the reason you don't know him now is because of the choices you made."

She was thinking about how he'd betrayed her, but the tightness in his expression warned her that he'd gone to a different place.

"You leave Rayanne out of this," he growled.

"I wasn't talking about her."

"You blame her."

She considered the question. "Not as much as you do."

"I don't blame her. She was my wife."

There was something about the way he said the words, she thought. She didn't know what it was. What secret or piece of information she was missing.

Before she could decide if she should hit him or walk away, he surprised her by touching her cheek with the back of his hand.

"I'm sorry," he said. "Sensitive topic."

"Apparently."

They stared at each other. Looking into his eyes was a little too much like looking at the sun. Do it for any length of time and there would be permanent consequences.

"I don't want to fight with you," he told her. "You're right. We need to come up with a plan."

The gentle stroking made her want to lean against him. "As if I'd trust you now."

"I don't want to hurt you, Liz."

She glanced away. "What do you want?"

He dropped his hand to his side. "I want a do-over. I want to be there when Tyler's born and watch him grow up."

There was raw honesty in his expression and anguish in his tone. Her chest tightened.

"I'm sorry, too," she said softly. "More sorry than I can tell you."

"I know."

Two little words that usually didn't mean much. But this time, spoken by him, they were the world.

"We can make this work," she reiterated. "I want you and Tyler to spend as much time together as possible."

"Hard to do when you live in San Francisco."

She wanted to say that if this was so damned important, he could be the one to move. He could run his businesses from there. Only she knew that wasn't possible or practical. That most people would say she should be the one to compromise. To turn her life upside down and move back to Fool's Gold. Because it would be better for everyone.

Everyone but her.

"I need to get back," she concluded. "I have to work before the kids get home from camp."

They walked to the parking lot together. Liz tried to think of something to say—another compromise that they could both live with. But it didn't exist.

When she pulled out the keys to her small SUV,

Ethan grabbed her arm. He pulled her around and there, in the middle of the afternoon, in an open parking lot, on a Thursday, he kissed her.

His mouth claimed hers with a combination of need, anger and determination she could relate to. Instead of pulling away, she leaned into him, kissing him back just as passionately, letting her emotions flow through her. Their lips clung, their bodies strained. He wrapped one arm around her waist, she put her free hand on his shoulder.

For a single moment, there was nothing but the heat of the sun and the man who held her. There was wanting and promise and in that space of time, anything was possible. Then sanity returned in the sharp honk of a horn, the sounds of traffic and the realization that this problem was bigger than a kiss.

Ethan released her. She stepped back. Without saying a word, they each got in their own car and drove away.

LIZ ARRIVED HOME KNOWING THAT if she wasn't expecting three children to walk in the front door in the next hour or so, she would give in to the theory that it was five o'clock somewhere and pour a big glass of wine. As it was, she changed into jeans and a T-shirt and medicated herself with Diet Coke and two peanut butter cookies. She'd barely taken her first bite, had yet to feel the sugar coursing through her body, when someone knocked on the front door.

She found herself hesitating before answering. In this town, unexpected company was rarely the good kind. A theory confirmed when she pulled open the door and found Ethan's mother standing there.

Liz did her best not to flinch. She knew better than to show fear in the face of a predator. Denise Hendrix smiled and held out a covered casserole dish.

"Mac and cheese," she said. "It was Ethan's favorite when he was growing up. Actually it was all my kids' favorite. What is it about children and cheese and pasta?"

Denise looked both friendly and hopeful.

Liz once again wished for wine or a margarita. When neither appeared, she stepped back to let the other woman in.

"You'll want to put this in the fridge," Denise continued. "It only needs to be heated. About forty minutes at three-fifty. Oh, and take off the foil."

"Thanks," Liz said, taking the dish and walking into the kitchen. "Can I get you anything?"

"No. I'm fine. Were you working? Am I interrupting?"

"I've been dealing with other things today," Liz said, wondering if she should mention the visit with the judge or leave that for Ethan to share. She wasn't completely sure about Denise's reason for stopping by. Somehow the food delivery seemed more like an excuse than a plan.

"Do you have deadlines?" Denise asked.

"Yes. I usually stay on top of them. This summer has been a challenge."

"You've been dealing with a lot."

Sympathy? Was it safe to trust it? "There are unique circumstances."

Denise leaned against the counter. "I know about the injunction and I'm sorry my son was such an idiot. I hope it went well with the judge."

So his mother already knew. Is that why she'd stopped by? But why not wait and get the story from her son? "We saw her this afternoon. It was interesting." Liz explained how she and Ethan had until the end of summer to come up with a plan.

"Do you know what you're going to agree on?" Denise asked.

"Not yet. I know what Ethan wants." Liz said the last sentence defiantly. Because it would be what Denise wanted, too.

"I'm sorry about what happened," the other woman told her. "That you had to go through having a baby on your own. I remember when I was pregnant with Ethan. I was terrified. You were younger and alone. That couldn't have been easy."

Liz forced herself to relax. She moved to the kitchen table and pulled out a chair, then waited for Denise to do the same before sitting.

"I had a few difficult moments," she admitted. "Luckily I found a shelter for pregnant girls. It was nice not to be completely by myself. I saw a doctor, got the right kind of food and vitamins."

"I wish we'd known," Denise offered. "I wish you'd come to me."

Liz stared at her. "I appreciate what you're saying but that would never have happened." It wouldn't have occurred to her. Not ever, but especially not after Ethan had rejected her so publicly.

"I understand. I wish I'd known the two of you were together. Maybe I would have thought to check on you."

Rather than say something she would regret, Liz pressed her lips together and nodded slightly.

"I knew what they were saying about you, back then," Denise told her. "I always felt so bad for you. I wish your mother had protected you more."

"She was the real problem. I wasn't doing those things. I wasn't that girl, but no one cared to look beyond the rumors. Well, except for Ethan and then, not so much."

Denise frowned. "What do you mean?"

"It doesn't matter. It was a long time ago."

"It matters to me." She leaned toward Liz. "Why did you leave that first time?"

Liz tried to be vague. This was Denise's son, after all. "We had a fight."

"I don't believe that's the only reason."

Liz drew in a breath. "You should ask him."

"I'm asking you." Denise gave her a faint smile. "Don't make me use my 'bad mom' voice. I have six kids and a lot of practice."

Fine. If the woman wanted to know, Liz would tell her.

"Ethan and I had been going out for two months. He

didn't want anyone to know. Despite how much he said he loved me, I think he was a little embarrassed by my reputation. I was going to join him at college, where no one would know about me. We were going to be together. I loved him. He was my first boyfriend. My first kiss. My first…" She cleared her throat. "You know."

"I can imagine. Then what happened?"

"I was working at the diner. Ethan was in with his friends, like always. I used to think it was so romantic that no one knew. It was our secret." Knowing Ethan loved her had made her feel special.

"Josh mentioned seeing us together. All Ethan's friends started going after him, wanting to know if he was 'doing me.'" She laced her fingers together, determined to stay in the moment, to not remember too much. "He said he barely knew who I was. That he would never be interested in someone like me."

Denise flinched. "Oh, Liz. I'm so sorry."

She shrugged. "I was humiliated and hurt. I could feel my heart breaking. I dumped a milk shake on his head and walked out. That was the last time we spoke. When I found out I was pregnant, I came back to tell him. I found him in bed with another girl."

"Oh, God." Denise touched her arm. "That's awful. I don't know what else to say."

"It's okay."

"No, it's not. Nothing about the situation is okay." Denise shook her head. "It's Ralph, and that damned idea of his that we're the Hendrixes. The family that founded Fool's Gold." She sounded frustrated. "Reputation is everything. Act right, do right, be right. Emotions be damned."

Denise sighed. "I loved my husband from the moment I first saw him, but he wasn't easy. And he passed all that righteousness onto Ethan."

Liz wasn't surprised. "He was the oldest."

"Exactly."

"Being with someone like me violated everything his father had ever said. I get it." Liz spoke as if the words didn't hurt her and hoped the other woman couldn't see the truth.

"For Ralph, the world was black and white. Reality is much more gray. I don't think Ethan was mature enough to see that."

Denise sounded sincere and conciliatory, which Liz appreciated, but it also made her uncomfortable.

"I'm fine," she said quickly. "The past is over. Tyler and I have been fine. I've taken good care of him."

"I don't doubt that," Denise assured her. "But while you've been busy taking care of your son, who's taken care of you?"

"I don't need anyone to take care of me."

Denise smiled gently. "Liz, we all need someone. And now you have us. I hope you'll accept me and my children into your family. You're a part of us now."

It was as if she could hear a door slam somewhere in the distance. No. Not a door—a gate. Denise was Tyler's grandmother. He had aunts and uncles. However far she might want to run, she was bound to these people forever, and for the life of her, she couldn't figure out if that was a good thing or a bad one.

CHAPTER THIRTEEN

LIZ HAD DONE HER BEST TO prepare Roy's daughters for the reality of seeing their father in prison, but words couldn't begin to explain the experience. Not only did Melissa and Liz have to leave their cell phones in the car, Abby wasn't allowed to bring gum. She'd had to tell the girls not to wear chambray shirts or jeans because the color was forbidden for visitors. It was what the prisoners wore. They all had to make sure their shirts had sleeves and that they would have to pass through a metal detector before they could see their father.

Their cheerful mood during the drive had faded, the closer they got to the prison, then disappeared when they stopped by the structure. Liz understood completely. There was no way to look at the forbidding building and feel anticipation.

They followed the other visitors to an open patio where Roy hovered. He looked both excited and nervous.

"You came," he said, when he saw them.

Abby rushed toward him and he embraced her, but Melissa hung back.

"It's all right," Liz told her.

Melissa shook her head. "It's not," she whispered. "He's not getting out of here, is he?"

Liz's throat tightened. "It will be a while."

"How could he do this? How could he leave us?"

Liz didn't know what to say.

"He's still your dad," she managed to murmur. "He still loves you."

Melissa swallowed. "Loving us isn't going to be enough."

She slowly approached her father, then hugged him.

The three of them settled on a picnic table. Liz hung back, wanting to give them private time together. She sat by herself, reading the book she'd brought, trying to ignore the other reunions going on around her. Some groups were happy, but others were quiet, marked with tears and obvious pain.

About an hour later, Roy walked over to sit next to her.

"They told me that you're having the house fixed up," he relayed, avoiding her gaze. "Thanks for that. I got the paperwork that lawyer sent. I've already signed it and sent it back."

She nodded. The house was being put into a trust for the girls.

"When it's finished, I'll talk to a real estate agent again and we'll figure out if it's better to sell it now and invest the money or keep it and rent it out."

Roy nodded. "Do whatever you think is best. You were always the smart one in the family."

"Either way they'll have money for their future." They wouldn't need it for college. If either of her nieces wanted to go, Liz would pay for it herself. She thought about saying that but thought Roy might think she was showing off. The situation was awkward enough already.

"I signed that other paper, too," her brother told her, looking at her for the first time. "The one making you their legal guardian. I told them that they have to do what you said. Mel's mad because you want to move them to San Francisco. I told her it was for the best."

"I doubt she believed you."

"She'll get over it. She's just a kid." He shifted uneasily. "I was thinking you probably shouldn't bring them back to see me again. It's too hard on them."

Liz had a feeling the person he was most concerned about was himself. "Are you going to write them?"

"Sure. Sure. I sent that one letter."

"They'll want to hear from you. You're their father."

"I know. I said I'd write."

"Okay," she murmured. "I'll make sure they write you, too, and let you know what's going on with them."

"Thanks, Liz."

"Sure."

He returned to his daughters. A few minutes later, the girls walked over to her.

There were tears in their eyes. Abby tried to smile but failed. Melissa, like her father, wouldn't look at Liz.

"Ready to go?" Liz asked.

Abby nodded.

They returned to the car. The afternoon was warm, the sky a cloudless blue. She cranked up the air conditioning until it blasted them, then headed for the freeway.

"Dad said you were our legal guardian now," Melissa reported as she stared out the window.

"I am." Liz clutched the steering wheel. "It's not that he doesn't love you. This just makes things easier. Like if you have to go to the doctor's, I can sign the paperwork."

"Or make us move," Melissa said bitterly. "You're not our mom."

"I'm not trying to be," Liz explained, refusing to take the attack personally.

"Can't we stay?" Abby asked softly from the backseat.

"No," Melissa told her, turning to glare at her. "We can't. Aunt Liz is going to make us move and we can't stop her. If we run away, the police will find us and bring us back. She can do anything she likes. Even dump us in foster care."

Liz merged onto the freeway. "Melissa, that's enough," she said sternly. "You can be mad at me if you want, but don't take it out on Abby. No one is going into foster care and you know it. You may not like the idea of moving, but in the few weeks you've known me I've done my best to take care of you."

"You might be able to make us move, but I'll never forgive you," Melissa announced. "I'll hate you forever."

"Something we'll both have to live with," Liz told her.

She glanced in the rearview mirror and saw Abby was crying. Melissa had her head turned away, so Liz wasn't sure how upset she was. Nothing about this situation was easy, she thought sadly. Nothing was the way it was supposed to be.

No one spoke. After a few minutes, she turned on the radio. A while later, Abby's tears stopped. She sniffed every now and then but otherwise was silent. Melissa sat stiffly in her seat. When they finally arrived back in Fool's Gold, Liz was actually relieved to be in town.

She drove directly to the house and had barely put the car in park before Melissa jumped out. Abby followed her sister.

Liz got out more slowly, then came to a stop when she saw Ethan at the top of the porch stairs.

He'd spent the morning with Tyler and no doubt wanted to complain about something or throw her under a nearby bus. She was too tired and drained for another fight, but telling him that felt like admitting weakness.

"I take it things didn't go well," he guessed as he approached her.

"Knowing their dad is in prison and seeing him there are two different things. They're upset."

He was tall and handsome and the fact that she

noticed made her want to stomp her foot in frustration. Why did he have to be the one man on the planet able to win her with a single look? Even now, with the injunction, the past and everything else between them, all she could think about was stepping into his strong embrace and letting him handle things for a little while.

"They took it out on you," he assumed, not asking a question.

"I'm an easy target."

He reached toward her. She thought about stepping back but instead braced herself. He tucked a strand of hair behind her ear.

The light brush of his fingers against her skin made her warm inside and a little stronger. Craziness, she told herself. Ethan might not be the enemy, but he wasn't exactly her friend.

"Let's go riding," he offered.

"What?"

"We'll rent bikes. For all of us. Getting out of the house will make Melissa and Abby feel better and you won't have to deal with them alone."

"It makes me nervous when you're nice," she admitted.

"I guess I should be nice more often so you get used to it."

"I find that unlikely."

He gave her a slow, sexy smile. "Don't sell yourself short."

"Very funny. I was trying to indicate I'm not sure you *can* be nice."

"Try me."

She would like to, even if that made her the local idiot. "I think a bike ride would be safer."

A HALF HOUR LATER, THEY HAD bikes and were making their way around the lake. Sunlight sparkled on the water where paddle boats glided. Families sat on the grass or under the trees. On the other side of the bike path, teenaged boys played with a Frisbee.

Ethan hung back, wanting to make sure that Melissa and Abby were both comfortable and safe as they rode. Abby stayed close to Liz, talking easily. Melissa was in front, her shoulders stiff, her pace determined. The teenager was obviously still angry.

Tyler was on the other side of his mother. Ethan watched his son weave back and forth, deliberately riding a serpentine course. Every now and then he took both hands off the handlebars, causing his mother to glance at him. Tyler grinned and returned his hands to the bars.

When a family on bikes came toward them on the wide, paved path, everyone moved to the side. Melissa wobbled a little and had to put her foot down to keep from falling. Ethan rode up to her.

"Been a long time," he said with a grin. "It'll come back to you."

"Riding bikes is for kids," she said, pouting.

"Ever hear of the Tour de France?"

She sniffed. "That's some big race."

"Right. Know what they ride?"

"Fine." She rolled her eyes. "Kids and weird people."

He held in a laugh.

They were a ways back from Liz and the kids. He lowered his voice.

"Who are you really mad at? Your dad for being in prison or Liz for wanting to move back to San Francisco?"

She turned away. "I'm mad at Liz."

"I don't believe that."

She glared at him, tears filling her eyes. "You don't know anything."

"I know some. I know this is hard. I know you're about the bravest person I know, taking care of your sister like that. And I know Liz dropped everything to come here the second she got your e-mail."

Melissa sucked in a breath. "Maybe."

He didn't know if she was talking about herself or Liz and decided not to push it.

"I don't want to leave here and she's going to make me," Melissa said.

Not a subject he could be neutral about, he thought. He didn't want Liz to go, either. But he also knew this was a chance for him to protect Liz's back and show her that he wasn't the bad guy in all of this.

"She's taking you away from all your friends and never letting you come back, huh?" he asked. "That sucks."

Melissa glanced at him. "She said I could still see my friends. You know, on the weekends Tyler's with you. And I'll have my cell phone."

He didn't say anything.

She sighed. "It won't be the same."

"That's part of growing up. Things change."

"But I don't want this."

"That happens, too."

There were a lot of things he didn't want. He didn't want to have missed the first eleven years of his son's life. But no matter how he yelled or complained or threatened, nothing about the situation would change.

"Sometimes you have to accept how things are," he said as much to himself as to Melissa. "You can make it easy on yourself, or you can make it hard. The choice is yours."

"Maybe I don't want to grow up," she argued.

"After what you've already been through?" He smiled. "Sorry, Melissa. It's happening and you're turning out great."

"Can we get ice cream?" Tyler asked, looking back at Ethan.

"I think ice cream is a good idea," Liz agreed. She pointed to the stand up ahead. "Something dipped in chocolate would be very nice."

Beside her, Abby laughed. "You really like choco-late."

"I do. It's a chick thing."

"Ice cream for everyone," Ethan concurred. He turned to Melissa. "You okay?"

She nodded.

Fifteen minutes later they were all stretched out on

the grass, in the shade, eating ice cream. Abby stayed close to Liz, as did Tyler. Melissa was a few feet away, by herself. Ethan found himself wishing Liz were leaning against him the way Abby leaned against her. Because being angry didn't mean he stopped wanting her.

It had always been that way, he reminded himself. It had been the first day of his senior year of school. He'd been walking down the hallway when he'd spotted Liz. She'd had that shy, terrified look that told him she was unprepared for the transition from junior high.

Even then she'd been beautiful. Tall and slim, with curves in the right places. There'd been something about the way she'd carried herself—with a warning that you could look but you couldn't touch. She didn't make eye contact with anyone.

One of Ethan's friends had nudged him.

"See that girl there? She's Liz Sutton. I've heard she puts out as much as her mom. I hope it's true."

Ethan didn't know what combination of events had started the rumors about Liz. Maybe the girls in school had resented how beautiful she was. Maybe the boys had hated that she wouldn't pay attention to them. But in a matter of weeks, everyone knew Liz Sutton had a reputation for being easy and cheap.

Even so, he'd been attracted to her. Not just for the potential sex, but because he'd seen something in her eyes. Something that called to him.

He'd spoken to her a few times that year. Or at least

he'd tried. She'd always turned away and disappeared with an ease that told him she was well practiced at vanishing. Then he'd graduated and gone off to college, nearly forgetting all about Liz.

Until the summer before his senior year. When he'd come home in May and literally run into her on the sidewalk. He'd taken one look at her and known he had to have her.

His initial interest had been about how she looked, but he'd quickly discovered there was a smart brain behind the green eyes. That Liz had a wicked sense of humor and yet a moral compass that appealed to him. He'd learned she was kind and self-aware and that no one else had ever kissed her. He'd been her first...for everything.

"Ethan, what are you thinking?" Liz asked. "You have the strangest look on your face."

He smiled. "I was remembering that you were the smartest girl in school."

Liz wrinkled her nose. "Hardly."

Abby and Tyler both looked at him. "Really?" Tyler asked. "Mom was smart?"

"Hey, kiddo. I'm plenty smart now," Liz pointed out.

He grinned at her, then turned back to Ethan.

"She was," he told them. "All As in her classes. A scholarship to college." Which she hadn't used because of him, he reminded himself.

"That was a long time ago," Liz reminded, avoiding his gaze. "School was easy for me. I liked to read. Books were my friends."

"Is that why you write now?" Melissa asked. "Because you used to read?"

"I'm sure that's part of it. One of the best ways to learn how to write is to read."

"How can you have a book for a friend?" Abby asked. "You can't talk to them."

"No, but they can take you away to another place. With books, the world feels safe."

Abby and Melissa looked at each other, then back at her.

"Could you give me the name of some books to read?" Abby asked quietly.

"Sure. We can go to the library later."

"I like to read, too," Tyler said.

"Are you going to be a writer?" Melissa asked. "When you grow up?"

Tyler shook his head. "I want to build stuff, like my dad."

Ethan happened to be looking at Liz as their son spoke. She didn't react at all, as if she'd already heard this. But to him, the information was new and filled him with a sense of pride. He waited for that to be followed by resentment—after all, he'd already lost so much.

The feelings were there, but not as intense as before. The loss, the anger was muted somehow. Less important. Liz had been right—he couldn't have a relationship in the present if he kept living in the past. What mattered with Tyler was today.

His gaze drifted over Liz's face. She was a part of

his son's life. He couldn't have one without dealing with the other. He'd loved Liz once—as much as he could at that age. With a limited life experience and nothing much ever required of him. He'd been a child in a man's body. He was older now. But all that life experience hadn't made him a whole lot smarter when it came to Liz.

THE AFTERNOON OF BIKE RIDING stretched into a dinner out, followed by a movie. By the time Ethan walked Liz and the kids home, it was after ten and everyone was tired.

Liz felt her own emotional exhaustion sucking at every step and knew the girls had to be ready to collapse, as well. For once, no one protested getting ready for bed. While she checked on the girls, Ethan said good-night to Tyler. They met downstairs. Liz was prepared to thank him for the day and show him the door, but something in his eyes stopped her. They were bright with an emotion she didn't recognize.

"I never got to do that before," he revealed quietly. "Put him to bed."

There was nothing accusatory in his tone, and still she felt as if he'd hit her in the stomach. Her body stiffened as guilt flooded her. Then like a montage in a movie, she saw her son's life as a series of pictures.

Somehow in the challenge of raising a baby alone, she'd forgotten about the magical moments Ethan had missed. The first smile, first step, first word. First day of school, first friend. But even more painful were the everyday things she took for granted. The moments that made a relationship.

"I'm sorry," she whispered and sank onto the sofa. "I'm so sorry."

He sat next to her and wrapped his arms around her. For once, she let herself lean on someone as everything crashed in on her. Being back in town, the stress with her nieces, the reality of dealing with Ethan again. He might be the cause, but he was also the only safe haven she'd ever known. While their time together had ended badly, that was for another time. This was about now and maybe what could have been.

"I never wanted it to be like this," she muttered, fighting tears.

He touched his fingers to her chin, easing her head up until they looked at each other.

"I know," he told her.

"It's mostly your fault," she declared with a sniff.

"I'll take some of the blame."

"I can't believe you married Rayanne."

She hadn't meant to say that and as soon as the words popped out, she covered her mouth.

"I take it back," she said quickly. "I'm sure she was lovely." After all, Pia had changed into a nice, normal person. Rayanne could have had the same sort of transformation.

He angled toward her, his hand resting on her shoulder. "You mean, why did I marry her?"

"I didn't ask you that. I'm assuming the normal kind of thing. Dating, falling in love, marriage."

His dark gaze held hers. "You know about my bike crash in my senior year of college?"

She nodded.

"It was a moment of bad judgment or bad luck. I zigged when I should have zagged." He shrugged. "I hit Josh's bike, but I was the one who went down. I was hurt bad enough that I couldn't race again."

"That must have changed everything." She remembered how he'd loved the sport. How winning mattered more than nearly anything. Without wanting to, she recalled the night he'd vowed that she was more important than anything else. How he loved her more than winning. She'd been young enough and foolish enough to want to believe him.

"I didn't take it well," he admitted. "I was angry and blamed Josh. He felt guilty enough that we didn't talk for over ten years."

That stunned her. "He was your best friend."

"Yeah, well, we can both be stubborn. Things are fine now."

"I hope so."

"You're too softhearted."

"I pretend-murder people for a living. How softhearted can I be?"

"I'll remember that." He reached for her hand with his. "I finished school and came back to town. I didn't know what I wanted to do with my life, but I wasn't going to do it here. A few weeks later, my dad dropped dead of a heart attack. I'm the oldest. Suddenly it was all up to me."

"The family business," she murmured. "You never wanted to go into construction."

"I didn't have a choice. There were six people depending on me. My mom fell apart. The girls were still in high school, my brothers needed to finish college. So I did what had to be done. But I didn't like it."

She hadn't liked being responsible for a newborn. Maybe that's what life was about—doing the things that had to be done without expecting anything in return.

"I grew up those first few years," he admitted. "Painfully, kicking and screaming. Then one day I realized I liked building things. I liked starting a project and seeing it through. By then nearly four years had gone by and I hadn't been out on a date. One day Rayanne walked into my office and asked me out. It shocked the hell out of me."

Because Ethan wouldn't see himself as sexy, smart and dependable. Three irresistible qualities when it came to picking a husband.

"We started dating," he said, averting his gaze. "One thing led to another. I liked her, but I knew she wasn't 'the one.' The day I planned to break up with her, she told me that she was pregnant."

Liz did her best to keep her expression neutral. To not give in to the churning emotions inside her.

Pia had already told her that he'd married Rayanne

because she was pregnant. But she couldn't help feeling annoyed. No, more than annoyed.

There was a voice in her demanding why Rayanne and not her? Reminding the voice he hadn't known she was pregnant didn't make her feel any better.

"You seem to have a track record of unplanned pregnancies," she told him. "Haven't you ever heard about birth control?"

One corner of his mouth turned up. "That's what my mom said. Only with a little more emotion."

"I would think so. If we weren't having this very nice moment, I'd smack you on the back of the head and tell you to be more careful."

"Yes, ma'am."

She sighed. "So you married her. And then I showed up and because you'd told her about our relationship, she felt threatened."

"Probably."

"We've both really messed up," she said.

"I guess we have."

They smiled at each other then, and she found herself getting lost in his gaze. When he shifted toward her, she moved the last few inches, bringing her mouth to his.

This kiss was more tender than the last one. His firm mouth teased hers, making her melt even as she wrapped her arms around him.

He pulled her closer, their legs tangling on the sofa. She parted her lips and he eased inside, his tongue stroking hers. Need blossomed, but she ignored the wanting. Not only were there three kids upstairs, she wasn't ready to make love with Ethan. Last time had been unplanned—an event driven by passion. She'd been able to walk away, only slightly scarred by the experience. This time would be different. This time there would be emotional complications and they were the last thing she needed.

Apparently he was feeling the same. They kissed again and again, but he didn't push things further. She savored the feel of his body next to hers, enjoyed the heat building inside. It had been a long time since she'd really wanted a man. Wanted this man. Because Ethan could do things to her no one else could.

He drew back and they stared at each other.

"I should probably go," he murmured.

She nodded, and shifted so he could stand. When she rose, he pulled her to him and kissed her again. After glancing at the ceiling, he exhaled slowly.

"You have a houseful of kids up there," he noted.

"I know."

He rested his forehead against hers. "Damn."

She touched his face, rubbing her fingers against the stubble. For a second she allowed herself to think what it would be like if they were alone. If there weren't other considerations. If she didn't have to worry about losing her heart to a man she couldn't trust.

He kissed her lightly, then walked to the door. "I'll see you soon."

She nodded and followed him onto the porch. He

walked down the steps, along the path, then turned onto the sidewalk. After he was gone, she stood there, looking up at the night sky, admiring the stars. Two months ago her life had been so routine, she thought. So predictable. Things had changed quickly, and she couldn't be sure where she would be two months from now.

There was something fun about the not knowing, she told herself. Then she leaned against the porch pillar and breathed in the scent of the night.

CHAPTER FOURTEEN

LIZ HAD NEVER BEEN TO A WAKE before and wasn't sure what to wear. And it was blisteringly hot, which limited her options. She settled on a green sleeveless dress and cream-colored sandals. Word of the celebration of Crystal's too-short life had come from Montana, who had phoned her two days before and asked her to bring a salad. Apparently the wake was a potluck.

As the type of salad hadn't been specified, Liz had settled on a favorite pasta and mixed lettuce salad that was both healthy and delicious. Normally, she enjoyed making the salad, but this morning her heart hadn't been in it. Crystal's death was just too sad, her life over too soon. Even though they hadn't been close in years, Liz felt the loss of someone she'd considered a friend.

She'd done her best to avoid thinking about where she was going and what would happen when she got there. She had a vision of a bunch of people sitting around in a quiet room, speaking softly, with everyone trying not to cry. Liz didn't want to share her emotions in public, that was for sure.

But when she got to Jo's Bar she was surprised to

find what sounded like a party going on. The main room was full of people laughing and talking. Music played in the background and a slide show of pictures of Crystal and a handsome young man in a marine uniform flashed on a big-screen TV.

"Hi. Thanks for coming. We're putting food in the back room," Montana greeted as Liz entered. "On the pool tables."

The tone was friendly but not especially welcoming. Sort of the way one spoke to a stranger.

Liz froze. After all this time, was Montana now blaming her for what happened with Ethan and Tyler? She felt stricken. It wasn't as if she had a lot of friends in town—she didn't want to lose one now.

"Are you…" she began, only to stop.

While the woman standing in front of her looked very much like Montana, there were differences. Shorter hair, a faint scar on the right cheek. A different way of standing.

Triplets, Liz thought in relief. Montana was one of three identical triplets.

"You're not who I thought," Liz explained.

"Who were you expecting?" the other woman asked.

"Montana. I'm Liz Sutton. We met at the girls' night at my house."

Ethan's sister smiled. "I remember. I'm Dakota."

"Hi."

"How are you holding up? It's got to be difficult, moving back here, dealing with Ethan and taking on Roy's kids."

"I'm handling it. Some days better than others."

"If you ever need anything, call me. I'm always up for babysitting or whatever."

"Thanks. That's really nice of you."

"Hey, you're family now."

"I appreciate that." She raised her bowl. "I'll put this with the other food."

"Great. Jo's serving pink grapefruit martinis at the bar. She and Crystal created them one night about a year ago and they're surprisingly good."

As it was barely two in the afternoon and she had three kids coming home around four, Liz agreed but privately told herself she would only have one.

She made her way through the bar, stopping to greet the few people she knew. She felt herself relaxing. It was unlikely anyone would verbally attack her at Crystal's wake. This was a time to focus on the young woman who had died. And Dakota's offer to help had been both unexpected and really nice.

After dropping off the salad next to several other dishes, she returned to the main room, where she saw Pia talking to a group of women.

Liz started to approach them, then stopped, not sure if she should join in. Pia made the decision for her by excusing herself from her friends and walking over to Liz.

"Hi," Pia said, her eyes red from tears. Her mascara was smudged, her face pale. "I'm a mess."

"You're missing a close friend," Liz stated, giving her an impulsive hug. "It's okay to be a mess."

Pia hugged her, then stepped back. "I guess. I can't believe she's gone. It's not a surprise, and yet I can't seem to get my mind around it."

"We never expect people to die, even when we know they're going to."

Pia nodded slowly. "You're right. But knowing that doesn't make it easier."

"I'm sorry. That will take time."

Pia's eyes filled with tears again. "It's so damned unfair, you know? Crystal was a sweetie. She'd already lost so much. And then to die like this."

Liz didn't know what Pia was talking about. "I thought she was sick."

"She was." Pia sniffed. "I meant the other part. She was married. He was a soldier in Iraq."

Liz looked around the room but didn't see any men who fit that description. "Is he still over there?"

Pia shook her head. "He died. Because they knew that would be a possibility, they decided to make sure there were children. They used IVF to create several embryos before he left, just in case."

Liz gasped. "Crystal has children?" That would make it worse.

"Not exactly. After her husband died, she went to have the embryos implanted. During a routine physical, she found out she had cancer." Pia's eyes filled again. "Can you imagine? She couldn't even have her husband's children. I don't know how she kept going every day. She was so nice. I'll never be that nice."

Liz hugged her friend again. "You're perfectly nice."

"Not really. I try. I was horrible in high school, but you know that. I want to be better. I have her cat and I swear I'll do everything possible to make that cat happy." She sniffed again. "I guess I should buy a book or something. 'Cat Happiness for Dummies.'"

Liz didn't mean to be insensitive, but she couldn't help laughing. "I'm not sure they have that title yet."

"I have to do something. I guess I should really be grateful she only left me the cat. She had those embryos. I don't know what arrangements she made for them."

Liz hadn't thought about that, but it made sense. Crystal would be concerned about her unborn children. "That would be a lot of responsibility," she conceded quietly.

"Figuring out what to do with them?" Pia asked.

"Sure. Implied in the gift is the request to have the babies, then raise them."

"I'm glad it's not me," Pia noted. "A cat is about all I could handle. I'm not very maternal."

"You don't know until you try."

"I have trouble keeping plants alive. I don't really do the nurturing thing."

Liz shook her head. "Do you think I was prepared to have Tyler? You do what's required. At first it's hard, but then it gets easier."

"I need a drink," Pia muttered. "Let's go see what Jo's pouring."

They made their way to the bar. Before they reached it, an older woman paused to glare at Liz.

She felt a sinking sensation in her stomach and wondered if she could escape out the back way. But before the plan formed, the woman spoke.

"You should have married him," the older woman snapped, her eyes nearly as blue as her hair. A shapeless floral print dress hung past her knees and her sensible shoes gave her an extra inch of height. "It's disgraceful. In my generation, if a girl got pregnant, she married the father of her child. Now young people have sex and don't worry about the consequences."

Liz opened her mouth, then closed it. What was there to say? Her mind was totally blank, except for the continual chanting of "Anywhere but here."

Pia stepped in front of her and waved her index finger at the woman. "Back off, Esmeralda. You don't know what you're talking about. Liz was a kid. If you're so concerned about what's right, why didn't you step in back then? Why didn't you talk like this to Liz's mother? Everyone knew what was happening at her house. Where was your moral code then?"

Esmeralda pressed her thin lips together. "Well, I never."

"Now you have," Pia declared firmly. "This is my friend's wake. Do you really think Crystal would want you talking like this here?"

Liz, feeling all warm and fuzzy and supported, expected the older woman to snap back at Pia.

"You're right," Esmeralda said primly. She turned to Liz. "I apologize. For Crystal's sake."

"Thank you," Liz acknowledged, stunned.

Pia linked arms with Liz and took her the rest of the way to the bar. "See? It's not so bad here."

"I can't always count on you to rescue me."

"I will if I'm there. And let me say for the record, that shows what an amazing person I am."

Liz accepted the drink Jo passed her. "Because I don't deserve you defending me?"

Pia took her drink, smiled her thanks, then turned back to Liz. "You walk really straight for someone with such a big chip on her shoulder. It's impressive."

Liz bristled. "I don't have a chip."

"Oh, please. It's huge. The size of a small car. Which must make sleeping difficult."

Liz narrowed her gaze. "Are you drunk?"

"No, but I plan to be." She took a big swallow of her martini. "My point was you're so damned perfect, I should hate you, but here I am taking your side. You should be grateful. And maybe buy me a diamond or something."

Liz had barely sipped her own drink, but her head was spinning. "I'm not perfect."

Pia rolled her eyes. "As if that's true. Look at you. You were gorgeous in high school, and now you're even more beautiful. Worse, you don't seem to notice. It's not like you go out of your way to be attractive. It just happens. Have you ever seen me in the morning? No.

Well, let me just say without some serious work, I can't walk out of the house. I would scar small children for life."

Liz didn't know if she should laugh or run for her life. "You're insane."

"Maybe, but it's true. Even more horrible, you're smart. Everyone knows it. Back in school, the teachers always talked about you. 'Why can't you be smart and dedicated like Liz?'" she repeated in a mocking tone. Pia took another sip. "You ruined it for all of us."

Now Liz couldn't help laughing. "I did not."

"Ya huh. You so did. And now. Look at you. You're a famous mystery-thriller writer person. You've got that damn scholarship in your name at the stupid community college. You have a great kid. What do I have? A cat who doesn't even like me and three dead houseplants."

Pia looked miserable and defiant and slightly tipsy. Liz took her free hand and squeezed her fingers. "I'm not all that, and you have so much more than you listed. You have a great job and a community and people who love you. Crystal loved you."

Pia wiped tears from her face. "She did and she was great. But you have character and I never did."

Liz kept a hold on her fingers. "You have enough character for all of us. Trust me."

Pia's wide eyes filled with tears again. "You promise?"

"Cross my heart."

ETHAN PUNCHED THE BUTTON TO increase the incline on the elliptical. It was midafternoon and the gym was quiet. A few high school guys worked out with the free weights and there was a yoga class going on in the glass-enclosed area at the far end of the building.

"This is how girls work out," Ethan grumbled as he wiped away sweat.

Josh grinned at him. "We could have gone bike riding."

"I didn't have time. Unlike you, I work for a living."

"I work," Josh protested. "Not very hard, but I work."

His friend had called to suggest they head to the gym together. They'd briefly discussed a thirty-mile bike ride, but Ethan had meetings later that afternoon. As much as he would have enjoyed the mountainous route, it would have to wait for another day.

"Maybe this weekend," Josh suggested. "If you're not too busy with Tyler."

"Why are you free on the weekend?" Ethan knew his friend, a recent newlywed, spent every free second with his wife.

"Charity and Mayor Marsha are going to San Francisco to shop for the baby's room."

Ethan grinned. "You don't want a say in colors and accessories?"

Josh shuddered visibly. "No, thanks. I just want the baby to be healthy."

"And a boy."

Josh chuckled. "I wouldn't say no to a boy. But

we're waiting to find out. Charity wants to be surprised."

Ethan felt the burn in his legs and increased the pace of his workout. "You scared?" he asked.

Josh shrugged, then nodded. "Sometimes. When I think about it. What do I know about being a father?"

Ethan could relate to that. The difference was Josh got to start small—with a newborn. Of course a baby was a whole different set of worries.

"I know what you mean," he said.

"How's it going with Tyler?"

"Good. Great. He's bright and funny. Athletic."

"You see yourself in him?"

"Yeah, but there's a lot of Liz, too."

"Is that bad?" Josh asked.

"Sometimes," Ethan admitted, wiping away sweat. "I'm dealing, not that I have a choice. But when I think too much about what she did…" He grabbed his water bottle and swallowed several gulps.

Going there, getting riled up, accomplished nothing, Ethan reminded himself. It was a waste of time and energy.

"She speaking to you?" Josh inquired.

"Sure. Why?"

"The injunction. I would have figured she'd come after you with something sharp."

"She wasn't happy," he commented. "I reacted. It wasn't smart. But it's done now."

"Can't you undo it?"

Ethan thought about the judge. She didn't seem like the type of person who would support him changing his mind. And he wasn't willing to test the theory and risk jail time.

"We'll figure out a plan," he declared.

"Charity said Pia told her Liz came back as soon as she found out she was pregnant. But you were otherwise engaged."

"I was asleep," Ethan protested.

"With Pia in your bed."

"Still."

Josh grabbed a towel and wiped his face. "Sorry to tell you this, but Liz pretty much gets a pass. She left town because you threw her under the bus and then you were in bed with another woman when she came back to tell you about the baby. There's no way you're the good guy."

"She kept my kid from me. Nothing excuses that." No matter what, Ethan had lost something unrecoverable.

"I'm not saying it's an excuse. I'm saying you're not blameless."

"Maybe." He didn't want to think about that. "Everything would have been different if she'd stuck around. Woken me up. Hit me with something."

"That's not her way."

"You know this how?" Ethan asked.

"She left. She was hurt and she went quietly. You might not want to admit it, but from what I can see, she did a hell of a job with her kid."

"I know." He had no complaints about Liz as a mother to his son.

"Maybe she's not the one you're mad at," Josh guessed.

Ethan's legs ached, his muscles shook slightly with the effort of his workout. He pushed harder, not wanting to hear his friend's words, let alone think about them. Then the machine beeped, indicating his thirty-minute program had ended. He slowed reluctantly.

"Sure Liz didn't tell you when she first found out," Josh continued. "But the real tough one is that she came back."

Ethan stepped off the machine and grabbed his towel. "Thanks for the update."

Josh ignored that. "Rayanne kept the truth from you. She was your wife. You should have been able to trust her more than anyone. You *did* trust her."

Ethan started to turn on his friend only to remember that Josh had also been betrayed by a woman. Big time. Maybe he knew what he was talking about.

"She felt threatened," Ethan admitted, reaching for his water. "She was pregnant when we got married."

"I figured," Josh told him.

Ethan raised his eyebrows.

"Come on," Josh said, spraying down the handles of the machine and wiping them off, then handing the disinfectant to Ethan. "She was never your type. I couldn't figure out how you two got together at all."

"I came up for air and she was there," Ethan detailed.

"I'd been working hard, learning the business, starting with the windmills. I hadn't had much time to date. One day Rayanne walked into the office and I was interested."

He didn't bother saying it wouldn't have lasted. Bad enough to admit that to Liz. For reasons he couldn't explain, he'd wanted her to know the truth. But no one else needed the information. Despite the circumstances, Rayanne had been his wife. She deserved his loyalty.

"She was only a few months along when Liz showed up," he recounted. "I was out of town. I'm sure the news frightened her. I'd talked about Liz some, so she had a clue about how serious things had been. Or maybe she would have imagined the worst regardless. Plus knowing I already had a son might have scared her into thinking I wouldn't care as much about our baby."

At least that was his assumption. He'd only been able to look at things from his perspective. Rayanne wasn't around to ask.

He wanted to give her the benefit of the doubt. Wanted to believe the best of her, but the bottom line was, she'd kept her secret until the very end. Even when they'd both known she was dying, she hadn't told him about Tyler. That was a tough thing to forgive.

"You're still pissed," Josh pointed out.

"Sometimes."

"Does it ever occur to you that because you can't get

things right with Rayanne that you're taking out all of it on Liz?"

Ethan stared at his friend. "What are you talking about?"

Josh shrugged. "I'm just saying that sure, Liz has some blame in all this, but so do you and so does Rayanne. Only Rayanne's not here. Being mad at the dead never plays well, even to ourselves. So what are you left with? Liz."

Ethan finished his bottle of water and tossed the empty container into the recycling bin, then dropped his towel across his shoulder and headed for the locker room. Josh fell into step beside him.

They walked downstairs and pushed through the swinging door. His friend's words made sense, which fried his ass.

"When did you get all insightful?" he asked.

"I have no idea," Josh admitted.

"I don't like it."

"Me, either. Makes me feel like a girl. Don't tell anyone."

SATURDAY DAWNED AS HOT AS THE rest of the week had been. By ten, it was close to eighty-five degrees. The air conditioning in the old house was questionable at best, which meant it was on the repair list. But so far, the subcontractor hadn't shown up. Something Liz would discuss with Ethan the next time she saw him. In the meantime, she had three kids to deal with.

Melissa and Abby were arguing about who got to use

the phone next, with Abby pointing out Melissa could just as easily use her cell phone, while Tyler resented the limit on his computer game time.

"Dad would let me play longer," he whined as she reached for the controller.

"You don't know that."

"Uh-huh. He let's me do lots of stuff you don't." Tyler's lower lip jutted out.

She didn't doubt that Ethan wasn't into things like limits right now. He was getting to know his son.

She told herself to be patient and understanding. That everything would even out eventually.

"I'm glad you're getting along with your dad, but right now your computer game time is up." She took the controller from him. "We're heading out, so please put on your swimsuit."

"I want to go see Dad instead."

She ignored that and walked to the stairs. "Fifteen minutes," she yelled over the girls' bickering. "Be ready or be left behind."

Abby ran to the landing. "Where are we going?"

"The pool. We'll spend the whole day there."

"Can we have hotdogs for lunch?" Abby asked.

"Yes."

Melissa joined her. "I'm too old for the pool."

Liz was less sure about leaving the teenager home alone. Not that she was afraid Melissa would get into trouble, but more because she would brood. Better for her to be out with people.

"Call one of your friends and invite her along," Liz offered. "Be ready in fifteen minutes. I mean it."

The two of them turned and ran down the hall. Liz went upstairs to put on her own bathing suit. She didn't have big plans to get in the water, but the odds of being splashed were huge. Better to be prepared.

Tyler slowly climbed the stairs, muttering something about preferring his father.

It took nearly a half hour to get out the door, but it was worth it. Although there were several families at the pool already, there were still plenty of spots in the shade.

"How about over there?" Liz asked, pointing.

"I see Jason," Tyler said, already moving away. "I'm going to see if he wants to go on the slide."

"Brittany's with her mom," Abby stated. "May I sit with them?"

"Madison's waiting for me by the snack bar." Melissa was already inching away.

Liz gave permission for Abby to visit with her friend and found herself carrying everything over to the bit of grass she'd selected and laying out towels. She put on sunscreen, plopped a hat on her head and opened the romance novel she'd brought with her. Less than a minute later, her cell phone rang.

"Hello?"

"It's Pia. I'm at your house. Where are you?"

"At the pool." She hadn't talked to Pia since Crystal's wake. "What's going on?"

"I have printouts of the posters," Pia explained. "I wanted to make sure they're okay with you. After all, you're our star."

Liz frowned. While she appreciated the concern, the posters weren't her business. Pia's job was to promote the entire signing and the town. Besides, Liz had seen the posters at the meeting.

Then she realized that maybe it wasn't about the posters at all, but about missing Crystal.

"I'd love to see them," Liz told her. "But I've got all three kids here. Why don't you put on a sassy bikini and join us?"

Pia sighed. "No, thanks. I'll just go home. I'm not feeling very well."

"All the more reason to slather on sunscreen and pretend to tan. Come on. I desperately need an adult to talk to."

Pia hesitated. "Maybe," she said. "Okay. I'll be there. Want me to bring anything?"

"Wine?"

Pia chuckled. "I don't think they'll let me open a bottle by the pool."

"Probably not. Then just bring yourself. See you soon."

Liz was concerned that Pia would change her mind, but in less than a half hour, the other woman had shown up with her towel and a cooler full of cold water.

As Pia peeled out of her shorts and tank top, Liz tried not to be envious of the other woman's long, lean legs.

Height was required to look that good, she decided. While she wasn't exactly vertically challenged, Pia topped her by a good three inches.

"This is nice," Pia said, settling on the towel next to her and looking around. "It's been years since I've hung out at the pool."

"I've been here on and off since school was out," Liz told her. "The hotdogs are good." She glanced at Pia. "How are you doing?"

"Okay. I miss Crystal a lot, but work is keeping me busy, so that's good. I bought a collar for Jake. Sort of as a way to let him know we're committed to each other, now that Crystal is gone."

Liz blinked at her, not sure what to say.

"I know he's a cat," Pia added with a smile. "We don't actually have those conversations."

"Good. Because I would have worried about you."

"I was all set to put the collar on him when Dakota scared me off." Pia paused. "She's one of Ethan's sisters."

"I've met her a couple of times."

"She said a friend of hers put a collar on a cat who'd never worn one and he about ripped his head off, scratching to remove it. He nicked a vein or something and there was blood everywhere. The last thing I need is to come home from work one day to a scene in a horror movie."

Liz winced. "Are you sure Dakota wasn't trying to be funny?"

"I don't think so. Anyway, Jake won't be getting his collar anytime soon."

"Probably a good plan." Liz thought about Ethan's sister. "Doesn't Dakota work at the camp?"

"She's the head counselor, which doesn't sound as important as it is. She has a PhD in childhood development. Raoul Moreno owns the camp. While it's just a summer place now, he wants to expand it into a year-round facility. Dakota is helping him with that."

Liz frowned. "Raoul Moreno. Why is that name familiar?"

Pia grinned. "Oh, honey, you haven't seen him? He and I haven't actually had a conversation, but I've spotted him around. Talk about yummy. Tall, dark and very pretty. In a macho, Latin kind of way. He played football for the Dallas Cowboys. Quarterback. Smart and athletic. Does it get better than that?"

"Sounds like someone has a bit of a crush."

"Only from afar. I'm not interested in having a relationship right now."

"Why not?"

Pia hesitated. "I'm not very good at them. I want to be. I want to be nurturing and know fifteen different ways to stylishly cut a sandwich. But it's not my thing. I like kids, in theory. I don't know much about them. But getting serious and having one of my own? I don't really think I'm the right person for that."

There was something about the way she said the words. As if there was more, but she wasn't comfortable telling the story. Liz didn't want to press. Her friendship with Pia was still new. But she couldn't help wondering what secrets her friend was keeping to herself.

"I don't think skilled sandwich cutting guarantees great nurturing," she said instead. "I only know two ways."

"That's one more than me. Besides, you're a natural parent. I've seen you with Tyler. You two have a great relationship."

"I'm a parent because I got pregnant," Liz told her. "I was eighteen. Instinct or not, I was a kid and I know I made a bunch of mistakes. I spent the first year terrified I was going to drop him or something. I think loving is a whole lot more important than anything. Children need to know they're wanted."

"That's true," Pia said. "Not being wanted sucks."

"I know."

"It's a nonissue," Pia said flatly. "I'm between men and I intend to keep it that way. I have Jake the cat and that's enough."

"At least he won't leave the toilet seat up."

"Exactly. I heard from Crystal's lawyer. She wants me to come in and talk in the next few weeks. She said there was no rush so I'm assuming there's something in Crystal's will about a formal transfer of ownership."

"Be sure to tell the city," Liz teased. "There's paperwork with pet transfers."

Pia lowered her sunglasses and glanced over them. "You're not all that. You know that, right?"

Liz laughed.

Pia smiled at her. "I'm glad you came back."

Liz groaned. "Don't say that."

"Still being harassed by the elderly?"

"They're not all old." Thinking about Fool's Gold left her feeling confused. "There are some things about being here that I really like and some that make me insane."

"Where does Ethan fall on the list?"

"He's on both sides."

"See? Men are a complication."

"Tell me about it," Liz grumbled. "I know he wants a relationship with Tyler and I encourage that. But then he goes and does something stupid like the injunction and I want to bitch slap him."

"Can I watch? It would be the highlight of my week."

Liz smiled faintly. "Probably not his." She sighed. "I just don't know what to do."

"Because you don't know how you feel about him? How could you? It's been years, but you were in love with him once and now you have Tyler together. It's got to be complicated. Trying to decide if you still love him."

Liz felt the world tilt to the right. She grabbed on to her towel to keep from sliding away. Only nothing was really moving—it was all happening inside of her.

"I don't love Ethan."

Pia's expression turned pitying. "Speaking as a professional, I can tell you that denial is a dangerous place to live. It really messes up any long-term planning. I'm not saying you love him, I'm saying you have to decide if you might."

"No. I don't accept that. He denied me in public—twice! He never tried to find me. I'm sure he hasn't thought about me in years."

"Interesting. So your feelings are dependent on his? I wouldn't have thought you were that shallow."

Liz sputtered. "Excuse me? That's not what I'm saying."

"It's what you said."

Liz sucked in a breath. "The point is I'm not interested in Ethan that way and he's not interested in me. We have a child together. There are details that have to be worked out. Nothing more."

Care about Ethan? Love Ethan? Not on this planet. She barely liked him. Okay, sure she wanted him, but that was different. Having a sexual connection was hardly significant.

"You're wrong," Liz added. "You couldn't be more wrong."

Pia picked up a bottle of water and opened it. "Isn't there a line in Shakespeare about protesting too much? I can't remember, but then, I'm not the literary one here."

"No. You're the crazy one."

Instead of getting upset, Pia only smiled.

Liz glared at her, then crossed her arms over her chest and stared out at the pool. Love? That was just plain stupid. She didn't love Ethan. She refused to do more than like him and that was just for her son's sake. Anyone who implied otherwise needed some serious mental therapy.

CHAPTER FIFTEEN

TALK ABOUT A BAD IDEA, LIZ thought as she stood in front of the house where Ethan had grown up. Denise had called to invite her and the kids over for dinner. Sort of a family bonding time. Liz had wanted to say no, but hadn't been able to think of an excuse. Ethan's brothers were out of town, but the triplets would be there. Which meant five members of the Hendrix clan to face down.

Liz kept telling herself that Denise had been perfectly friendly the last time they'd talked. That everything would be fine. The problem was she couldn't quite believe herself.

She clutched the flowers she held tightly, then led the way to the front door and rang the bell. The children clustered behind her, talking about the newly installed shower in the upstairs bath back home. For reasons Liz couldn't understand, the glass blocks around the window had been a big hit.

The door opened.

"You made it," Ethan said.

"Was there any doubt?" she asked, trying not to let her nervousness show.

"We were taking bets."

"Great."

"I'm kidding," he corrected, stepping back. "Come on in."

She walked inside. Tyler came after her and hugged his father, while Abby and Melissa huddled together. Denise appeared, looking relaxed and pretty in a matching light green crop pant and T-shirt set. There was a rhinestone pink flamingo filling the front of her shirt, and she had pink sparkles on her flip-flops.

"Come in, come in," the older woman urged as she hugged first Tyler, then the girls. She took the flowers Liz offered. "Aren't you sweet? They're beautiful and I have just the right vase for them." She frowned. "But it's up high and I can't reach it. Melissa, honey, can you get it for me?"

"Um, sure." The teen followed her into the kitchen.

"I always wanted to be tall," she could hear Denise saying. "You're so pretty. I don't even want to think about all the boys you have interested in you."

"Me, either," Liz agreed, allowing Ethan to ease her down the hallway toward the large kitchen. Abby and Tyler trailed after them.

The kitchen was light and bright, obviously the center of the home. The blue floor tiles warmed up the white cabinets and dark granite. There were stainless steel appliances and lots of storage space. It was the perfect kitchen for a large family.

Through the far door, Liz saw the table in the dining

room had been set for nine and there was still plenty of room. Ethan's family had always been large.

"We're keeping it simple tonight," Denise announced as she put the flowers in water. "Barbecued chicken and salads. I made a few fresh pies earlier today, so we have them for dessert. Now let's go into the family room. It's more comfortable there."

She led the way into a big open space filled with comfortable-looking sofas and chairs, plenty of small tables scattered around a fireplace. A long bar stood against the far wall and a big TV was mounted on the opposite wall.

Ethan's sisters were already in the family room. They stood as Liz and the kids entered, moving next to each other.

"Sweet," Tyler said as he stared at them. "You're really Dad's sisters?"

"Uh-huh," Montana said. "Which means we're your aunts. Very cool. I know I'd like me for an aunt. I'm Montana. You've seen me at the library and I babysat once." She pointed to her head. "Long hair. I'm the pretty one, in case you hadn't noticed."

"You're a lot of things," Dakota muttered. "Hi. I'm Dakota, Tyler. This is a lot to take in, huh? Don't worry. You'll get used to there being three of us. This is Nevada."

"Long hair, medium hair, short hair," Tyler said. "That works."

Liz put her hands on his shoulders. "Don't get used to it too much. Women tend to change their hair."

"We might," Montana acknowledged. "Nevada just cut hers. She says this cut is more sensible."

Nevada, the quietest of the triplets, only smiled. "I'm not out there looking for attention."

"Or a man," Montana added. "It wouldn't kill you to date."

"Like you go out every weekend?" Nevada quipped.

"I'm waiting for the right guy," Montana explained.

"You mean the perfect guy," Nevada said. "He doesn't exist."

"You're all making me so proud," Denise said with a shake of her head. She turned to Abby and Melissa. "You two are sisters. Do you fight?"

Abby grinned. "A lot. But it's okay. We still love each other."

"She can be a pain, but I'm used to it," Melissa conceded.

"That's encouraging." Denise motioned to the sofas. "Everyone have a seat. Ethan, you're in charge of the bar tonight. There's lemonade for those not yet of drinking age. I made a very nice fruit sangria for the adults. Or we have the usual drink fixings."

"Sangria sounds nice," Liz said, taking a seat on one of the sofas. Both Melissa and Abby settled next to her. Tyler wandered over to the bar and sat on one of the stools. Everyone else found a place in the room.

The girls kept glancing at Ethan's sisters. Finally Melissa asked, "What's it like to be a triplet?"

"Easier now," Dakota told her. "We have our own

lives. We're close but because we're interested in different things, we don't have the same friends, hang out at the same places."

"Back in school, almost no one could tell us apart," Montana said with a laugh. "We used that to our advantage."

"Your names are nice." Abby's voice was low and shy.

Denise brought the girls each a lemonade. "And not my fault," she stated. "Just remember that."

"What do you mean?" Liz asked.

Denise sighed. "Giving birth to triplets isn't easy and I had a very hard time recovering. The boys were scared and being very difficult for their grandparents. To make them feel better and give them a distraction, their father promised they could name the girls anything they wanted."

Liz laughed. "That's giving away a lot of power."

"I know," Denise agreed. "When I found out, I nearly had a fit. But by then, it was done."

"I like their names," Abby said.

"I like yours," Dakota told her.

"Would you like to see their baby pictures?" Denise asked.

Melissa and Abby both nodded.

Montana groaned. "Mom, please. Not the baby pictures."

"I was on bed rest for nearly four months with you three. I can do anything I want."

She opened several cabinets in the storage unit below the TV and pulled out albums. Melissa and Abby joined her, as did Tyler. The triplets exchanged a glance and slowly moved over to where Denise had the albums open. Liz got up and walked to the bar.

"Does she do this a lot?" she asked.

Ethan grinned. "More than she should. It was worse when my sisters were in high school and starting to date. They had to bring the guys home to meet the folks, but ran the risk of the pictures coming out. My younger brothers made money by distracting her."

"It's almost enough to make me grateful for my inattentive mother."

"Don't get too comfortable," he warned. "Any second now she'll start lamenting her lack of grandchildren. I'll be off the hook for a while because of Tyler, but my sisters are feeling the pressure."

Even though she was standing in the room and seeing it all as it happened, there was a part of her that wondered if any of this was real. Were there actually families that interacted with each other? That laughed and fought and made up for years and still had that loving connection? While she and Tyler were close, it was just the two of them.

Or it had been, she thought, correcting herself. Her small family had just doubled in size with the addition of Melissa and Abby.

Liz felt her chest tighten and she had to consciously suck in air.

"You okay?" Ethan asked.

"I guess." She looked at him. "I'm responsible for them. Melissa and Abby. They're living with me permanently."

He seemed confused. "That's not news."

"I know. Roy asked, I agreed. I never thought about saying no. It's just...I never really put the pieces together before now. They're my responsibility. I'm going to have to take care of them. Doctors and dentists and schoolwork and talking about boys. Until now it's all been theoretical. I'm not prepared for teenage girls. Technically Abby's not yet a teen, but still."

He walked around the bar and sat next to her. "You're doing great. Just keep with the plan."

"I don't have a plan. I don't have anything. What if I mess up?"

"You'll say you're sorry and then you'll start over."

That seemed too simplistic. The responsibility was suddenly overwhelming. She'd gone from being a single mom of one child to being responsible for three. How could she have missed that?

What now? What would be best for them?

She turned toward the far wall and saw Denise bending over a coffee table, flipping pages in a photo album. Tyler, Melissa and Abby were clustered around her. The triplets hovered nearby, correcting or adding to the stories.

This was good for them, Liz thought. Seeing a big family in action. Feeling a part of something. They'd already been through so much. Not a thought designed to make her feel good about her decisions. Because in a few weeks her plan was to take her nieces from everything they'd ever known and move them to San Francisco.

She knew the argument. Her life was there. The schools were great, the house big enough. They would adjust. Kids did it all the time. But she couldn't escape the voice whispering that staying here would make things easier for everyone. Well, everyone but her.

Tyler wouldn't mind being uprooted. He might protest about leaving behind his friends, but the truth was he loved Fool's Gold. And she had a feeling he would gladly trade time with his friends for time with his dad.

"Earth to Liz. You okay in there?"

"Don't distract me with the facts," she snapped.

He held up both his hands, as if to show he was unarmed. "I'm not the enemy here and you're not making sense."

"I know. I'm sorry. I'm confused by all of this." And at the core of it, she was confused by him.

"Can I do anything to help?" he asked.

"Spike my drink?"

He grinned. "You got it."

DINNER AT THE HENDRIX HOUSE was loud and fun and delicious. By the time the kitchen had been cleaned up—a job complicated by too many people trying to help—dessert eaten and more pictures viewed—this time of Ethan as a boy—it was nearly ten.

Ethan insisted on walking them all home. There were hugs for Denise and the triplets, promises to do this again soon, and then they were out in the cool, clear night.

Once they arrived, Liz herded the kids upstairs to get ready for bed, then turned to Ethan.

"We all had a great time," she began. "Please thank your mom for the—"

Anything else she'd been planning to say was cut off when he kissed her. He cupped her face in both his hands, then pressed his mouth to hers. She reacted instinctively, moving closer, parting her lips and hanging on because kissing Ethan was always a hell of a ride.

He didn't disappoint. After dropping his hands to her waist, he hauled her against him. His tongue invaded, taking and teasing, exploring and exciting. She felt the heat pouring through her body, the wanting. Just being near him was tempting enough, but actually touching him made her knees weak. She was hungry, but not just for sex. What burned inside her was need for this specific man.

She leaned into him and deepened the kiss. He responded in kind, their tongues stroking frantically. He moved his hands to her breasts and cupped the curves. His thumbs brushed against her tight, sensitive nipples, making her groan.

There was a noise from upstairs. As if something had fallen. They weren't alone.

Reluctantly, she pulled back and he let her go. They stared into each other's eyes, their breathing hard.

"Damn," he murmured.

"Double damn."

She thought he might ask to come back later, but he didn't, which relieved her. Given the fact that she was still sleeping on the sofa, that there wasn't any privacy in the house and that things were still unresolved, she knew making love would be a mistake.

"I should go," he said.

She nodded.

"I had a good time tonight," he told her.

"Me, too. And I didn't expect to."

He grinned. "I won't tell my mother."

"Thanks." She raised herself up on tiptoes and brushed her mouth against his. "I'll see you soon."

"I look forward to it."

He released her and left. She waited until she was sure he was gone, then stepped out on the porch into the darkness.

The night air cooled her heated skin. She brushed her fingers against her lips, as if she could recreate the feelings. But nothing would be the same as kissing Ethan. Reluctantly, she went back inside and started up the stairs to say good-night to her family.

SUNDAY MORNING LIZ DUG OUT AN old waffle maker and mixed batter. Tyler rose early, as he always did, while the girls slept in.

"Last night was fun," he commented as he set the table, then carefully poured juice. "Did you see those old pictures of Dad? I really look like him."

"I know. That's what I thought when you were a baby—that you looked just like your dad."

"We're going riding later," her son continued with a grin. "He's showing me some really sweet tricks and stuff. He says I've got talent. I don't know if I want to get serious and race professionally, but it's so much fun."

Tyler glanced down, then back at her. "In a couple of years, I'll be old enough to go to racing school. Dad knows Josh Golden. He's this really famous racer and he runs the school and everything."

Hero-worship, she thought wryly. That was new. "I know Josh. I went to high school with him."

Tyler's mouth drooped. "So he's like really old, huh?"

Liz winced. "Hey, not so old. Although he's a couple years older than me."

"But he could still teach me stuff. Only if we don't live here, I guess I couldn't go."

Great. So now it wasn't just Melissa and Abby who didn't want to move. "You can't go to the school for a few years, so let's not worry about that now."

Tyler hesitated. "But if we moved here, I could."

"Yes. I get it. Let's move on."

Her son sighed, then nodded. "Dad says because I'm so good in math and science, that I could study a lot of different things in college. Like engineering or maybe do research."

They were discussing his college plans?

"Maybe you should think about finishing high school first."

"Oh, Mom. Plans are important. And goals. It's a guy thing."

"Girls don't have goals?" she asked as she poured the batter into the heated grid.

"I guess some do, but some just want to be pretty."

"And some guys are only into playing video games and partying."

"Sure, but that's different."

Her son, the sexist, she thought, faintly annoyed. Apparently there needed to be more conversations about equality and tolerance. Perhaps Ethan should be the one doing the explaining. Then he could be more than the fun parent.

While she appreciated that Ethan and Tyler got along so well, she knew they were a long way from being father and son. Right now Ethan was entertaining and new. He'd yet to have to make any hard decisions, to stand up to Tyler or punish him.

"How is it different?" she asked.

"Guys don't care about how they look and girls don't care about computer games. Melissa takes forever in the bathroom."

"Abby plays with you."

"But there are more girls like Melissa than there are like Abby."

"You know this how? Did you take a survey?"

He frowned. "You're mad. Why?"

She checked on the cooking waffles. "Because you're making statements about people that may or may not be true. You're assuming a lot. It's easy to say a group of people always acts a certain way, but it's not accurate."

"But why does it matter?"

"Because people are a lot more alike than they are different. The biggest problems we have in this world are because of what we assume about each other. People make decisions based on appearance or gender or race, without getting to know anyone in that group. Or they have a very limited sample. Then they say things and other people hear them and start to believe them. Pretty soon we have a cultural bias that affects all kinds of decisions."

Tyler stared at her blankly.

Liz shook her head. "Let me try it another way. When Melissa and Abby move to San Francisco with us, Abby will be in your school, right?"

He nodded.

"She's from a small town. Let's say a few students and teachers think that people from small towns are stupid. So they find out about Abby transferring and they tell everyone at the school that Abby is stupid. Is that right or fair?"

Tyler's eyes widened. "Abby's not stupid. She's really smart and nice and fun. She's my friend."

"I understand that, but so what? You said it didn't

matter if you said something about someone that wasn't true."

He was quiet for a few seconds. "They'll hurt Abby's feelings and I'll get mad. And if I act out because I'm mad, I could get into trouble. And all my friends will help me and they'll get in trouble."

"That's a big mess," Liz said as she used a fork to pop the waffle onto a plate. "All because someone believed something that wasn't true."

"I guess it does matter what we say, huh?"

"Yeah. And a little word can have a big impact. The difference between *all* and *some*. 'All girls don't care about computer games' is really different than 'Some girls don't care about computer games.'"

"Okay. So when I said girls don't have goals, I was wrong. Some boys don't have goals."

"Exactly." She passed him the waffle.

He grinned at her. "You're really smart."

"Thank you."

"You're probably the smartest mom in the whole world."

She laughed. "That's very possibly true."

LIZ HAD LIVED THROUGH CABINETS being torn out, carpet being ripped up, drywall installation and insistent banging of hardwood floors being laid. But the noise that finally drove her out of the house was the high-pitched scream of a tile saw.

She took her laptop and a blanket to the far end of

the yard and stretched out in the shade of a tree. The sound was still intense, but not so distracting.

She glanced up at the house. Even from here, she could see the changes. What had once been poured foundation and a few attempts at framing had become a real room attached to the house. The master suite was nearly complete. When it was, she might think about moving off the sofa.

Inside, the kitchen gleamed, the fresh paint added a brightness and the carpet was plush. The house had come a long way since she'd first arrived in town. It was practically new.

But no matter how many changes occurred, she couldn't seem to shake the sense of doom and defeat when she walked inside. Maybe the memories were just too strong. Whatever the cause, this house would never be her home. Staying or leaving, she would move out as soon as possible.

She returned her attention to her computer. After loading her word processing program, she started to read the pages she'd finished the previous day.

It only took a few minutes to get back into the story. She glanced at her plotting notes, then began to type. The serial killer in this book targeted teenaged boys. The scene took place at a high school basketball game and she closed her eyes to imagine what it would sound like and feel like to be in that gym during an important game.

Two hours later, she leaned against the tree. The scene was nearly finished, her back ached from the uncomfortable position and the tile saw had grown mercifully silent. All in all, a pretty decent morning's work.

The back door of her house opened and Ethan stepped onto the patio. He had a bottle of water in each hand.

God, he looked good, she thought as she took in the faded jeans, the long legs and narrow hips. He moved with an easy masculine grace—a man comfortable in his own skin.

"Couldn't stand the noise?" he guessed.

"They defeated me with the tile saw."

"And here I thought you were indestructible." He offered her a bottle, then settled across from her on the blanket.

"Not all the time." She glanced at the house. "They're doing great work. Thank you for that."

"You're welcome. I have a good team." He pointed at her computer. "How's the book going?"

"Good. I'm finally into it enough to make the writing easier. The beginning is always a nightmare. Figuring out who everyone is, why they're doing what they do. That sort of thing."

"You make it sound like work," he teased.

She mock glared at him. "Don't make me hurt you. We both know I could."

"I'm trembling in fear."

They smiled at each other and she felt a quiver low in her belly.

"Are you going to keep killing me?" he asked.

"I wasn't, but I've changed my mind."

"What did I do?" he inquired, looking all innocent.

"What didn't you do? You're raising my son to be sexist and judgmental when it comes to women."

Ethan stared at her. "What are you talking about?"

"Girls don't have goals? Since when? I know he got that from you."

Ethan groaned. "I didn't mean it like that. We were talking about how important it is to set goals. To figure out what you want and just go for it."

"And?"

He shrugged. "I might have said something about girls not being interested in anything but fashion and talking on the phone."

"If I didn't need my laptop, I'd throw it at you."

"I'm sorry. It was just one of those things guys say to each other."

"Tyler isn't a guy. He's a kid and he adores you. As far as he's concerned, everything you said to him is ultimate truth."

Ethan looked both pleased and chagrined. "Okay. You're right. I need to think before I speak."

She opened her mouth to say more, then closed it. "Excuse me?"

"You're right. I shouldn't have said that. In fact there's a lot of things I regret. Like the injunction. I should have talked to you first. I was upset. That's not the best time to make an important decision."

"Well, damn. If you're going to take responsibility and express regret, how can I keep yelling at you?"

One corner of his mouth turned up. "You'll find a reason. Then you can kill me off in your book again."

She smirked, raising her eyebrows. "Maybe I already did."

He laughed, then took a drink of water. "You're good, you know. Those books. They're extraordinary."

His compliment warmed her. "Thank you."

"You have a detective you talk to?"

She nodded. "I met her at Tyler's preschool. She was picking up her daughter and we started talking. She reads my manuscripts and tells me where I get it wrong."

"She's a mother?"

Liz put aside her laptop, stretched out her arm and slapped him on the shoulder. "What is it with you? Nevada is female and she's an engineer. Why is that okay but you're a pig about other women?"

He grabbed her hand and pulled her onto the blanket next to him, then rolled her onto her back.

"I don't have a problem with women," he said leaning over her. "I said mother not woman. I never thought of a detective as having a family."

"You wouldn't. They usually don't show the home life on TV."

"Are you saying I'm shallow?" he asked with a grin. "You're awfully arrogant for someone completely in my power."

"You only think I'm in your power."

"Keep telling yourself that."

They stared at each other. His mouth hovered inches from hers. She did her best not to react to the feel of his body against hers.

"What are the odds of one of my crew watching out the window?" he theorized.

"Better than fifty percent."

"That's what I thought, too. Damn." He rolled off her. "Change of subject. Has being here made you late with your book?"

"I'm not too behind."

"This summer can't have helped with your deadline."

"That's true, but I tend to plan ahead. Usually I have less time to write in the summer because Tyler's home, so I'm still okay."

He shifted so he faced her and brushed the hair from her face. "What were you doing before you were a writer?" he asked.

"I waited on tables. Same as here. That's what I did when I first moved to San Francisco. When I got big enough that I walked slow, I was a cashier, where I could sit during my shift. After Tyler was born, I got work at a nicer restaurant where the tips were better."

"Don't take this wrong," he suggested slowly, "but I would have helped."

"If you'd known."

He nodded.

She considered the words. He was right—he would have helped.

She thought about the long, lonely evenings after she'd brought Tyler home from the hospital. Her terror at being alone with a newborn. She had checked out a few books from the library, but had no real working knowledge of what to do. She'd never really been around babies and there was no one to ask. Help would have been nice.

Loss made her throat tighten. Everything could have been different, she thought. Looking back, she wasn't sure if it would have been better, if they would have lasted as a couple. She wasn't sure she would have ever started writing. After all, her first short stories had all been about killing Ethan in an assortment of creative ways.

Regardless, she was sure, given the choice, he would want the chance to know his son from birth.

"I'm sorry," she whispered.

"Me, too."

She rolled toward him. He leaned in and lightly kissed her mouth, then they stared at each other for a long time.

She read a world of ache in his eyes. Saw the place where the past should have been. In that moment, she knew she had never stopped loving Ethan, never stopped missing him, had never moved on. And if she stayed here too long, she was in danger of him discovering that particular truth.

CHAPTER SIXTEEN

THE BANQUET ROOM AT THE HOTEL had a view of the mountain that filled the window. Concentrating on the lush colors of the plant-life seemed much easier than making small-talk with people she didn't know at a luncheon she didn't want to attend. But here she was.

The purpose—to award scholarship recipients—made perfect sense. But knowing these women were getting scholarships in her name made her feel as if she was having an out-of-body experience.

Betty Higgins, the clerk from the community college, waved from another table. Liz waved back. There were about fifteen tables in all—and nearly one hundred people at the event. Lunch had been pleasant—a delicious salad and warm sourdough bread. But after the hot fudge brownie had been delivered, Dana Marton, the president of the college, stood to address everyone.

"Thank you so much for coming," Dana, an attractive, slender woman said with a smile. She'd introduced several members of the faculty, a few significant donors, then had shifted to Liz.

"Everyone here has been brought together by a single person of extraordinary talent. Liz Sutton left Fool's Gold only a few months after graduating high school. She went away, had a baby, supported herself and her child, then started writing a detective novel. That first book, published nearly six years ago, made it to the top of the bestseller lists. Not only are her characters real and smart and sympathetic, they remind us of people we know. And for me, that's writing at its best."

Dana glanced down at her notes, then back at the people listening. "But the significance of Liz's story lies elsewhere. Yes, she managed to overcome tremendous odds and adversity. But the most amazing part of her journey is that it had to happen somewhere else. Not here, in the town we love so much."

Dana drew in a breath. "In a town that prides itself on caring, Liz slipped through the cracks. While we all noticed she was neglected at home, no one acted. Maybe it's because she was so mature for her age. Her grades never suffered, she was always on time to school. Maybe it was because we weren't as sensitized to disenfranchised children years ago. But when we, as a community, could have helped, there was silence."

Liz felt the heat on her cheeks and did her best not to give in to the need to bolt for the closest door. They were talking about her life as if everyone knew. She'd become a sad and tragic legend.

"While the outcome of Liz's story is a happy one,

not every ignored child is so successful," Dana continued. "Not every child has the skills and determination
and character to survive. While we are proud of Liz and
her life, we must not lose sight of this opportunity to
learn from our mistakes. To do better next time so no
child ever slips through the cracks again."

There was a round of applause. Liz felt everyone
glancing in her direction and did her best to appear
calm and engaged. Because panic was just so unattractive.

"When Liz disappeared, we were left with a small
scholarship," Dana went on. "It should have been hers.
The first suggestion was to simply fold the money back
into the scholarship fund. But before we could do that,
someone sent in a few dollars in Liz's name. More
checks arrived. As someone once told me, fifty dollars
can't change a life, but when everyone gives a little, we
can change the world."

Dana smiled at Liz. "That is how the Elizabeth Marie
Sutton Scholarship was born. To date there have been
nearly thirty recipients and most of them are here
today."

To Liz's astonishment, several people stood. Then
more joined them. There were exactly twenty-eight
woman clapping and smiling at her. Beaming as if she'd
actually done something for them.

When the women were seated, Dana invited the four
women who would be receiving the money this year to
speak. Each of them talked about how she wanted to go

to college and how this money made it possible. They thanked Liz, which made her want to point out her big act had been to run away. But maybe this wasn't the time.

There were a few more speeches, then the luncheon ended. Liz found herself shaking hands with people and accepting their thanks. As much as she wanted to say she didn't deserve their praise, she was glad that her story had become symbolic of something bigger.

Only in Fool's Gold, she thought as a teenager was explaining how her mother was sick and the girl had to take care of her younger three brothers. That meant paying for college wasn't possible. But at Fool's Gold Community College, she could get a start on her education. All thanks to Liz.

It took a while to work through the crowd. Liz finally made her way to the college president.

"It's so nice to meet you," Dana said warmly. "I only moved here a few years ago, so I missed the formative years of the scholarship. However, I'm happy to tell you more women apply for this money than any other scholarship we have."

"I'm happy to hear that," Liz stated, pulling a business size envelope out of her purse and handing it over. "I want to make a donation, but please don't say anything."

"I won't," Dana promised, then opened the envelope and glanced at the ten thousand dollar check. "Oh, my."

Liz glanced around warily. "Not a word."

"But you're being so generous."

"I want to give back."

A few weeks ago, Liz would have laughed at the idea of giving back. To a town that had ignored her? But things had changed. Sure, Fool's Gold wasn't perfect. No place was. There were good things and bad things, the same with the people. She might have slipped through the cracks, as Dana had described it, but that was as much a symptom of the time. Back then, how you raised your children was a more private matter. People looked away, rather than get involved. She realized it was more important to see that the people in town had tried to change. And in doing so, they'd helped others.

"Maybe you'd like to come speak to our students in the fall," Dana suggested. "We have a lecture series that's very popular. I know you'd draw a crowd."

Liz hesitated. "I'm not sure of my travel plans this fall," she explained, which was mostly true. "I usually go on a book tour."

"We could work around that."

"Maybe," Liz said, doing her best to sound doubtful. "I'll think about it."

Come back here and lecture? She didn't want to have to make a special trip. Although if she was still living here…

No, she told herself. Not here. She couldn't let herself be lulled by a few good days. Did she really want to spend the rest of her life in a place where people felt free to judge her when they didn't know what they were talking about?

Never, she thought with a firm nod.

"I CAN GET YOU A DISCOUNT," Ethan murmured.

Liz stared at the dresser made entirely of twigs. Not logs, not sticks, but twigs. Lots of twigs.

"How does he do that?" she reflected in a low voice. "How is it staying together?"

"You don't want to know."

The book festival took place in the main park in town, but as Liz and Ethan walked with Abby and Tyler, she saw there was a lot more than books for sale.

The booths were clustered by subject. All the crafts together, the cooking across from the travel section. Novels were at the far end, but Liz wasn't due there for half an hour.

"She has a great crowd," Liz noted, pointing to a large group of people surging toward a booth.

"Cookies," he told her, grabbing her hand and keeping her close. "She writes a cookbook and offers samples."

"Great idea. I should do that." She frowned. "Although I'm not sure what sample I would offer."

"Blood," Tyler teased cheerfully from Ethan's other side.

"Or dead bodies," Abby said with a giggle. The preteen walked next to her. Melissa had gone off with a couple of girlfriends.

"Very nice," Liz said. "Where do you two get your ideas?"

They both laughed.

This was fun, she thought as they stopped for lemon-

ade at a stand, then strolled by the quilting demonstra-
tion. Part party, part county fair. So far everyone had
been friendly enough, calling out to her. No one had
said anything bad about her or Tyler.

"Is that a llama?" Ethan asked, pointing.

Liz squinted, then stopped when she saw a small
llama in the shade. "Don't they spit?"

"That's what I heard."

"It's not a llama," Tyler stated importantly. "It's an
alpaca."

"They're like sheep," Abby added. "Their fibers are
like wool and can be made into a lot of different things.
Some of the fibers are really soft."

"Llamas have ears shaped like bananas," Tyler
informed. "Alpaca ears are straight."

Liz glanced at both of them. "Excuse me?"

The kids grinned. "A lady brought alpacas to camp
last week," Abby told her. "We spent a morning
learning about them."

"Impressive," Liz said.

Ethan ruffled Tyler's hair. "Nicely done."

The boy shrugged, but looked proud.

They continued toward the far end of the park. The
crowd got thicker and Liz noticed big posters featuring
her books. It was strange to see huge publicity photos
hanging from trees.

"Is that you?" an older woman asked, stopping her.
"You're Liz Sutton?"

Liz smiled. "Yes."

"Oh, I'm such a fan. I can't wait to have you sign my books. I drove in from Tahoe this morning. I told my Edgar that we were spending the day in Fool's Gold and that I was going to meet you."

The woman smiled at Ethan. "Hello."

"Hi."

Liz separated herself from Ethan and the kids and moved toward the woman. "I'm signing from one to three, then from four to six," she said. An impossibly long time, but Montana had insisted. Now that Liz saw the crowd, she had an idea that maybe she would be selling books for that long.

"I think the lines are going to be long," Liz continued. "Did you bring a book with you? If so, I can sign it now."

The woman beamed. "Would you? That would be so nice. Edgar wants to get home before dark." She sighed. "You know how men are."

Liz nodded and got a pen out of her purse. She took the offered book. "What's your name?"

"Patricia."

Liz wrote a note, then signed the book and handed it back. Patricia patted her arm.

"You're lovely. I knew you would be." She winked at Ethan. "And your husband is very handsome. No wonder you have such nice-looking children."

"Thank you," Liz said.

Patricia excused herself and left.

"Why did she say that?" Tyler asked. "Dad isn't your husband. You should have told her."

Liz crouched in front of him. "She was trying to be nice. Sometimes it's easier to accept the compliment than explain. Besides, both you and Abby *are* nice looking."

"Jason's parents are married," Tyler declared.

She stayed where she was, eye level with her son. "Yes, they are."

"You and Dad aren't married."

"No, we're not."

"You didn't get a divorce."

"That's right."

She could feel Ethan hovering, sensed that he wanted to help. But what was there to say? Eventually Tyler was going to figure out that she and his dad hadn't followed a traditional path.

"You didn't get married at all." The words sounded like an accusation.

"It's complicated," Ethan described, drawing Liz to her feet and putting his hand on Tyler's shoulders. "There were extenuating circumstances."

"I don't care about that," Tyler argued stubbornly.

Abby looked uncomfortable. Liz took her hand and smiled reassuringly.

"You should be married," their son announced.

Liz held in a groan. "An interesting idea," she said lightly. "But not one we're going to discuss right now and certainly not here."

"But I—"

"You heard your mother," Ethan reiterated firmly. "She has a signing. This isn't the time to deal with the subject. We'll talk later."

"I want to talk now!"

"Come on, Tyler," Ethan said firmly. He glanced at her. "All right with you?"

She nodded and Ethan led Tyler away.

Abby hovered close by. "Should I go?"

"I thought you wanted to be with me for the first part of the signing. It's okay. Really. Why don't you come with me until you meet with your friends at one-thirty?"

"Okay."

They walked toward the booths at the far end of the park.

"Tyler's mad," Abby observed.

"I know."

"He said he always wanted a dad, but you wouldn't talk about his. He didn't know how to make you. Sometimes he got really sad and stuff."

Liz didn't know if she wanted to hear more or not. "I remember he would ask a lot. It's complicated."

"Grown-ups always say that, but if you don't tell us stuff, how can we learn?"

Liz smiled. "You're pretty smart."

"I know." Abby grinned.

The preteen's point was a good one. Maybe it was time to explain the truth to Tyler. That Liz hadn't exactly pressed for Ethan to know about his son, and later fate, in the form of Rayanne, had intervened. She would discuss the idea with Ethan later.

Liz saw the signs pointing toward the signing area and was surprised at how many people had already lined up. Rather than go through the crowd, she and Abby went around, down by the lake, then back up through the trees.

"Do I have leaves in my hair?" Liz asked as they broke through several bushes and came out behind the booth where she would be signing. "I don't want to look—"

She came to a stop and stared at the stacks of boxes from her publisher. There were at least a dozen. Maybe more. Both hardcovers and paperbacks.

Liz held in a groan. Montana seemed to have gotten ahead of herself. Enthusiasm was great, but if a significant percentage of the books didn't sell, Liz's publisher wasn't going to be happy.

She saw her assistant Peggy waiting by the table and hugged her. "You came."

"How could I miss this?" Peggy asked. "The great book signing caper. This is a lot of inventory."

"Tell me about it."

Liz introduced Peggy and Abby.

"I was feeling guilty about wanting to look at the quilts," Peggy conceded with a laugh, "but you're going to be busy for a while."

"Yes, there's plenty of time to come back later."

"You're here," Montana said, rushing up to greet

her. "I think we should start a little early. The lines are so long. Hey, Abby." She hugged Liz, then the girl and introduced herself to Peggy. "I have water and pens. We're going to take turns holding the books open for you to speed things along."

Liz couldn't seem to tear her eyes away from the book boxes. "Don't you think you got a little ambitious with the ordering?"

Montana laughed. "Trust me, Liz. I know what I'm doing."

"I've never sold that many copies in a single signing before. Not even close."

"Then we're going to break a record, aren't we?" She patted Liz's arm, then turned to Abby. "Want to take the first shift with holding open the books? I'll show you how."

"Okay," Abby agreed cheerfully.

They walked toward the booth. The people in line began to clap and call out to her. Liz eyed the crowd and felt a little better. There had to be at least sixty people waiting. If they each bought a book, maybe she wouldn't embarrass herself with poor sales. But someone had to have a serious talk with Montana. Optimism was great, but one had to be practical, too.

"I OWE YOU AN APOLOGY," LIZ said, nearly five hours later as she approached the end of the signing. Her right arm ached, her fingers had cramped two hundred books ago and she was exhausted.

Montana laughed. "Never doubt the power of positive thinking."

"Or great advertising."

They'd gone through box after box of books and the crowd had never seemed to get smaller. Liz hadn't had the hour break in the schedule, instead she'd signed straight through, talking to fans, posing for pictures and answering questions about various story lines.

"Has it occurred to you that people love your books?" Montana asked.

"Not this much. I need to ask for more money."

Montana laughed, then turned to the next person in line.

Liz sipped water, then threw herself into author mode, focusing on the reader. Each one mattered. She wanted to know what they thought of her stories, what moved them the most. They were the reason she wrote.

A half hour later, the line had dwindled. She could actually see the end of it, which was great because she was close to running out of books. She'd half expected Ethan to bring Tyler by but she hadn't seen either of them. As she glanced up to scan the crowd, she noticed a tall, thin man waiting at the end of the line.

What caught her attention was his intense gaze. He stared at her with a focused expression that made her uncomfortable. After a few seconds, she looked away.

She shook off her uneasiness and smiled at the woman next in line. The signing continued. It was well after six when Montana murmured, "Here's the last one."

"Hello, Liz."

She looked up and saw the thin man who had creeped her out earlier. He had medium brown hair and watery blue eyes. His skin was pale and there was something about his expression that made her uncomfortable.

"Hi," she greeted, forcing herself to sound cheerful. "I hope you weren't standing in line too long."

"Not at all. I wanted to see you. To talk to you. I would have waited forever."

Talk about icky, she thought, grateful she wasn't alone with the guy.

"Thank you," she said. "So, can I sign a book for you?"

"I already have all your books." He eased closer. "I thought we could end the day together." His voice lingered on the last word, as if making a point. "Would you like that?"

Liz glanced around for Montana but her friend had been pulled aside by one of the volunteers. No one else seemed to be paying attention to what was happening.

Which was fine, she told herself. Every writer had a few crazy fans. The important thing was not to overreact to the situation.

"I appreciate the offer, but I have plans," she answered smoothly. "Are you sure you don't want me to sign a book?"

Something flashed in his eyes. Anger. No, that wasn't right. It went beyond anger.

"How about a picture?" he asked.

"Sure."

She rose, then hesitated. Normally she walked around the booth to stand next to the fan, but this time that didn't feel right.

"You're going to take one of me by myself," she said, more command than question.

"Sure."

But instead of pulling out a camera, he grabbed her arm. The action was so unexpected, she didn't even react. She simply stared at his hand closing over her skin.

"We're going to be together," he told her. "Forever."

In the nanosecond it took the words to sink in, her brain finally reacted.

"Get the hell away from me," she screamed as loud as she could and wrenched free of his grip.

He grabbed for her again, lunging toward her. She picked up one of her last hardcovers and struck him.

"Get away!" she yelled again, hitting his shoulder, his hands, his head. "Stop it."

He plowed into her and knocked her down. "Shut up," he hissed, slamming her head onto the grass. "Shut up, shut up, shut up."

Suddenly there were people everywhere. Dark shapes flew at her, then the air was thick and she couldn't breathe. The man let go of her. Coughing and gagging, she sat up, shifting so she was on her hands and knees, desperately trying to suck in air. Her throat burned, as did her eyes.

A familiar voice told her to try to relax. Ethan.

She turned to him, his outline blurry through her tears. "W-what?" she asked in a croak.

"Pepper spray," he said, lightly touching her back. "Give it a second."

"Pepper spray?"

"You were a casualty of your own rescue."

He pointed and she turned to look at the scene behind her. Over a dozen old ladies were beating the man with their purses and dousing him with pepper spray. Several police officers hovered nearby, as if they couldn't get close enough to help the guy. They didn't look like they were trying very hard.

"What kind of sicko pervert are you?" one woman demanded. "Liz Sutton is one of us. You try to hurt her, you answer to all of us. You got that?"

"Seniors to the rescue," Ethan told her.

Liz straightened and started to laugh. Laughing made her cough, then she couldn't stop either. Not until Ethan pulled her close and held her.

"You okay?" he asked.

"I will be."

CHAPTER SEVENTEEN

IT WAS CLOSE TO TEN BEFORE life calmed down. Liz had been taken to the hospital to be checked out. Less for the pepper spray than for the swelling around her jaw and the bump on her head. When she'd been pronounced healthy and ready to go home, Ethan had brought her to his place rather than hers.

"My mom is with the kids," he explained. "They're worried but fine. Why don't you call home and talk to them?"

She'd done as he'd suggested, reassuring all three of them that she was fine. Then Ethan had sent her to shower followed by a long bath. The former to wash away any residual spray, the latter to help her relax.

As she stretched out in the tub, bubbles to her chin, she found herself unable to shake off the feeling of being watched. A sensation that would take time to erase, she told herself. A few minutes later, Ethan knocked on the door.

"Come in."

He opened the door a few inches. "If I bring wine

and promise to behave like a perfect gentleman, may I come in?"

Even if he didn't promise, she thought but didn't say. "Sure."

He stepped into the steamy room, an open bottle of wine and two glasses in his hands. He poured one for each of them, then settled on the tile surround by the tub.

"How are you feeling?" he asked, looking just above her head, as if not wanting to look directly at her.

"Okay. A little weird."

"Your eyes still burning?"

"No. They're fine. The toxin wears off in about an hour." She managed a smile. "That was the damnedest rescue I've ever seen."

"Don't mess with our seniors."

"Apparently not." She glanced at him. "Did you hear from the sheriff?"

He nodded. "The guy is Bradley Flowers, age thirty-six. He has an assortment of arrest warrants, three convictions for some fairly nasty crimes. Just his being here is a violation of his parole. The attempted kidnapping won't help his case, either. He's in jail, waiting extradition back to Colorado. The D.A. is still figuring out the best way to charge him. He'll probably be tried here, serve out his sentence there, then come back to finish up with prison time for kidnapping."

"How much time does he have left in Colorado?"

"Fifty years."

"Oh."

The thought of an eighty-six-year-old stalker was a little less frightening.

He stroked her cheek, finally staring into her eyes. "Try not to think about it. You'll have plenty of time to deal with it later."

She nodded. "I've never had anyone come after me like that. Some of my fans are intense, but they're not scary. A lot of them are cops."

"So I should make sure I stay in line."

She smiled. "Probably." She held up her free hand. "At least I'm not shaking anymore."

"It's okay if you are. You've been through a lot."

She sipped her wine. If she wasn't careful, she could find herself reliving the moment. Not exactly the best way to spend an evening. The doctor at the hospital had given her a short-term prescription to help her sleep. Normally she wasn't big on prescription drugs, but this time she might make an exception.

"Everything happened so fast," she murmured. "I wasn't prepared for him to attack me."

"Why would you be?"

"I guess I wouldn't be, but it was weird and so quick. He creeped me out. I guess it's good I paid attention to that." She thought about the flying handbags and zealous hits of pepper spray. "It must have been surreal to see the old ladies go on the attack."

"Not something I'm going to forget." He shrugged.

She noticed something intense in his expression. "What?"

"I wanted to kill him."

The words were spoken evenly, calmly, but with a certainty that told her Ethan wasn't kidding.

Before she could react, he continued.

"Tyler nearly went crazy trying to get to you." There was pride in his voice now. "He wanted to take the guy down."

She felt a little warmer on the inside, knowing the men in her life wanted to protect her. That there were…

Wait a minute. Men in her life?

"Maybe it's not so bad here," Ethan said.

"Maybe not," she admitted, turning her attention back to the stalker and away from Ethan.

She wasn't sure what would have happened if her crazed stalker had struck in a big town. While the police would have still dragged him away, she wasn't sure she would have been so well protected by other people who just happened to be there.

"We should stop talking about this," he suggested. "You need to relax, not relive the event." He rose. "I'll leave you to your bath."

Not sure if she wanted him to stay or not, she watched him leave. After placing her glass of wine on the tile surround, she settled back in the water and closed her eyes.

As she did, she remembered the feel of the man's hand on her arm, the rush of air as he barreled into her, pushing her to the ground. She reached up and lightly touched the left side of her face. It was painful and swollen but not too bad. It could have been a lot worse.

She drew in a deep breath and tried to relax. This time when she closed her eyes, she saw Ethan, which was a much better picture. She smiled, thinking about *him* smiling. She thought about how he was with both Tyler and her nieces. How he looked after his mom and sisters. He had a strong sense of family. A need to belong to a community. He was his father's son.

He'd gotten Rayanne pregnant and had done the right thing. That's who he was. He would do the right thing now. She knew the character of the man and was willing to admit that twelve years ago, he'd still been a kid. Not mature enough to stand up for the woman he claimed to love. Or maybe he hadn't loved her enough. But that was the past and if they were to work anything out, she had to be willing to let it go. The fact that he might not have cared about her as much as she'd cared about him didn't change the fact that they had a son together and decisions had to be made.

It also didn't change the fact that she loved him more now than ever. Time had allowed her to pretend it was over, but she'd been fooling herself. So what was it to be? A second chance with the only man she'd ever loved? Did she allow pride and mistakes to keep them apart forever? There was no guarantee that Ethan felt the same way, but maybe it was time to find out.

She pulled the plug on the tub and stood. After drying off, she wrapped herself in the bathrobe he'd left for her and walked out into the master bedroom.

Ethan stood by the fireplace, staring at the flames.

He didn't hear her, didn't turn. She was able to study the handsome lines of his face, the stiffness in his body, as if he were forcing himself to do something he didn't want to do.

Or preventing himself from doing something he did. "Ethan?"

He visibly shuddered, but didn't turn to look at her. "I'll drive you home."

"Isn't your mom expecting me to stay here tonight?"

"It's not a good idea." He swore under his breath. "You were attacked today. Attacked. He hit you. All I can think about is how I want to beat the shit out of him. And when I'm not thinking about that, I keep seeing you in the tub. I keep wanting…"

He swallowed. "I'm sorry."

"For what? For wanting me?"

He looked at her, then. "Doesn't that make me the biggest jerk ever? A totally insensitive guy only interested in taking?"

"Would you only be taking?"

"You know what I mean."

His guilt was charming, she thought. His feeling bad only made her want to be with him more.

She whispered his name. When he turned to face her, she slowly, deliberately, shrugged out of her bathrobe, letting it fall to the floor. She stood naked in front of him.

His intake of air was audible in the quiet room, then he moved toward her. Lunged was more like it. When he reached her, he touched the uninjured side of her face with one hand and placed his other hand on her waist. He didn't have to draw her to him. She went willingly, surrendering with the first kiss.

His mouth was hot and hungry, his lips pressing against hers. Her mouth parted for him immediately. He swept into her mouth, their kisses both arousing and achingly familiar.

She felt the soft brush of his well-washed jeans against her thighs. Her breasts flattened against his shirt. Wanting heated her blood and made her long for him to touch her everywhere. She tilted her head and wrapped her arms around his neck.

His tongue stroked against hers. She closed her lips around him and sucked gently, causing him to groan. When he did the same to her, she felt the tug clear down to her belly. Her breasts swelled, as did that place between her legs.

He dropped both hands to her waist, then moved them lower, gliding over bare skin. He explored the curve of her hips before slipping around to graze his fingertips along the curve of her butt. The sensation was as ticklish as it was exciting and she shivered.

He kissed his way down the side of her neck. Warm, damp lips teased her skin. He licked the skin just below her earlobe, then nipped and made her gasp. Then he bent lower and took her left nipple in his mouth. He licked the tight tip, before sucking deeply, pulling her into his mouth.

The tugging sensation wove its way through her whole body. She had to hold on to Ethan to stay standing. Over and over he sucked and licked and then blew on her damp skin. She shuddered in response. As he moved to the other breast, he slipped his hand between her legs and found her damp, waiting center.

She immediately parted her legs. He moved his fingers against her, circling that one swollen spot over and over. Then he dropped to his knees, parted her with his fingers and kissed her intimately.

His tongue brushed against her with just the right amount of pressure. The steady rhythm made it impossible to breathe. Her legs shook and she could barely stand. When he thrust a finger inside her, she had to bend over and put her hand on his shoulders to stay upright.

Stop. He had to stop. They could go to the bed and lie down and then she would…

Only she didn't want him to stop. Not when everything about the moment was so perfect. Not when her muscles tensed and the wanting grew and she knew she was closer and closer. There was only the man and how he made her feel. There was only the sensation and pressure and tension and need. He closed his mouth over her clit and sucked. At the same time he pushed deep inside of her, curving his finger slightly and stroking the very center of her body.

She came with an explosion that made her gasp his

name. Shudders of release claimed her. He touched her until she had drawn the last drop of pleasure, then caught her as she collapsed into his arms.

"It's all right," he whispered into her hair.

"Easy for you to say," she murmured. "You're not the one who's naked."

"I can change that."

She looked into his dark eyes and smiled. "Would you?"

In the time it took her to get to her feet and walk to the bed, he had pulled off his clothes. Together they drew back the covers, then she patted the mattress.

"Right here," she told him.

"What are you going to do to me?" he asked, his eyes bright with humor and anticipation.

"Everything."

LIZ AND ETHAN ARRIVED BACK AT her place about eight the following morning. If Denise suspected how they'd spent the night, she didn't say anything.

"Everyone slept fine," she relayed as she collected her purse.

"Did you?" Ethan asked.

"I did okay. I wanted to check on them a few times in the night, just to make sure no one was having night-mares." She yawned. "All right. Maybe I didn't exactly get my full eight hours. I'm heading home now. After church I plan to doze in my chair. It will be good practice for when I'm old."

Ethan kissed her cheek. "You'll never be old."

"I wish."

"Thanks for staying here," Liz said, hugging her.

"After what you'd been through, you needed a break. I'm happy I could help."

Sunday was a lazy day of strolling around town, followed by lunch and a movie. Ethan hung out with them. Liz did her best to act normal so none of the kids would suspect that she and Ethan had behaved like more than friends the night before. At least thinking about sex meant she didn't have to think about her attacker.

Since she didn't know what making love with Ethan had meant, there was no reason to talk about it. Not that she would anyway. But it was difficult not to think about it or try to assign various meanings to their time together. It was a bit stressful, so by Monday she was ready to have her life back.

Unfortunately, the town didn't cooperate. She spent the day fielding visitors who stopped by to check on her. About ten-thirty, after her doorbell rang for the fifth time, she accepted the fact that she wasn't going to get any work done. At least not that day.

She already had a collection of casseroles in the freezer, salads in the refrigerator and enough cookies to make the kids do the happy dance for weeks. When the doorbell rang again, she braced herself for yet another visit where they would discuss her stalker fan, relive the attack, her rescue and crow over the fact that because she'd been in

Fool's Gold when it had happened, all was well. She wasn't expecting to find Dakota and Tyler on the porch.

"What's going on?" she asked.

Dakota held up a hand. "Don't panic. Everything is fine. I was heading into town when Tyler said he wanted to come home and talk to you."

Liz looked at her son. He stared more at the ground than her, but there was something about the set of his shoulders that made her worry.

"Okay. That's fine." She opened the door wider.

Dakota looked curious, but only said, "You can take him back to camp later if you want or have him stay home. Just phone the office and let us know which."

"I will," Liz promised.

Dakota waved and left.

Liz followed her son into the living room. Instead of sitting he turned to face her.

His dark eyes, so like Ethan's, were bright with emotion. He pressed his lips together, as if gathering his thoughts, then spoke.

"You should have married Dad."

She held in a groan. Not exactly a turn she expected the conversation to take, and not a concept she looked forward to explaining.

"Is this about what that woman said on Saturday?" she asked, doing her best to sound calm.

"Sort of. Parents get married."

"Some do. Some don't."

Tyler glared at her. "I wanted to know my dad. I kept

asking and asking and you wouldn't tell me. You wouldn't say anything. It's not fair." His voice escalated exponentially.

"Okay, if we're going to have this conversation, we're going to sit down and we're going to speak calmly. If you're going to get upset and yell, I'm not talking to you."

"Fine," he grumbled and collapsed on the sofa, his arms folded across his chest.

She sat on the coffee table in front of him, so they were facing each other.

"When I found out I was pregnant, I was terrified. I was only four years older than Melissa. Do you think she's ready to be a mom?"

He shook his head but didn't speak.

"I came back to tell your dad, but he was with someone else. A girl. And I was hurt and confused, so I left."

"You should have stayed. You should have tried harder."

"I know."

"You should have," Tyler repeated, his voice getting louder again. "He would have married you. I asked him and he said he would have married you. We would have been a family."

She drew in a breath. "Tyler, please. I know you're upset, but I meant what I said. I'm not having a screaming match with you." Especially not about this.

She reached out to touch his hand, but he jerked it

back. That hurt more than the questions, more than the accusations.

"He would have been my dad," her son said more quietly.

What was she supposed to say to that? How could she explain?

"I was very young."

"You keep saying that. I don't care. You were wrong." His eyes filled with tears. "You kept me from my dad."

Which is what this was about.

How was she supposed to explain about hurt pride and a bruised heart? Maybe she didn't.

"You're right," she said again softly. "I did keep you from him. That wasn't my intent. I didn't mean to hurt either of you, but that's what happened and I'm sorry."

"That's not good enough." A tear slipped down his cheek. He looked away. "I needed my dad and he wasn't there."

She thought about pointing out how she'd tried again five years ago, but fate, in the form of Rayanne, had intervened. Information Tyler would need at some point, but not now.

"I can't change the past," she stated, feeling sick to her stomach.

"He would have come to get me," Tyler told her, his voice fierce with emotion. "He would have wanted me with him." He turned to glare at her. "I want to live with him. I want to live with my dad and not you."

CHAPTER EIGHTEEN

HELL CAME IN THE FORM OF A pain that wouldn't go away. Ethan's rejection was nothing when compared with her only child telling her that he didn't want to live with her anymore. It was as if Tyler reached into her chest and pulled out her still-beating heart and threw it in the trash. She couldn't think, couldn't breathe. All she knew was that she couldn't cry in front of him because it might upset him. An irrational, maternal response that came from instinct.

She stood, amazed that her legs still worked, then walked into the kitchen.

"Did you hear me?" he yelled, following her. "I don't want to live with you. I want to live with my dad."

Each breath sliced through her like a knife. She half expected to see blood pouring out of her body, pooling at her feet. It felt like she was dying. Truly no death could be worse.

After finding Denise's phone number, she turned to Tyler.

"I heard you," she said quietly. "I need to make a call, then we're leaving."

"I don't want to go back to camp."

"Good, because you're not." Liz couldn't imagine making the drive. She was in no shape to negotiate the mountain road and surely shouldn't be behind the wheel of anything dangerous.

She punched in the phone number, then waited until Ethan's mother answered.

"Hello?"

"Hi, Denise. It's Liz."

"Oh, hi. How are you?"

Talk about a question she couldn't answer. "I know it's really short notice, but could you please take Tyler for a couple hours? He's not sick or anything."

"Of course. He's not at camp?"

"Not right now. May I bring him over now?"

"Sure. Is everything all right?"

No. Nothing was all right. Nothing would ever be all right again. "May I bring him now?"

There was a pause. "I'll be here."

"Good."

Liz grabbed her cell phone and her house keys. "Let's go," she told Tyler and walked out of the house.

It took less than fifteen minutes to get to Denise's place. Tyler didn't speak and Liz was grateful. When they reached the welcoming home, she stopped on the sidewalk.

"Go on in," she said. "I'll wait here. I'll be by to pick you up later."

Her son, the child she had given birth to, worried over and loved with her whole heart, looked at her with angry eyes. "I want to live with my dad."

"I got that."

"I'll run away if you don't let me."

More wounds, she thought sadly. More pain. A few short weeks ago she and Tyler had been so close. She would never have believed he could speak to her like this. That he would want to drive her out of his life. He was only eleven. How could he not love her?

The front door opened and Denise stood there. The other woman probably wanted to ask what was wrong, but instead she gave Liz an encouraging smile, then turned to Tyler.

"Hi. Have you had lunch?"

"I'm not hungry," Tyler groused.

"Then we've got a problem because I just ordered a pizza."

Tyler smiled slowly. "With pepperoni?"

"It's not pizza if there's no pepperoni."

"Sweet!" He hurried up the walkway and entered the house.

Liz watched him go, waiting for him to turn around, and say something to her. To run to her, wrap his arms around her and tell her that he was sorry. He didn't. He didn't look back at all.

"Are you all right?" Denise asked.

Liz shook her head. "I have to go," she said, struggling not to cry. "I'll be back later."

She hurried away.

Her arms folded, her shoulders hunched, she made her way to Ethan's office. Now that Tyler was with Denise, Liz could allow herself to think about the man responsible for all this. The man who had turned her child from her.

It had been his plan from the beginning. She realized that now. He'd been angry and hurt and desperate to get what he wanted. She was in the way, and he'd been determined to make her irrelevant.

Why hadn't she seen it? The truth was here—clearly visible in everything he did. Could reality be any bigger than the injunction? He'd played her from the beginning and she'd let him. She'd thought she was in love with him. Talk about stupid. Following her heart, letting herself trust and love again had cost her the only thing that had ever mattered.

Her son.

She pushed through the door into Ethan's construction company. The receptionist at the front desk looked up and smiled.

"May I help you?"

"No," Liz said and headed for Ethan's private office.

The young woman got up and followed her. They reached Ethan's door at about the same time.

"You don't want to get in the middle of this," Liz told her.

Ethan hung up the phone and stood. He took one look at Liz, then turned to the girl. "It's all right, Cindy."

Liz stepped into the office and carefully closed the door behind her. Now that she was here, she couldn't think of a single thing to say. She'd thought she might want to throw things, to scream, to threaten. She'd worried if she had access to a weapon, she would use it. But all her energy was gone, bled away in the open wound of her missing heart.

"You don't know what it means to love a child," she said softly. "To be willing to die to protect him. Loving a child isn't about winning. You don't deserve him. But you can't see that. You wanted to punish me. Well, congratulations. You have. You may think you've won, but you haven't. Because for now, you're a bright, shiny new toy. Eventually Tyler will see that. And then he'll come home."

At least that's what she was telling herself with every breath. That her son would come back to her. That he would love her again. That he loved her now…still…he was just too angry to see it.

Ethan moved toward her, stopping in front of her. "What are you talking about?"

The question sounded genuine. He looked more confused than upset.

No. It was another trick. All of it. She couldn't trust him. He was the enemy—she'd been the fool who'd forgotten that.

"Tyler told me that he wants to live with you," she

repeated flatly. "Don't pretend this wasn't part of your plan."

"What?" Ethan took a step back. "Jesus, Liz. What are you saying? Tyler's not living with me."

He sounded so sincere, she thought. Of course he'd made love with her as if she was important to him. As if she mattered.

"You've played me from the beginning," she revealed. "I let you, so I suppose the blame is as much mine. You pretended to want what was best for everyone. You kissed me and touched me, all the while knowing you were going to do this. You must not have a conscience. At least the guy who tried to kidnap me was honest in his intentions."

"Wait a minute. Stop this." He grabbed her upper arms. "Look at me. I'm not trying to hurt you. I never talked to Tyler about coming to live with me."

Maybe that was true. Maybe Tyler thought of that on his own, but he would have had help getting there. "Didn't you tell him that if you'd known I was pregnant that you would have married me?"

"Yes, but—"

"Didn't you talk about all the time you've missed with him? Didn't you blame me?"

"At first. I was angry. But not recently. Liz, I want what's best for him and that means you. You're great with him."

"What was it you said that first week? That I'd had him eleven years, so you should get the rest of his childhood?"

He tightened his grip. "No. I didn't do this."

The worst part was she wanted to believe him. "I trusted you. Even when I knew what you'd done to me before, I believed in you."

He stared into her eyes. "Don't stop believing in me. Please, Liz. We can make this work." He sucked in a breath. "Marry me."

If he hadn't been holding on to her, she would have fallen. "What?"

"Marry me. It solves everything. Then we both get Tyler. It would be better for the girls, too. They could stay here with their friends. Marry me."

She pulled free of his grip and crossed to the sofa. After collapsing, she rested her elbows on her knees and dropped her face to her hands.

It was too much, she thought. She was physically and emotionally drained. That was the only reason she hadn't run screaming into the afternoon. Or hurled a lamp at him.

Marriage as a practical solution?

"We have a child together," he continued. "It makes sense."

Of course it did. Because why would love enter into it? He'd married Rayanne because she was pregnant—why wouldn't he marry her because they had a child together?

She straightened. "No."

He sat on the sofa and angled toward her. "Come on, Liz. Why not?"

Where was she supposed to start? "We don't love each other."

Only a half truth. She loved him, but this was hardly the time to go into that.

"We like each other," he stated. "We get along. And it's better for the kids. You said being a good parent was all about making sacrifices."

"Not those kind." She rose.

"Wait." He stood. "We have to figure this out."

"No, we don't. *I* have to."

"Tyler is my son, too."

"You've made that very clear—to all of us."

She left.

Ethan stared after her, not sure if he should follow her or give her time to sort things out. He still couldn't believe what Tyler had done. The kid hadn't warned him that he was about to tell his mother he wanted to live with Ethan.

His son wanted to live with him. Ethan couldn't help feeling excited at the idea of really getting to know his son. They could have so much fun together—really bond. Not that he wanted Liz hurt.

His office door opened and Nevada stood there.

Nevada was the quietest of the triplets, the most practical. She'd studied engineering, had come to work for him and did a helluva good job. Customers liked her, the other employees respected her. When he wasn't around, she also ran things.

Now she stared at him with a combination of pity and amusement.

"You really are the stupidest man on the planet," she said.

"What do you mean?"

"I would have thought the statement was self-explanatory." She leaned against the door frame. "I just passed Liz and asked how she was. She said you asked her to marry you for practical reasons. Tell me that she's lying."

"It's not like that."

Nevada raised her eyebrows. "Then what's it like?"

He explained about Tyler and Liz being hurt and how getting married would solve all their problems.

"Very romantic, too," she quipped sarcastically.

"This isn't about romance. It's about doing the right thing."

Nevada stared at him for a long time. "I think it's about you getting what you want. You're not thinking about Liz. Why does she need to marry you?"

"Tyler needs a father."

"Sure. But what does that have to do with Liz?"

"She's his mother."

"Yeah. I knew that. You're not answering the question. What does Liz get out of marrying you? It's not like she needs a second income. Or housing. Most people get married because they're in love and want to be together, but you already took that off the table. So why exactly should she marry you?"

"I, ah…" He swore silently.

Something he'd never considered. Why *would* Liz

want to be with him? He blurted out the proposal without thinking. Because it was the right thing.

Just like with Rayanne, he thought. Was that so wrong?

While he knew it wasn't, he couldn't escape a nagging sense of having screwed up in the worst way possible.

Nevada shook her head. "I'll give you a hint because you're my brother. The only thing Liz needs and wants from you is for you to love her."

"You can't know that."

"Of course I can. It's what every woman wants. Why else would she put up with your crap? She didn't have to be this nice. She didn't have to tell you about Tyler. She could have taken her nieces back to San Francisco that first night and you would never have known. Liz has been giving you chances since she got here and I'm going to guess you've blown every single one of them."

"No," he retorted, even as he wondered if Nevada was right.

"Here's the thing, Ethan. You have a very limited window of time to make this right. Assuming you want to. Because if you're trying to convince Liz to stay with you, you're going about it all wrong."

Then Nevada walked out, leaving him staring after her.

Wait. She couldn't leave like that. He had more questions. Damn.

As he stood alone in his office, he realized that

maybe his sister's point was that he had to figure it out himself.

"I'm not the bad guy," he spoke into the silence. "I'm doing the right thing."

But for the first time in his life, he wondered if doing the right thing was going to be enough.

LIZ WALKED THROUGH TOWN. THERE were plenty of tourists on the street and she had to weave between them. Summer was a busy time, with visitors flooding the area to check out the wineries, hike in the mountains and spend time on the lake. To anyone who didn't have a gaping hole in her chest, Fool's Gold probably looked really good. She knew better. It was her own personal, living nightmare. It was the place where she'd lost both her heart and her son.

She turned onto a residential street and reminded herself that she hadn't truly lost Tyler. It only felt that way. He would come around. What she didn't know was how long it would take and she wasn't completely sure she trusted Ethan to be impartial. A part of him had to love the fact that his son wanted to live with him.

But being a parent was about more than saying yes. It could be difficult and frustrating. There were lessons every child had to learn. If someone didn't teach the kid right while he was young, life lessons were that much harder to grasp later.

Would Ethan get that? Would he look past his need to connect with Tyler to what was best for the boy?

Even as she asked the question, a part of her knew she was searching for reasons to be able to tell Tyler and herself why spending more time—maybe even living with his dad—wasn't possible.

Because the truth was, Ethan would be a great dad. He'd always been responsible. When his father had died, he'd taken over the family business. Because it was the right thing to do. He'd helped his mom, his brothers and sisters. He'd…

She stopped on the sidewalk and replayed the words in her mind. Because it was the right thing to do. That had always defined Ethan. He hadn't loved Rayanne. He'd married her because she was pregnant. He'd claimed he would have done the same with Liz, and she believed him.

Had Ethan ever declared himself? Had he ever truly loved anyone?

There had been a time, when she'd been eighteen, she would have sworn he had loved her. Had she just been fooling herself? He'd admitted that he'd been too young then. Neither of them could have possibly known if they could make it. But he would have tried.

There was more to a relationship than just giving one's heart. There was caring and commitment and doing the right thing. There was being a good person. Ethan had all those qualities.

But he didn't love her.

That was why his offer of a practical marriage had hurt her so much. Why she couldn't accept. She loved him too much to accept a half life, even if it was the right thing to do.

Which left her with a dilemma. What happened now?

As there was no easy answer, she kept walking. When she got close to Denise's house, she saw Ethan's mother sitting on the front porch, obviously watching for her.

"Tyler told me what happened," the other woman said as Liz approached. "I'm so sorry."

Liz found herself fighting the need to give in to tears. "Me, too. It's not that I mind Tyler spending more time with his dad…" She had to stop and clear her throat.

"It's that he's rejecting you along the way," Denise summarized softly, then patted the step. "Come sit down."

Liz joined her. She felt sick and confused and lost.

Denise moved close and put her arm around her. The gesture was oddly comforting.

"This isn't about you," Denise began. "I know it feels like it, but it's not. You're a great mom. We can all see that. We don't even have to watch you with Tyler to get it. Just being around him tells us. He's bright and confident and curious. Open and friendly, but with plenty of common sense. He cares about other people. You did that. You raised a great son."

Liz pressed her lips together and nodded. Her throat was too tight for her to speak.

"He's also still a kid and he has no idea how he's hurting you. He genuinely can't see that."

"I know," she whispered, then had to wipe away several tears. "I keep telling myself it's not about me. He's angry about his dad and Ethan is new and exciting."

"Exactly. If only knowing made it hurt less."

Liz looked at her and nodded.

"Oh, honey, I wish I could make it better," Denise told her.

"Thanks." She swallowed and tried to get the tears under control. "Want to guess Ethan's response?"

Denise sighed. "I do love my son, but he's just a man, so I'm going to guess he was an idiot."

"He thinks we should get married. That will solve all the problems. Isn't it practical? I'll stay here and he can see Tyler all the time and hey, even help with the girls."

As soon as she spoke, Liz realized it was probably a mistake. Denise was Ethan's mother. Of course she would take her son's side. No doubt the other woman would enjoy having her grandson around more.

Denise sighed. "Is this where I tell you Ethan takes after his father?"

Liz glanced at her. "You don't think it's a good idea?"

"The words *practical* and *marriage* don't belong in the same conversation. Nothing about marriage is practical. It's wonderful and difficult and amazing and demanding. Besides, no one wants a proposal like that. We want to hear that the man in question is madly in love with us. We want to be swept away. Not compared to a really good microfiber dust cloth. Attractive and practical. That's going to make your heart beat faster."

Liz leaned her head against the other woman's shoulder. "Thank you," she whispered, wishing she could have known Denise years ago. Maybe if they'd had a chance to form a relationship, things would have been different. She could have come and talked to her and—

Liz straightened, then scrambled to her feet. "You're not surprised he proposed. You know we've been..." *Sleeping* seemed like the wrong word. "Seeing each other?"

Denise laughed. "Yes. It's fairly obvious. Ethan is many things, but subtle isn't one of them. He was furious at first, but now you're getting along. I assumed things were progressing."

Denise paused. "I wasn't sure at first. I always felt so badly about how you grew up. I could see how difficult it was for you. I have three daughters myself. Yet I couldn't seem to reach out to you. I never knew how or what to say."

Liz hugged her arms across her chest. "That doesn't matter now."

"It matters a lot. All your life the people you care about have hurt you. Including Tyler. Now my son proposed in a way designed to make sure you know you're not special to him." Her voice softened. "For what it's worth, I think he does care about you."

Liz appreciated the support, but the words didn't change anything. "Caring isn't enough."

"I know." Denise looked as if she was going to say more on the subject, then sighed. "Please don't take this wrong, but I think you should let Ethan have Tyler for the rest of the week and through the weekend."

Liz froze. She eyed the door and wondered if she could go inside and grab her son and get out before Denise stopped her.

"Ethan and Tyler both have an unrealistic view of their relationship," Denise continued. "I have six kids. I know what it's like and sure, from the outside, it's easy. He doesn't have a clue as to the reality. Tyler doesn't, either. Maybe you should let them find out."

"I can't," she breathed.

Denise rose and moved toward her. They stared at each other.

"I give you my word Tyler will be safe. Ethan isn't going to disappear with him. You know that. Let them find out just how boring everyday life can be. Your son loves you. Give him a chance to miss you."

The words were impossible to hear, but Liz knew they were accurate. Her gut told her this was exactly what had to happen. Not that she could imagine even a day without her son. Although he'd been gone overnight before—to camp, with friends—this was different. This terrified her.

Slowly, she nodded. "Okay. Through the weekend."

Denise pulled her close. "It will be all right. You'll see."

"I hope so."

She hugged the other woman and was held in return. For a second she closed her eyes and absorbed the loving support.

"It's not supposed to be this hard."

Denise patted her back. "It's not supposed to be a lot of things, but still we get through it. You'll get through this."

"I know." She straightened. "I'm going to go home and pack his things. Would you mind calling Ethan and telling him the plan?"

"Not at all. Don't you want Tyler to pack for himself?"

"No. If he's so ready to move out, let's start now."

Denise touched her arm. "I feel your pain, honey. Hang in there."

"I will," Liz promised. After all, she didn't have a choice.

CHAPTER NINETEEN

"WHAT ARE WE GOING TO DO tonight?" Tyler asked, cutting into his steak. "We could watch a movie."

Ethan thought about his collection of action movies—most of which were rated R—and knew they would be a bad choice. "We'll check out pay-per-view."

"Sweet! Mom only lets me watch movies on the weekend."

Something Ethan hadn't known. "Why?"

"I dunno. She wants me to read and stuff. Play outside. I wish she'd brought my Xbox."

Ethan had a feeling that there was a specific reason for that. Liz had wanted him to spend as much time with his son as possible.

"How's your steak?" Ethan asked.

"Good." Tyler glanced at him. "Are you going to cook something else for dinner tomorrow?"

Because this was the second time in four nights he'd barbecued steaks. The other two nights they'd gone out.

Usually Ethan grabbed something on the way home, or his mother dropped off a casserole for him to heat up in the microwave. Since he'd taken Tyler, she hadn't been anywhere to be seen and neither had his sisters. He'd left messages for all of them and while they'd called back, they'd managed to miss him both at the office and home. He had a feeling they were doing that on purpose.

The catering service he used when he had company was at the hotel for the week. Something about a big corporate retreat.

His cooking skills were limited at best, but there had to be something he could make.

"What would you like?" he asked.

"Lasagna."

Pasta, meat and sauce. How hard could it be?

"Sure. I'll swing by the grocery store tomorrow and we'll have it tomorrow night."

"We're out of milk, too, and could we have a different cereal?"

"We'll make a list after dinner."

"Okay." Tyler chewed another bite. "I don't have any more clean clothes."

"What?"

"I have socks and shorts, but no T-shirts or underwear. And I'm supposed to make a poster for camp tomorrow."

Ethan stared at him. "What kind of poster?"

"Like for a movie. You have poster board, right?"

"Not exactly." He frowned. Who knew summer camp had homework? "If you have to make a poster, we can't watch a movie."

"But you said we could."

"That was before you told me about the poster. School comes first."

"But this isn't school, it's camp."

Ethan felt the beginnings of a headache. He was tired. Not because he wasn't sleeping well, but because his mornings were starting earlier. Tyler didn't like getting up and moved at the speed of an exhausted snail. With the extra errands he had to run, there was no time to get to the gym. Now instead of a quiet evening watching a movie, they were going to the office supply store, to buy poster board and markers, then get through making a poster.

"When did you get the assignment about the poster?"

"Monday."

"And you didn't mention it until now?"

"Mom always asks."

Of course she did.

"Is there anything for dessert?" Tyler looked expectant.

Ethan held in a groan. "We'll stop on our way back from getting the art supplies."

"We could bake cookies."

"Maybe tomorrow."

"We're riding bikes on the weekend, right? With Josh?"

Ethan nodded.

"What else are we going to do?"

It was then Ethan realized he'd only ever had his son

four or five hours at a time. Blocks that were easy to fill. Suddenly the weekend seemed like an endless parade of empty hours. They mocked him and made him think he should have opened a bottle of wine with dinner. Or a case.

"We'll have to come up with some ideas," he said, leaning back in his chair.

"We could go hiking. Or out on the lake. Or swimming. Maybe Abby can come with us. She's really cool, for a girl. Or the park…"

Tyler kept talking. A steady buzz of ideas and questions and statements. Ethan watched his son and wondered how on earth Liz had done it by herself. He didn't know that he would have managed, let alone done as good a job. The hell of it was, loving Tyler didn't guarantee getting it right. Having someone like Liz to watch his back would make all the difference.

She hadn't had anyone. Because he'd never bothered to go after her. Hurt pride had kept him from following her. Hurt pride had cost him more than he could ever recover.

"To the stupidity of men," Dakota said, raising a glass. "And my brother, who is their king."

"To Ethan," Montana said.

Liz, Nevada and Denise also raised their margaritas and toasted.

After a dinner of delicious Mexican food, Melissa had gone to a friend's house for a sleepover and Abby had danced off to watch the latest Hannah Montana movie out on DVD. Liz and the Hendrix women were in the backyard, sprawled on lawn chairs, slowly getting drunk.

Word had quickly spread through the family and to Liz's surprise, Ethan's sisters had rallied around her as much as Denise had. They'd been appalled at the proposal, insulted by his refusal to declare his love and disappointed by her physical restraint in not at least throwing something at his head.

"He's having a tough time with Tyler," Denise informed, leaning back and staring up at the stars. "His phone messages are getting more and more desperate. Apparently he tried to make lasagna." She giggled. "It didn't go well."

"Lasagna? That's a lot of work."

"His first message was something about pasta and sauce and how it wouldn't be that hard. The second one was to ask what a lasagna pan looked like. Then there was something about did he really have to cook the pasta noodles first. The last message said they were eating out."

Liz tried to laugh with everyone else, but she mostly felt sad. Having Tyler gone was getting harder, not easier.

Dakota turned to her. "He's asking about you. Today he came into my office and wanted to call you. I know he misses you."

"I hope so." She desperately wanted to talk to her son, but knew the plan was the best way to go. Ethan would return Tyler to her Sunday night. Then they would talk. The three of them.

In the meantime, she had women she could depend on. Friends, and that felt nice.

It was close to ten when everyone left. She rinsed out the glasses and put them on the counter. Washing could wait until morning. While she was enjoying her pleasant margarita-induced buzz, she didn't think that it was a good match for a soap-slicked glass.

She turned off the lights in the kitchen and walked back into the living room. Abby sat on the bottom stair.

"I thought you were going to bed," Liz said. "Is everything all right?"

Abby shook her head.

Liz pointed to the sofa. "Want to have a seat?"

"Okay."

The preteen got up and walked to the sofa. Liz settled next to her, put an arm around her and kissed the top of Abby's head.

"Tell me what's going on," she coaxed gently. "You feeling all right?"

"I'm okay." The girl snuggled close. "Don't be mad, but I don't want to go."

Go? As in… "You don't want to move to San Francisco?"

Abby nodded. "Can't we stay here? I like it here. I feel safe. I have friends and Melissa has friends. Tyler likes it, too. Everybody wants to stay here but you."

Talk about a kick in the stomach.

The worst of it was, Abby told the truth. Everyone *did* want to stay here. It would make things easier for

Tyler and Ethan. Technically, Liz could work anywhere. The town accepted her—with the occasional dig at her choices. But they'd also come to her rescue. She had a past here, and while that wasn't necessarily a good thing, maybe it was something she couldn't escape. Maybe she should stop trying.

But staying meant facing Ethan and now that she was willing to accept what seemed like her fate, she could also be honest. At first leaving had been about not belonging, but later she'd wanted to go to get away from him. Being around him when she loved him was like living with an open wound.

"We'll be really, really good," Abby promised.

Liz wrapped her other arm around the girl. "You're already that. I know it would mean a lot to both of you if we stayed here. I guess…" She drew in a breath. "I guess we can do that."

Abby sat up and beamed at her. "Really?"

Liz nodded.

"I can't believe it. Are we going to live in this house? If we do, you need a real bed and we need another bedroom. Or do you want me and Melissa to share? We can. She won't like it, but I don't mind."

Liz hadn't gotten that far. Given the choice, she would prefer a house without so many memories. "Moving might be easier."

"We can move. We'll help pack." Abby threw both her arms around Liz and hung on. "Thank you so much, Liz. I love you."

"I love you, too."

Abby rose and spun in a circle, her bright red hair flying around her face. "I'm so happy! We're staying. We're staying!"

Liz reached for her cell phone and handed it to the girl. "Why don't you text your sister and tell her?"

"Can I? Thanks. I will. This is the best."

Liz wondered how long it would take Abby to wind down enough to sleep. Staying in Fool's Gold. Who would have thought? When Ethan returned Tyler, she would tell them both. Then Ethan could take back his stupid, thoughtless, practical proposal. The town was small enough that she and Ethan could co-parent their son. He could spend equal time with each of them. That should satisfy Ethan and the judge.

It was, she told herself, the right thing to do.

ETHAN STOOD IN TYLER'S ROOM at his house and watched his son sleep. After a morning of bike riding and afternoon of failing to get peanut butter cookies to bake right and an evening of watching the first two Harry Potter movies back to back, Tyler had fallen asleep on the sofa.

Now, as he stared at his son, he felt a warmth in his chest. Love was there. Real love, born of time and frustration and a sense of being a complete failure as a dad, but still wanting to get it right. Tyler was everything he'd wanted his son to be—and he wasn't easy. He got the latter from his mother.

Ethan stepped out of the room and went downstairs. In the quiet living room, he sank onto the couch and tried to figure out what he was going to do next.

He missed Liz.

He hadn't realized how much he'd gotten used to having her in his life until she was gone. He missed talking to her, seeing her, having her smile at him. He missed her in his bed, but that was the least of it. While he would want her until the day he died, the ache inside him wasn't just about getting laid. It was about having a conversation, hearing her laugh, watching her with Tyler and Melissa and Abby.

He wanted her in his life. He wanted her to be his family.

He wasn't the only one. Tyler had gone from being mad at his mom to talking about her all the time. Today he'd regularly counted down the number of hours until he saw her again. Both of them had learned a lesson in the past few days. Which was probably the point.

Tyler had learned to show his mother a little more respect and Ethan had learned that Liz was everything to him. His eyes sank closed as he realized he loved her.

What should have been a stellar moment in his life made him instead want to put a fist through the wall. He loved Liz. He *loved* her. And instead of making her feel like a princess, instead of promising to love and adore her forever, he'd offered marriage as a practical solution.

"Oh, crap."

He rolled onto his side, his face in the cushion. Talk about stupid.

He lay there, mentally beating himself up, then straightened. Fine. He'd screwed up. He would fix it. There had to be a way. Liz was a great woman—and he would fight for her. Figure out how to do it right. How to be the man she deserved. She'd loved him once, maybe she could again. Everything wasn't lost.

He understood what she didn't like about Fool's Gold. While he didn't like the idea of leaving everything behind, it didn't have to be like that. He could run his business from San Francisco. Make a few trips in a week. Maybe they could have a second house here and spend summers in town. That would be a good compromise. Liz wasn't looking to make him miserable. She would meet him halfway.

As long as she was willing to give him another chance.

She had to, he told himself. He would convince her. Somehow he would show her that they belonged together.

The decision made, he rose and started for the front door. Halfway across the porch, he stopped. Showing up at her house in the middle of the night probably wasn't smart. Nor was leaving Tyler home alone. So Ethan would wait. He could come up with a plan and this time, he would get it right.

LIZ WATCHED THE CLOCK anxiously. Ethan was supposed to bring Tyler home on Sunday. It was only a little after eleven. At this rate, she would give herself a heart attack in the next hour. She needed to keep busy.

Both Melissa and Abby had run off to spend the morning with friends, celebrating her decision to keep them in town. They were beyond happy and seeing their joy confirmed that she'd made the right decision. Tyler would appreciate it, too. The chance to be with his dad more, and with his family.

She'd wanted to call Denise but had decided that Ethan and Tyler should hear it first. So she'd spent a restless night and a bad morning. Writing would be impossible. There was no way she could focus.

The thought of cleaning made her shudder, so she grabbed a big straw hat and a few garden tools from the back porch then went outside to see what she could do to spruce up the garden. She'd barely begun weeding when she heard someone calling for her.

"Mom? Mom? Where are you?"

Still on her knees, she straightened. Her heartbeat thundered in her chest as her son burst through the back door and raced toward her.

"Mom!"

He flew into her arms and hugged her so hard, she couldn't breathe. She held on to him, doing her best not to cry, letting the familiar feel of his body ease her fears that she'd lost him forever.

"Hey, you," she whispered, when he'd released her and stepped back. She pulled off her gardening gloves and shoved them into her pocket.

He stared into her eyes, then hugged her again. "I really missed you."

"I missed you, too."

He glanced back at his father and then at her. "Maybe I could still live here, you know. More of the time."

"I think that could be arranged. Your dad and I will work things out."

"Yeah?" His dark eyes—Ethan's eyes—lit up.

She stood and ruffled his hair. "It'll be a grown-up thing. Melissa and Abby will be back soon and we're going to the pool. Want to get changed and go with us?"

"Sure."

He dashed toward the house, then paused and looked at his dad. He ran back, hugged Ethan, then took off again.

Liz stared after him, feeling her world right itself. Denise had called it exactly as everything had played out. At least from Tyler's point of view.

She turned to Ethan. "How did it go?"

He shoved his hands into his pockets. "Damn, I missed you, Liz."

She thought about their last conversation. How he'd hurt her with his thoughtless words. It wasn't his fault, she told herself. Why would he offer more? She'd never bothered to tell him how she felt and now she never would. Not when she was staying in town.

"Did you two get along okay?" she asked.

He shrugged. "Great. He's a good kid. But there's a whole lot more work involved than I realized. A few hours here and there is easier than taking care of him full-time."

"I know."

"I don't think I'm nearly as exciting as he thought I'd be. Regular life taught us both something."

"That was the point."

He moved closer. "Liz, I never wanted to take him from you. Okay, maybe at first, but not now. I care about you both. We have to work something out."

She held up a hand to stop him. It was oddly difficult to be this close to him, to hear him talk. Probably because as much as she'd hated how he'd proposed, there was a part of her that couldn't help dreaming about how it could have been. If he'd loved her back.

"We have to talk about it," he continued, ignoring her gesture to stop. "We meet with the judge next week."

"It won't be a problem," she said. "I'm staying in Fool's Gold."

He stared at her. "What about your life in San Francisco?"

"I'll sell the house and move here. It won't be that difficult. Tyler wants to stay, as do the girls. If I'm here, you and I can co-parent him. I won't live in this house, so I'll make sure I buy something close to you. Tyler can spend alternating weeks with each of us. That should satisfy the judge and you'll both be happy."

She had already talked to Peggy, who was interested in moving to small-town America. "It should only take me a week or so to get things organized back there. If you'll take Tyler, I'll ask your Mom and Montana to split duties with the girls while I get everything settled. I'll make sure I'm back before everyone starts school."

"What do you get out of the deal?" he asked.

"I get to make my family happy. There are things I don't like about this place, but the good far outweighs the bad. Eventually people will stop telling me whether or not they support what I did with you and Tyler. I'm a writer, Ethan. I can work anywhere."

"Then why do you look so sad?"

Because being close to him, knowing that she'd never been able to forget him or get over him, wasn't her idea of a good time. Because the love inside of her seemed to grow bigger every day. Eventually he would find someone. Who wouldn't love Ethan? And then she would have to smile and pretend she was happy while he went off with someone else.

"I'm tired," she answered. "I missed having Tyler around." She glanced toward the house. "I need to get inside. We're going to the pool."

She started past him. He grabbed her wrist and held her in place.

"Wait." He stared into her eyes. "Liz, we belong together. We've always belonged together."

She had a bad feeling about where he was going and she didn't think she could survive it again. "Don't."

"Hear me out. I'm sorry about what I said before. I don't want to marry you because it's practical. I want to marry you because I love you."

He released her then, as if confident the words were enough to keep her where he wanted her.

"We can be a family together. The five of us. I was going to tell you that I'd move to San Francisco to be with you. But this is better. This is home, Liz, for all of us."

They were good words, she admitted, feeling the sadness pour through her. Nice words. Telling her that he would move added a little touch of sacrifice. Playing the kid card was good, too. Easy enough now that she was staying.

"No," she said and started for the house.

"What?" He came after her. "Why not?"

She paused by the back porch and looked at him. "I don't believe you. Oh, I think you want to marry me. It makes everything tidy. Besides, I'm the mother of your child and it's the right thing to do. But love? You never loved me. Not then, not now."

She drew her gardening gloves from her pocket and squeezed them in her hand. "You haven't loved anyone outside of your family. I'm not sure why that is. If you're afraid to care that much or if there's no need. You've always been blessed with everything you want. Even now, you're getting your son with very little effort on your part."

"Is that what this is about? I haven't suffered enough?"

"No. It's about risking everything. Putting your heart on the line, even when you don't know what's going to happen. It's risking having the person you love rip it out and stomp all over it in public."

"You're never going to let that go, are you?"

"I loved you, Ethan. I gave you everything I had. Not just my heart and my soul, but my body. I'd spent years being called a whore and being propositioned and lied about, so I protected myself. I didn't care about anyone. Until you. I was a virgin and you called me a slut in front of your friends. You said I wasn't worthy."

"I know. I'm the one who wasn't worthy. I never have been."

Hearing that didn't make her feel any better. "It doesn't matter now. I'm letting the past go. This is the last time we'll talk about it. I loved you then and I still love you. But I won't marry you. I won't be one more thing you got right. We'll raise Tyler together, in this town. That's going to have to be enough."

She walked up the steps to the porch, crossed the refinished wood and stepped into the house.

For a second she allowed herself to hope. To believe that he would come after her, tell her that she was wrong. That of course he loved her. He'd always loved her. He would beg and plead and she would allow herself to be convinced because that's all it would take. A little effort on his part.

But there was nothing. Finally she turned around and he was gone.

CHAPTER TWENTY

"HOW DRUNK DO YOU WANT TO get?" Raoul asked as he poured another Scotch and handed it to Ethan.

"I'll let you know when I've had enough."

"Not a great plan," Josh told him from his place on the opposite sofa. "You're already going to feel plenty of pain in the morning."

The three men were sprawled in Ethan's living room. It wasn't even dark and they were already plastered. At least Ethan was—he couldn't speak for his friends. They were probably being more careful.

As for a hangover, bring it on. Maybe a pounding head would help him forget what Liz had said to him that morning.

"She doesn't believe I love her," he mumbled into his drink.

"Liz Sutton," Josh said to Raoul. "It's a long story."

"Not long," Ethan replied. "I got her pregnant, turned my back on her and didn't love her enough." He frowned. "I didn't know she was pregnant. If I'd known, I woulda married her. Which makes me the bad guy. Doing the right thing is wrong. You two know that?"

"She's not mad because you would have married her," Josh explained.

"Then why?"

His friend shifted on the sofa. "Women are complicated."

"She said I don't love her. I do. Always did. I never saw that before." He gulped more Scotch. "There was always something about her."

"What did you say?" Raoul asked. "When you said you loved her?"

Ethan squinted at the other man, trying to bring him into focus. "I said I loved her. That I wanted to marry her and it wasn't because it was prac…" He cleared his throat. "Practical."

"When did you say it was practical?" Josh asked.

Ethan waved. "You know. Before."

"Before what?"

"The lasht time I proposed." Was it him or did his words sound funny? "Before I knew I loved her. Said we should get married because it's the right thing to do."

His face had gone numb, he thought, poking his cheek a few times. And his brain felt boiled. Or was it pickled? Maybe it was pickled.

"Keep her in town. With the kids. So I could be with Tyler."

"You are so screwed," Josh said conversationally. "You shouldn't have said that."

"Maybe not. But I love her and she doesn't care. How can she not care?"

"Maybe she cares too much," Raoul told him. "You've been acting like a jerk for a while now. What if she's loved you all along? She's been waiting for you to notice and instead you offered a business arrangement."

"And took her kid from her," Josh added.

"Didn't *take*. It was just a few days. Kids are hard. Women make it look so easy, but it's hard." Ethan closed his eyes and leaned back in the sofa leather.

His fingers relaxed on the glass. He heard someone get up suddenly and then the glass was gone.

"You're about ready to pass out," Raoul said.

"Gotta talk to Liz."

"You need to give Liz some time," Josh told him. "And you need a plan. You've blown it from the beginning. You need to make a big gesture."

"Liz isn't the big gesture type," Ethan mumbled, feeling himself start to drift. "I think she wants to be left alone. I should give her what she wants."

"The woman wants to be swept away," Raoul corrected him. "I know about these things."

"Not Liz."

There was the pain the other men had promised, but it wasn't from the alcohol. Instead it came from his heart—in knowing he could never have Liz. Maybe there'd been a chance, but he'd blown it too many times.

She'd said she loved him. That was nice of her. Kind. He would hold onto those words always, knowing that if he'd been smarter... If he'd understood more sooner, he could have had her.

"Love Liz," he mumbled.

"We got that," Josh said. "You should tell her."

"Too late. Way too late."

And then the world went dark.

LIZ CLOSED UP HER HOUSE IN San Francisco quicker than she would have thought. She ended up leaving all three kids with Denise. For some reason she'd been unable to get Ethan on the phone later that Sunday. Denise had said everything was fine, but wouldn't go into details.

After making the drive to the beautiful city by the bay, she'd spent two days with Peggy, sorting through the items she and Tyler would need in the next couple of months and what they could live without.

The must-have items were packed up and marked for the shipping company to pick up at the end of the week. Peggy would arrange for movers to take care of the rest.

Selling the house proved to be beyond easy. Liz had called a friend who was in real estate. Heidi had admitted that she and her husband had always loved the house, had decided to start a family and were desperate to get out of their apartment. Negotiations took less than an hour, the inspection was on Tuesday and by Wednesday morning, they were in escrow for a quick close. Peggy planned to come to Fool's Gold the week after Labor Day, to see if she wanted to move there.

With everything settled, Thursday morning, Liz started back for Fool's Gold. She and Ethan had an appointment with the judge the next day. With her settling in town and with plans to co-parent Tyler, they could meet the judge's requirements and both avoid jail.

After picking up the kids, they went out to the Fox and Hound for lunch.

"School starts on Tuesday," Melissa said as soon as they'd slid into the booth. "We all need clothes and supplies. We're really behind on our shopping."

Liz laughed. "Are we?"

"There's three of us now, Mom," Tyler indicated. "It's gonna take longer."

"You're right. When we get home, you can all make lists of what you need. We'll head out later and start the shopping. We'll do clothes tonight, then school supplies tomorrow. I have to be in court at nine, but it shouldn't take long."

Tyler grinned. "Are you going to talk to the judge and tell her that you're staying in town?"

"Yes. That should make her happy."

Melissa's phone chirped, indicating she had a text message. She glanced at the screen, then slid the phone back into her pocket before Liz could remind her no phones were allowed at the table.

"Are you staying in Fool's Gold because of us?" Abby asked quietly.

"Maybe a little. And so Tyler can be near his dad."

Abby bit her lower lip. "You've been really good to us." She glanced at her lap, then up at Liz. "Can I call you Mom?"

The unexpected question slammed into Liz like a

warm, gooey feel-good truck. Tears filled her eyes and she found it really hard to speak.

"I asked Tyler if he minded," Abby added quickly. "He said it was fine."

Liz put her arm around the girl and hugged her. "I'd like that," she said. "And saying it doesn't take away from your real mom. I know you love her."

Abby snuggled close.

Liz glanced at Melissa who was staring out the window. "It's okay. You don't have to."

The teen flushed. "Sometimes I want to, but…" She swallowed. "I don't know."

"'Liz' is fine."

"Maybe, you know. Later."

"Whatever makes you comfortable."

The waitress came by and they ordered. The kids started talking about the End-of-Summer festival that weekend and how they had to get all the back-to-school shopping finished so they could go.

Liz listened and smiled, feeling content. She might always miss Ethan, always love him, but as far as the rest of her family went—it was perfect. Maybe doing the right thing wasn't such a bad idea after all.

LIZ MET ETHAN OUTSIDE OF THE courthouse. He looked good, she thought, trying not to stare. Too good. Maybe with time she would get used to seeing him and her body would stop reacting to his presence. Maybe things would get easier between them. A girl could hope.

"Hi," he greeted as she approached. "How was your trip to San Francisco?"

"Good. Everything's underway. I sold the house."

He held open the door to the courthouse and they walked inside. "That's fast. You're going to look for something here?"

She nodded, hoping she didn't look as disappointed as she felt.

She'd thought he might bring up their last meeting. Say something, hint that he'd meant what he said. If only he *did* love her and want them to be together for the right reasons.

Instead they walked in silence toward the judge's chambers.

Fifteen minutes later, Judge Powers announced she was pleased with their decision to co-parent Tyler, warned them not to waste her time again and excused them.

"Tyler said you're going to the summer festival tomorrow," Ethan said.

"All the kids want to go. There's some band playing at noon. Apparently it's a big deal. I have no idea who they are and that makes me feel old."

"You're not old."

"Thanks."

They walked out into the sunny morning and headed for the parking lot. Ethan paused by her SUV.

"I want you to be happy, Liz," he said. "You've given up a lot to be here."

"Not that much," she countered. "It's important to take care of the kids and keep them happy. That's what I'm doing."

"Who takes care of you?"

His dark eyes seemed to see inside her. She wanted to squirm, to look away so he couldn't tell how much she loved him. Concern was one thing, but pity was just too sad.

"I'm pretty tough."

"Because you had to be," he commented. "I want to help any way I can."

Love me, she thought desperately. *Swear I'm the best part of your life.*

But he didn't say the words and she didn't have the courage to ask him to.

They looked at each other, then he turned and walked away.

THE END OF SUMMER FESTIVAL was part county fair, part farmer's market, part party for the parents at the thought of school starting in a few days.

Liz arrived with all three kids by ten Saturday morning and by ten-fifteen, she found herself alone. Melissa went off with a group of her girlfriends, while Tyler and Abby met up with kids from camp. Liz purchased ride tickets for the younger two and made them all promise to meet her at eleven-thirty for lunch. Then she stood in the center of the crowd, wondering what to do next.

She explored the booths in the makeshift market-place. There were crafts for sale, including some printed T-shirts she bought for the kids.

Denise Hendrix found her looking at candles.

"The jasmine scented ones are great," Ethan's mother said with a smile. "I have them all over my bathroom. How's it going?"

"Good." She held up the bag of T-shirts. "I'm doing my bit for the economy."

"And the economy thanks you." Denise pointed to a shaved ice stand. "Come on. I'm buying."

They walked to the stand and got in line. "You doing all right?"

"I'm fine. I'm starting house hunting next week."

Denise sighed. "My son's an idiot."

"Why?"

"Because it's obvious the two of you are crazy about each other. You should be together."

"Ethan's not in love with me. He's interested in duty rather than love and I'm not interested in settling."

"Not even if walking away breaks your heart?"

Liz sighed. "You loved Ethan's dad, right?"

"Constantly and to this day."

"Would you have settled for anything less than all he had?"

"No." Denise smiled sadly. "You're making the right decision. My head tells me that. My heart wants you to have a happy ending."

"I'm happy. Or I will be. I have three great kids, a

job I love and hey, I'm staying in Fool's Gold. Won't that be perfect."

Denise laughed. "Are you still worried about the town?"

"No. I don't like that people are so free with their opinions, but the good really outweighs the bad. I know that if I'm attacked by a crazed stalker, everyone will come to my rescue. The kids are safe here. We can all be happy. That's what matters."

There was a crackling noise, as if someone had flipped on the sound system. Liz and Denise both turned toward the stage at the far end of the park. Liz saw someone holding a microphone, but she couldn't see who it was.

"Hi, everyone," a familiar voice said.

Liz blinked. That sounded like Ethan.

"I'd like to have your attention for a minute."

Denise put a hand to her chest. "Is that Ethan?"

"I think so."

"What is he doing?"

"I have no idea."

"This won't take long," Ethan continued. "If you could move closer to the stage. I need to make an announcement."

Liz and Denise got out of line and walked toward the stage.

"For those of you who don't know me, I'm Ethan Hendrix."

"We know who you are," a man in the crowd yelled.

Ethan chuckled nervously, shifting from foot to foot. "Good. I need your help with something, and you're going to have to keep it a secret."

Several people laughed.

"You really think that's going to happen?" a woman asked.

"I hope so. Here's the thing. Someone really important to me is moving back to Fool's Gold. Her name is Liz Sutton. A few of you know her."

"She's that writer."

"That's her," Ethan confirmed.

Liz glanced at Denise who looked confused.

"Don't ask me," the other woman said. "I have no idea what he's up to."

Ethan was going to talk about her to the whole town? Why? What on earth was he going to say?

She walked a little faster toward the stage.

"Liz grew up here, like me. Unlike most of us, she didn't have an easy time of it. Her mother was indifferent at best and abusive at worst. Some of you might remember her. She had a reputation for being a drunk and…" He hesitated.

The crowd went quiet.

"In high school, Liz was smart and beautiful and sweet. But almost no one bothered to notice. Instead the other kids said terrible things about her. Things that weren't true."

Liz didn't know if she should walk faster or disappear into the crowd. Humiliation burned her cheeks.

"It was all a lie," Ethan continued. "I know, because I was her first boyfriend. Her first kiss. Her first."

"We know about the kid, Ethan," someone called.

"Right. But what you don't know is that I made a promise to Liz back then. I told her that I loved her. I said we'd go off to college together. And then when my friend asked me if I was dating Liz, I lied and said she wasn't anyone I would spend time with. I denied I even knew her and I did it in front of all my friends and in front of Liz."

There was an audible gasp.

Liz wove through the ever-growing crowd. She could see the stage more clearly now, could see Ethan. He stood alone, facing the town.

"I betrayed her and broke her heart," he said quietly. "I denied her and I denied myself. Because I did love her. But I was young and stupid and more worried about what my friends thought than her. I didn't deserve her."

"You can say that again," someone urged.

Liz reached the side of the stage, where the steps were. But now that she was there, she didn't know what she was supposed to do. Stop him? Listen? This was the most surreal moment of her life.

"Liz took off. Who can blame her? About three weeks later, she found out she was pregnant. She came back to tell me and I was, ah, otherwise occupied."

"What does that mean?" someone asked.

"He was in bed with someone else," a guy in the back hollered.

Several people laughed. A few groaned.

"Not smart," a woman said.

"Tell me about it," Ethan agreed. "Flash forward six years. Liz came back again to tell me about my son. This time, she was determined I would know. But someone got in the way and kept the information from me."

He drew in a breath. "The reason I'm telling you all this is that Liz is staying in town. She's moving here so I can be with my son and her nieces can live in a familiar place. She's a helluva woman."

"Hey. We've got kids here."

"Oh, sorry." Ethan looked chagrined. "She's amazing. So for those of you who want to say something bad about her, you're going to answer to me. No more stopping her on the street or in a store and saying she was wrong to keep Tyler from me. No more making her feel bad. Liz deserves better and we're all going to give it to her. Understand?"

There were several murmurs of agreement.

Liz felt as if she were taking part in a play. Or watching a movie. This couldn't be happening.

"If she's all that and you're obviously in love with her, why aren't you marrying her?"

The question came from down in front. Liz stiffened, not sure she wanted to hear the answer.

Ethan sighed. "Hi, Mom."

The crowd laughed.

"Answer the question," Denise insisted.

Liz held her breath.

"I want to. Liz is my world. But I've been an idiot one too many times. I asked her to marry me because it was the right thing to do."

"You really are stupid," a woman commented.

Everyone laughed.

"Did you tell her that you're sorry?" a boy offered.

Liz turned toward the speaker and saw Tyler standing next to Denise. Abby and Melissa were nearby, all looking at Ethan, all hopeful.

"She likes it when you apologize after you've done something wrong. And she always gives you a second chance," Tyler informed.

"Not this time, buddy," Ethan argued.

"But if you love her," Melissa said, "you should tell her again. Tell her like you mean it."

"Kiss her like they do in the movies," Abby added.

"It's not going to be enough. Liz deserves better than me."

"Darlin', if we only married who we deserved, then the world would be filled with single women," an older woman said.

There was more laughter.

"I do love her," Ethan told the crowd. "But sometimes love isn't enough."

Liz stared at the man who had always been in her heart and knew she'd been given the most precious gift of all. A second chance. Whatever doubts she'd had faded away in the face of Ethan humbling himself before everyone he knew—just to protect her and make her feel safe.

She felt his love, his caring, his support. The road they shared might not always be easy, but it was where they both belonged.

"Love is always enough," Liz said.

He turned, looking stunned. "I thought you weren't going to be here until noon. I thought the kids had come on their own."

"The band goes on at noon. We got here a while ago."

He dropped the microphone to his side. "How much did you hear?"

She climbed the stairs to the stage. "All of it."

"I do love you, Liz. I mean that."

"I believe you."

"What's he saying?" someone in the crowd asked.

A person up front shushed him. "We'll tell you later," the woman said.

Ethan set the microphone back in the stand and moved toward her. "I want us to get married. I want us to be a family. But only because I want to spend my life with you, making you happy. I want to be the man you deserve, but I'm going to need your help to get there."

"You got that right," she said with a smile.

"Is that a yes?" he asked.

She stepped into his embrace.

"Yes," she whispered, right before his mouth pressed against hers.

"They're kissing like in the movies," Abby crowed. "I love it when that happens."